AF491181

FREE
FALL

FREE FALL

A SONNY ROJAS ROCK AND ROLL THRILLER

LAWRENCE KELTER

First published by Level Best Books/Historia 2026

Copyright © 2026 by Lawrence Kelter

All rights reserved. No part of this publication may be reproduced, stored, or transmitted in any form or by any means, electronic, mechanical, photocopying, recording, scanning, or otherwise without written permission from the publisher. It is illegal to copy this book, post it to a website, or distribute it by any other means without permission.

This novel is entirely a work of fiction. The names, characters, and incidents portrayed in it are the work of the author's imagination. Any resemblance to actual persons, living or dead, events, or localities is entirely coincidental.

Lawrence Kelter asserts the moral right to be identified as the author of this work.

First edition

ISBN: 979-8-89820-081-7

Cover art by Level Best Designs

This book was professionally typeset on Reedsy.
Find out more at reedsy.com

For Robert and Lee Elliott

I

PART ONE - SLAM

Chapter One

Fresh from three weeks of Jump School and a handful of missions since being deployed to Vietnam, the lessons embedded in my brain were still vivid. But the continuous throbbing dread that began when I boarded the C-130 transport had rammed them against the back of my skull with such force that I couldn't touch them, couldn't get close.

Every man in my squad had come out of basic with a snarl and an upturned lip, trained to kill or be killed. We were taught to survive on our youthful arrogance and the tidal wave of testosterone surging through our veins. My name, Sonny Rojas. At nineteen, I was the oldest soldier in the group, but I wasn't the biggest. Before they shaved my head down to the scalp, I weighed in at maybe one hundred and thirty pounds.

I tried not to read my men's minds, worry about them, or feel guilty about leading them into danger. I knew what they were thinking, the unknown they feared. Being captured. The finality of death was a distant second in their minds. VC imprisonment was the true and absolute monster, a fate more ominous than death, an outcome blacker than the darkest pit of hell.

Our mission commander approached and addressed the paratroopers that were seated down the middle of the plane and against the hull, shouting at the top of his lungs so that he could be heard over the roar of the C-130's engines. "Suck it up, Marines. Same shit, different day. Combat jump. Seven-hundred-foot elevation. Nothing to it." The mission was a low-altitude night jump to slip into the jungle unobserved, just within enemy lines. Get in and report the VC's position, then proceed to the extraction site at the greatest possible speed. It should've been a walk in the park. Nine of us in, nine of us out. Easy peasy. The commander's eyes settled on me, the intelligence officer in charge of a platoon of reconnaissance Marines. No words, just an attaboy wink as potent as a syringe of adrenaline to the heart as he moved to the side door, anticipating our arrival over the drop site.

I shouldn't have been standing, but I was too fidgety to sit, and I momentarily lost my balance as the big airship banked. The popping in my ears told me we were descending, and I could feel my physiology changing. I was in touch with every hair on the surface of my skin and could feel my nerve endings sizzle. My neck was stiff, my muscles were tight, and my heart was beating just hard enough to make its discontentment known, signals that triggered cold, hard realization. No words needed. In plain English, fear.

"Here we go, Rojas." He pointed to me and popped a robust thumbs-up. "You ready, Marine?"

I saluted and barked my response like an attack-trained dog, "Yes, Sir. Born ready, Sir."

He turned to face the platoon. Cupping his hands, he boomed, "Outboard personnel, stand up."

I watched four platoon members sitting against the fuselage get to their feet.

My heart knocked double-time, not continuously, just for a few seconds or so, then it settled back into rhythm.

"Inboard personnel, stand up."

I wasn't five feet from the door when it opened and could feel oppressively hot air blast into the hold along with the pungent tang of the engine's kerosene-laden exhaust. 700 feet below us, Viet Cong snipers would be watching and waiting for the plane to expel us into the night like a live-bearing fish giving birth to its fry. They'd listen for the sound of deploying parachutes—at such a low altitude, the ruffle of the nylon chutes would not be missed. They'd site the parachute canopies and aim below them, hoping to pick us off before we hit the ground. Pulses pounding, they'd fire off continuous bursts, hoping to turn the members of my team into plunging corpses. The thought made my heart drop. It was in my stomach, and I could feel it thudding against my combat pack. I turned to look at the Marine standing behind me, who seemed every bit as tense, every ounce as focused as I was. We were of the same mind, taught to push past our nerves and brainwashed to fight through fear, to execute our orders without reservation. Somehow, the notion of two hardened Marines sharing the same worry seemed oddly comforting. And we were Marines—no way any of us would chicken out, ever! Still, there was that perception of mortality residing in the back of our minds, screaming out, "You're only flesh and blood. Marines bleed as easily as anyone else."

"Hook up," the CO said.

We hooked up to the static line and checked our equipment.

"One minute!" he shouted.

My heartbeat accelerated like a thoroughbred's bursting from the starting gate, wildly, recklessly. *Breathe, Marine. Slow and steady*, I told myself, then hummed a guitar riff, over and over, one I had played a hundred times. The muscles in my hand had memorized every note and I could play it back blindfolded. I pictured my fingers on the fret board, bending strings, hammering, muting, blues notes singing from a Marshall amp, sweet as honey. Calmness swept over me momentarily, but it didn't last.

"Thirty seconds!"

I glanced out the hatch. At 700-feet, I thought I'd see something, anything, but I was wrong. In the gaps between the plane's strobe, the night was pitch-black. Somewhere below us, blackened metal rifle muzzles were waiting, tracking the C-130 and eager for the first parachute to deploy.

"Stand by!"

I moved to the door, facing out, ready to launch myself from the platform.

"Green light! *Go!*"

I made eye contact with the mission commander, handed him my static line, and turned. Step, kick...

Chapter Two

I left the aircraft and was hit with a wall of air against my chest that felt like a Joe Frazier left hook. Darkness screamed past me as I plunged, my lungs still inflated with the same breath I took when I jumped. My heart hadn't beat once since I lunged from the C-130 and didn't feel as if it was going to but then it kicked back to life. Adrenaline surging, heart pounding, I was out-of-my-mind terrified. I felt a pop in my ears, and the gears in my head finally began to turn. I counted: *one thousand*, before I was blown into a horizontal position and carried away from the plane. *Two thousand.* The force of the air shifted my helmet about my head, and I was still travelling flat out in a horizontal path, away from the bird, not down but sideways. *Three thousand.* With my chin tucked into my chest, my hands clutched the sides of my reserve parachute. *Four thousand…five thousand.* I felt the tug of the deploying parachute catching air. *Six thousand.* Grabbing the risers, the straps that connected the parachute to the harness on my body, I looked up to inspect the canopy, make sure it had fully deployed, and that there were no tears or broken suspension lines.

As best I could see in the cloud-blanketed moonlight, there was no damage, but if there was, I'd just have to deal with it. All went quiet as I drifted downward, but something didn't feel right. My parachute was open, but it had twisted. I grabbed the risers and pulled them outward and away from me. Kicking my legs, I spun a couple times until the lines were free and the parachute was fully opened.

For an instant, it felt as if I was hovering, then the wind took me again. There wasn't much noise. I felt thankful that the twang of rifle fire was absent. Thank God. Had we taken the VC by surprise? Caught them sleeping? All I could hear was the sound of my breathing becoming even and regular as adrenaline ebbed. I looked down. Seven hundred feet. I should almost be—

I gasped. *Shit.* No way this was seven hundred feet. The gust that hit me when I left the plane must have taken me further than I realized, far away from the drop zone, and drifting somewhere over the Quezon Valley. With only my gut and instincts to guide me, wind buffeted against me like a barrage of body blows and I was traveling further and further off course. There was no instructor, no buddy, just me, blackness, and that sinking feeling that everything had gone wrong. I'd been falling too long and with every fleeting millisecond anticipated a barrage of VC rounds whizzing by me, so many rounds that one would certainly find its mark.

Below me, the jungle exploded in my eyes. Treetops illuminated by moonlight loomed like razor-sharpened bayonets, poised to punch through me and tear me to shreds. My fists were clenched so tightly I could feel them throbbing as a fierce gust carried me further still. I looked around for the other eight paratroopers, the Marines under my command, but there weren't any in sight. *Fifteen hundred feet? Two thousand?* They were my wild-ass guesses about the altitude we had actually jumped from but I'm sure closer to correct than the 700-foot elevation we were originally told. Looking down, rolling moonlit reflected off moving water. *Water landing,* screamed in my head, and I knew I had to get my boots off before I hit the water, get them off or drown. I had to jettison the combat pack and do it before it was too late. Pack away, I tugged at my boots as I approached the looming water. For all I knew it might only have been a couple of feet deep and a PLF landing might still be possible, but there was no time to do anything but follow protocol. I had one boot off and the other in my hands as I smacked down. A hard thud against my back. Pain like nothing I'd ever felt before, deep bone pain ignited and coursed through me as muddy putrid water ran into my gaping mouth. My heart pounded and with every powerful contraction reminded me I was still alive. Although long moments had elapsed since I left the C-130, in my heart I felt that I had never fallen so far so fast. What I didn't know was that the bottom was nowhere in sight.

Coming to after apparently blacking out, I sensed boots sloshing through the mud nearby and the slicing sound a body makes as it whips through chest-high thickets. The spasms shooting through my back and trunk were unbearable. Crippling pain made it almost impossible to draw breath. Were the VC on me? Was my life over? It was better to die here and now than be taken a prisoner. *Better than enduring that hell.* The thudding of my heart that caused my body to judder began to ebb. Numbness, like a fog, began to creep over me and as it spread I felt myself slipping away.

II

PART TWO - JAM

Chapter Three

Cu Chi, Vietnam

Four days later

Pilot's helmet under his arm, Warrant Officer John Roswell proceeded slowly into the building that made up the 12th Evacuation Hospital. The Huey pilot thought he'd become accustomed to sweltering temperatures and humidity but was overwhelmed by the staggering heat that bombarded him when he entered the steel arched-roof Quonset hut. The air was still and dank, thick enough to cut with a knife, and the metallic smell of blood was enough to make him gag. A soldier in the first bed had two bandaged stumps for legs. The wounded soldier looked like a corpse, but the subtle rising and falling of his chest proved otherwise. The man in the next bed had blood oozing from beneath his bandaged eye. A soldier in the third bed was in traction, his leg suspended by a rope tied to a sandbag for ballast. Roswell's concern for his own personal well-being evaporated. *Poor bastards*, he thought. It was only by God's grace that he wasn't among them. He knew that good luck might run out at any moment. The building was lined with beds against each wall, every one of them full. Men moaning. Writhing. Barely clinging to life. He shuddered and took a shallow breath of putrid air.

A diminutive, stick-thin brunette in fatigues and combat boots looked toward him as she switched out an IV bag. Her hair was tucked under a cap, her forehead dripping sweat, her gaze far from welcoming. "You need something?" she asked, irritated by the intrusion.

He meandered toward her, his gait faltering.

"Don't waste my time, Slick." She scanned the building from end to end. "You can see I've got a full house—there are a lot of really sick men here, and you're upright and moving under your own steam. What can I do you for?"

He waited a beat to scan her name tag before responding. "Nurse Hannigan, I was hoping you could hook me up with—"

"Talk up, would you?" she barked. "Half the men in here are sleeping. The rest are blasted out of their minds on morphine. Whatever your deep dark secret, it's safe from them."

"I…need some Vitamin P."

"Excuse me?"

"You know, Vitamin *P*."

Outside, the beating of helicopter blades grew from a far-off warble to an intrusive whomping noise. "That's the sound of chopper blades bringing incoming wounded. I'll step right over you to get to those injured men when they arrive. So, spell it out for me, would ya?"

The word stuck to his tongue. "Penicillin."

Her expression flashed disbelief. "You've got some balls, man. You caught something from one of the Lindas, and now you need meds from me to make the burning stop."

"Lindas?" he asked.

"Don't play dumb, they're all Linda. Somehow, every Vietnamese hooker got it into her head that all American women are named Linda. Or maybe that's the only name that comes to mind when the backs of their skulls are getting slammed against a headboard." She shook her head. "Well, you know what? Tough shit. I've got two dozen men flat on their backs, amputees, trauma patients, some with gunshot wounds, you name it. I'm on my feet twelve hours plus, and you want to take me away from my boys because you boned an Asian whore and picked up the clap? Nuh-uh. You can wait your turn at the infirmary like all the other horny GIs. You fucking men, is there a single one of you who can make it from sunup to sundown without sticking your dick where it doesn't belong?"

Somehow her fiery rant fell on deaf ears. He caught a glimpse of a patient in dire shape and turned away.

"Hey, shithead," she bellowed. "I'm talking to you."

"How's this one doing?" Roswell asked.

"What?"

He was standing at the foot of a soldier's bed. "Him." He pointed to the man asleep in front of him. "His name is Rojas, right? A Paramarine. First one I've seen since I deployed. I thought the Marine airborne forces campaign was kaput and I almost shit myself in the Huey when I spotted his parachute. I brought him in a few days ago. He doing okay?"

"Santiago Rojas," she said as she moved to his bedside and reviewed the chart. "Goes by Sonny. He's in a world of pain like everyone else in here. Shattered pelvis, exploded discs: he's pumping enough morphine to cold-cock a rogue elephant. He'll be here just until it's safe to move him to a real hospital for spinal surgery."

"He doesn't look like he's in pain."

"Oh, he's in pain, darlin', he just don't know it. If I don't shoot him up smack dab on schedule, he'll be screaming like a banshee." She read concern in Roswell's eyes. "But at least he's alive, right? And he's got his arms and legs, which is a hell of a lot more than I can say for some of these poor men. With God's help and a shit ton of rehab, he may even walk again." Her eyes widened when Roswell crossed himself. "That's sweet," she said. "These boys need all the prayers they can get and then some."

"Total fluke that I found him. I was on the way back from a hash and trash run delivering rations when I saw his open chute in a stream. It was first light when the sun comes in at just the right angle and turns the water into silver. I dropped down and saw this dark speck lying face up on a boulder in the stream—and there he was, still tethered to his chute. These guys are trained to gather up their chutes pronto, so they're not spotted by the VC reconnaissance planes. He must've gone lights out the minute he smacked down. I actually thought he was dead, but he moaned when I touched him. Then, he was dead silent again in the Huey the whole time we were in the air. I thought sure I'd lose him before we made it back."

Nurse Hannigan turned her gaze to Roswell. The steel in her eyes was gone. "You brought your helo down in broad daylight to save a man you figured was already dead?"

He pulled off his cap and lowered his head. "I'd hope another pilot would do the same for me." He ran the back of his hand against his forehead. "Shit, it's hot as hell in here. Why don't you have any fans?"

"We used to, but they needed them in the ER, and we can't have surgeons passing out from heat prostration while they're wrists-deep in a soldier's chest cavity."

"No, ma'am, I guess you surely can't," he said as he gritted his teeth. He smiled weakly when a tuft of hair fell from under her cap. "It's nice to see you haven't cut your hair like a lot of the other enlisted women."

She pushed her hair back under the brim. "You best believe I'm thinking about it. It's so fucking hot in here, about the only time of day I'm happy is when I'm in the shower. Yesterday morning, two gals had to drag me out of there just to get their turn." She placed the diaphragm of her stethoscope on Rojas's chest and listened to his heart. "He's way under. Way, *way* under. I could tap dance on his chest, and he wouldn't feel a thing." She pulled the stethoscope tips from her ears and was silent for a long moment. "I must be crazy."

"Why?"

"You win the Barb Hannigan Sympathy Award. Wander over to the supply cabinet when you're done with your reunion, and I'll hit you up with a dose of GI Clap Killer."

"No shit?

That's right, Sherlock, no shit."

"Thanks."

"You're welcome. Just don't go poking any of the enlisted women for a solid ten days. In case you haven't heard, condoms are free. So keep that bad boy wrapped, and you can plug every Linda between here and Ho Chi Min City and still sleep nights." She took a last sad look at Rojas, "I wonder what he's dreaming about?"

Roswell shrugged. "Don't know, but wherever he's at, I hope it's a far better place than here."

Chapter Four

RKO Theater, New York, NY

Six months earlier - March 26, 1967, about 3:00 AM

Sitting backstage, I was mesmerized as The Who's Keith Moon jackhammered his drums as if he was possessed. Pete Townshend slashed at guitar strings like the Demon Barber of Fleet Street with a guitar pick in hand in place of a straight razor. Seconds later, Townshend spun the guitar in the air before driving it into the stage floor like a logger wielding an axe. The audience was bombed, either blitzed on booze or stoned on weed, reveling in the havoc taking place on stage before them. John Entwistle plucked bazooka charges on the bass, and Roger Daltrey screamed like a banshee set afire. Security rushed the stage. Didn't know what to do. The Who ignored them. And the band played on, running amok, their unchoreographed mayhem continuing unbridled. I'd never seen The Who play live—to date, no one in America had seen the British band in the flesh. Seeing them up close, I felt lightning bolts of electricity coursing through my veins.

Exhausted and still panting minutes later, Townshend took one last glimpse at the shimmering silver backdrop curtain before reluctantly heading offstage. The audience was still lit and on fire, chanting, "More! More! More!" It killed Townshend to leave them wanting, but the group had been told in no uncertain terms to play the set list and clear the stage for the next act. The card was full, not full but jampacked. Murray the K's Music in the Fifth Dimension Extravaganza was sold out and featured well-known names as well as rising stars, The Who, Cream, Simon and Garfunkel, Mitch Ryder and the Detroit Wheels, the Rascals, Blues Project, and the Blues Magoos.

John Dazzle, the stage manager, had just handed me Eric Clapton's guitar to be tuned for Cream's performance when he saw Townshend hesitating as he crossed the backstage area on his way to the dressing rooms. "Take good care of it, Sonny," Dazzle said. "I hear this Clapton fella is a real fanatic." His eyes were still following Townshend, who stopped and looked as if he was about to call out to his bandmates before they disappeared from sight. Dazzle knew what was coming, and his job was to put the kibosh on Townshend's plan, stop that shit dead cold before the band stole back onstage. He could see that The Who's lead guitarist was aching for an encore to give the fans more of the music they were dying to hear.

"Leave 'em hungry," Dazzle said with a heavy hand on Townshend's shoulder. Dazzle was a dapper-looking gent with coiffed gray hair and a deep tan. He wore a checkered sports coat he likely swiped from a used car salesman. "Seven top acts, five shows a day for nine days…believe you me, young Mr. Townshend, the fans will get their money's worth and then some. Murray will make sure they do."

Townshend was tall and lanky with long brown hair. He leaned in, embarrassed to be overheard. "It's our first gig stateside, mate. We need to show 'em everything we've got."

"Oh? And you think recreating the Battle of the Bulge didn't leave an impression? I'm surprised you didn't roll a cruiser tank on stage."

"Is it really gonna kill you to let us do one more quick little number?"

"Murray was clear about that. No encores. No extras. No nothing. You and your bandmates are alright enough, but some of these established acts make a hell of a lot of demands: the size of their dressing rooms and how the bar is stocked. It goes on and on. They want their asses kissed, powdered, and pampered before they'll ever consider performing, and they don't want to be upstaged by a bunch of kids out of…?" His thought derailed, and he angled his head, directing Townshend's gaze toward a group of go-go dancers, lined up in a row and ready to take the stage. The troop leader's eyes were on the DJ as he dropped the needle on a spinning 45 and the intro to "These Boots Are Made for Walking" roared over the PA system. Nancy Sinatra's voice filled the auditorium as the mini-skirted showgirls took the stage. Heels thundering, the house lights bounced off their white patent leather go-go boots with enough intensity to cause snow blindness.

"Now, that's hot," Townshend said. "That lead dancer in particular."

"Avert your eyes, lad," Dazzle said. "That's Murray's wife, Jackie, heading up that chorus line, and he's insanely jealous. He catches you eyeballing his lady, and your set time will get cut in half. Those gals don't get pushed back for nobody."

"Uncool, man. I'm not stupid. Jackie of Jackie and the K Girls is the big boss's bird. Message received. What's K stand for anyway, king? He's running this bleeding event like a damn tyrant."

"It stands for Kaufman," Dazzle said. "Her name is Jackie Hayes, but she goes by Jackie the K." He cloaked his mouth. "Between you and me, king is more appropriate than Kaufman. In the world of rock 'n roll, Murray and Jackie are royalty, and you'd be smart not to forget it."

"He's treating us like we're all indentured servants," Townshend said. "He don't even let us leave the theater between sets. We're all going stark raving mad. It's absolute chaos backstage. Everyone pulling pranks on one another just to cut the boredom."

"No shit. Tell your drummer if he flushes another M-80 down the john, I'm gonna drag him all the way to the airport and kick his lily-white ass back across the pond."

"My mate's just having a little fun. If we wanted to be barked at by a drill sergeant, we would've joined the bleedin' British Army."

"England still got an army back in...where did you tell me you were from anyway?" he asked, his earlier thought careening back onto the rails.

"Shepherd's Bush, mate, and yeah, we've still got an army, a goddamn good one. What's so bleedin' hard to remember?"

"Townshend, you get to my age and things don't stick the first time around.

Maybe not even the second. I need to hear things a few times before I remember them, so don't take it personally. Now, your name? That's easy because I know what you look like. Townshend, I think, that's the tall skinny Brit with the big schnoz."

Townshend's middle finger sprang erect like a loose plank stepped on at the wrong end.

"Anyway, that's in London, right? Shepherd's Bush?"

Townshend nodded.

"Like I said, I'm sorry, kid, but everyone wants the stage, and if I let you back out there, I'll have to let everyone do an encore, and we'll be here until the 4th of July."

Townshend shrugged. "What's the 4th of July, the day after the 3rd of July?"

Dazzle shook his head. "Cut the cheeky shit, Townshend. You fucking Brits—suck it up for God's sake. You lost, we won, and Independence Day marks the day we showed your puny nation the door. End of story. Anyway, five shows a day, you'll get plenty of face time with the audience. Take a well-earned rest and save some energy for the chickadees."

"Don't you worry, mate. I've had more than my fair share of lusty birds."

"Trust me, limey, you haven't been laid until you've bumped uglies with an eighteen-year-old Bronx chick. They're a whole 'nother species. Ten minutes and you'll swear off every girl in Shepherd's Pie."

"That's Bush."

"Say what?"

"Bush. Shepherd's Bush." Angry, Townshend shook his head, then abruptly dropped on one knee and clasped his hands dramatically. "One song. Come on, one bloody song. Three minutes and we're off. Who's up next, anyway?"

"Cream just arrived, *finally*. Travel delays. They've been in the air all night."

Townshend's plea died a sudden death. "Fuck me—Clapton's up?"

"Came straight here from JFK. You should see how he's dressed, shiny pink checkered pants, permed hair—very sedate."

"That's Eric, changes his look as often as his socks."

Dazzle chuckled. "Says the man wearing a tailored British flag after smashing a Telecaster on stage. You buy guitars in bulk or something? Isn't an instrument supposed to be a work of art? Something to be cherished. I mean—"

Townshend cut his eyes at Dazzle. "It's rock and roll, man. Image is everything. The fans want aggressive, I give them aggressive. They want art they can pony up their hard-earned money and buy tickets to the Philharmonic."

"Yeah, but pink pants? He afraid he won't be noticed?"

"Trust me, Eric Clapton doesn't have to be seen to be noticed. He can stand backstage behind the curtain, and everyone will know it's him. No one can cover his licks because he never plays anything the same way twice. He's a genuine improvisational genius. Once he starts wailing on his—" Townshend glanced around the backstage area to see if he could spot his friend. "What's he playing tonight?"

Dazzle looked around and pointed to me. "See that baby-faced guitar technician, sitting on a drummer's stool with his ear to the neck of a black Gibson Les Paul?" Dazzle's comment didn't bother me. If it wasn't for my long sideburns, I'd look as if I hadn't reached puberty.

Townshend zeroed in on me. "Should've recognized it—I love that fucking guitar."

"That one gonna get smashed to bits too?" Dazzle asked.

"No, man, that's my thing, not Eric's. He doesn't have to. Are you telling me you've never heard him play?"

"I've heard some of The Yardbirds tracks, but they change guitarists as often as I change my jockey shorts. I'm never sure who's playing lead."

"Never heard Cream before they appeared on the lineup tonight?"

"Their cover of Willie Dixon's 'Spoonful' is pretty tasty. I dig it and all, but I can't say I lose my mind over it."

"Dig it? That's Eric playing with both hands tied behind his back. If he leaves it all out on the stage tonight you're going to see girl's white knickers sailing through the air like a flock of bleedin' seagulls."

"Yeah? Look, I'm from Missouri."

Townshend smirked. "Where the hell is that?"

Dazzle flashed a playful backhand. "Get the hell out of here, will ya? Clapton's drummer has a monster double-bass kit, and we've got to swap his for Moon's before they can go on, Marshall and Fender stacks too. All you Brit rockers lug them big ass amps around with you, or just the ones from Shepherd's Bush?"

Townshend shook his head and trudged off.

"Don't take it personally," Dazzle said, "That's the music biz—take it or leave it."

Chapter Five

As he walked backstage, Townshend couldn't help but stop to check out the black Les Paul he so admired. I was still tuning it, playing subtle licks at low volume and paused to adjust the tune. He listened to me play a sweet riff and smiled at the soulful and beautifully sustained notes. He applauded softly, then turned up the volume knob on the Fender amp.

"Holy shit, you're—" I said.

"A rocker, mate, just like you."

"I was told to keep the amp turned down."

The thunder of the audience stomping their feet was building as they waited for Cream to take the stage. "No worries, mate," Townshend said. "You've got an entire music-starved auditorium just dying for rock and roll. Once all those high-kicking girlies are off the stage, no one's gonna bitch about some sweet notes sailing through the air. And that riff you just played, that was magic. Nothing like I'd play but juicy all the same. You're playing the blues, but your sense of timing, it sounds Latin, and I don't hear a lot of vibrato. That kind of music move you, mate?"

I nodded and tapped my heart. *"Duende,"* I said.

Townshend was given pause, then his eyes gleamed knowingly. "Ahh. I get it. It touches you. Is that it?"

"Exactly. The passion. I feel it."

"You do any gigging?"

"Yeah, I've got a band, but they're back home in Florida. I came here—"

"Because New York is the scene," Townshend said, "and Florida is where the early bird special is the high point of the day."

"Something like that," I said.

"Play something else. Give me some more of those smoldering Latin trills."

Pausing to compose my thoughts, I switched gears and launched into an incendiary rant that sent Townshend back on his heels. I fired notes off the guitar like boulders from a medieval catapult, hitting grace tones, hammering up to higher notes, then back down the scale.

"Now that's me," Townshend said. "That's fucking me. Trying to impress me, are you?" He reached for the guitar, rested his foot on a stool, and played with the Gibson resting on the meaty portion of his leg. He mimicked what I just played, stripping out some of the Latin flavor and adding power chords, bright and brassy.

"Hey, that's—"

"Familiar? Yeah, mate, I bloody-well hope so." Townshend said, his glance taunting me.

Recognizing the chord, I nodded. Townshend's signature lick was immediately familiar.

"I use it a lot. Been fooling around with it as an intro to something I'm fiddling around with, a song about a blind kid playing pinball, if you can believe it. Got a long way to go on it yet." Townshend rolled his neck. "The point being you can hear the difference. What you played was great, fresh, bold. But I just made it my own. Thanks, lad," he said with a sly wink.

"Hey, are you ripping me off?"

"That's how it works, m'boy—you hear something, give it a tweak, and bang it out for all it's worth. Besides, if I play your guitar riff on stage...Well, young sir, you should be damn well honored." He smiled warmly. "Say, mate, you got a name?" Townshend asked.

"Sonny," I said, beyond thrilled to be acknowledged by the British rock star. "Sonny Rojas."

Chapter Six

Two hours later

Standing in the wings, I was awestruck. The electricity banging out of the amps ran right through my body, setting it ablaze. Hearing Cream live was like the first time a girl let me go all the way. Their music was raw, frenzied, insane, and culminated in an explosive finale. The volume blasting from the amplifier stacks was deafening, and each song featured an extended guitar solo. It was nothing like the two-minute songs I heard on the radio. Hearing Cream on vinyl was great, but live…? It was like rock and roll on steroids, orgasmic, and I couldn't get enough. Ginger Baker pounded the drum kit like King Kong beating his chest after snatching a fighter plane out of the air from atop the Empire State Building. And while Jack Bruce plucked bass notes with the ferocity of an artillery gunner, Clapton launched into one frenzied guitar solo after another. He was fast, fast as hell, but it wasn't about the speed. It was the melodies he peeled off, one riff transitioning into the next, then the next, then the next, effortlessly, seamlessly…endlessly, not one bad note, not one. It was as if he was channeling the blues straight from heaven, his Gibson guitar the antenna pulling harmonies out of the air. They played seven songs with extended jams and opened with a soon-to-be-released single they called "Sunshine of Your Love." I'd never heard anything like it before. Bruce's raw vocals, Baker's tribal beats, and Clapton's volatile guitar—standing offstage, I realized I was about twenty feet from heaven. Nothing I'd ever heard before was as awesome or inspiring.

They finished with "Toad," which was nothing more than a thinly veiled vehicle for Ginger Baker's drum solo. The man was a force of nature, a wild man with each hand and foot moving independently, hammering out rhythms with the accuracy of a Swiss watch while somehow tethering Bruce and Clapton to the beat, rooting the song forward from beginning to end. I was emotionally spent by the time they walked off the stage. Clapton handed me the Gibson as he walked by. He was about three strides past me when he turned around.

"Say, is your name Sonny?" Clapton asked with a distinctive British accent. He was dripping sweat, his shirt soaked through and through, yet had no difficulty managing a warm smile.

I nodded, like a puppy eager for a treat. He extended his hand. *Holy shit. Holy-fucking-shit.* This was Eric Clapton after all, who had been the lead guitarist for The Yardbirds and John Mayall's Blues Breakers before joining Bruce and Baker to form Cream. He was the guitarist British fans were calling God, a man idolized by every rock-and-roll fan around the globe. *And he's about to shake my hand.*

"Pete Townshend said you're good. So good he nicked one of your riffs. Is that right?"

All I could do was shrug. I mean, who was I to rat out Pete Townshend, me, a nineteen-year-old kid from Florida who had to bum a ride off a traveling vacuum salesman to get from Florida to New York? I had thirty-six dollars in my wallet, an all-time high. "I guess."

"He does it all the time," Clapton said. "We all do to some extent. You nick a riff here, a riff there, and spin it in a way that's a bit different. You know, change the tempo, break off into a different scale. It all comes from the same place, southern blues, guys like Muddy Waters and 'Big' Bill Broonzy, Robert Johnson, and T-Bone Walker. One day you'll do the same thing." I could see that he was tired, but he remained good-natured. "We're going to breakfast, then up to my place to jam for a bit. Care to join us?"

Me, have breakfast with him? I was so excited I practically peed myself. I'd just been invited to breakfast by Eric-fucking-Clapton. At that moment, someone left through the backstage door, and I could see it was already growing light outside. "S-sure. You mean…now?"

"Yeah, mate. I'm going to hit the loo first and have a bit of a wash up, but yeah. I've got a loft nearby. Do you wanna come over and jam? I've got amplifiers up there, a nice bit of equipment."

I'm gonna jam with Clapton? Oh my God, somebody snap a Polaroid. "Shoot, I don't have my guitar."

He smiled ear-to-ear. "You're not intimidated, are you?"

"Uh-*yeah*. I mean—"

"You're not auditioning for the Royal Academy of Music, Sonny," he said in a fatherly tone. "Just a bunch of guys playing music. I've got a Gibson SG at my place you can use. Bring the Les Paul." Placing his hand on my shoulder, he said, "This is the way it works, Sonny. We spot talent, and we bring it into the fold." He checked his watch. "You good, then?"

"Yeah, I'm great."

"Be back in a tick," he said. "We'll stop along the way and pick up Jimi." He turned, leaving me with a blank stare on my face.

Jimmy, I thought. *Who's Jimmy?*

Chapter Seven

Filmore Auditorium, San Francisco, CA

June 20, 1967

Chas Chandler was a giant with a mop of hair and a round face. I'd met him in New York, but we'd never found the time to have a real conversation. Everyone was talking about how Jimi Hendrix had exploded onto the music scene. Chas was the guy who lit the fuse. "Jimi had a guitar in his hand from the moment he woke up this morning, Sonny. He's super excited to play this show, and you know how he is, a bleedin' perfectionist. The fanatic he is, he's going to wear his fingers down to the nubs before he hits the stage."

Chas and I were standing backstage at the Filmore. He was one of those guys with a lot to say, and once he got started… "I first saw Jimi at the Café Wha in Greenwich Village. He was going by the name Jimmy James back then, but you know what they say about a rose, don't you?"

"That they're red and violets are blue?"

He playfully slapped the back of my head with his big mitt. "No, you daft colonist punk. 'A rose by any other name would smell as sweet' is how it goes. I mean, it's Shakespeare. It's basic." He shook his head with dismay. "Didn't you learn anything in school? Isn't Shakespeare taught in your yank schools?" Chandler had a long, lumbering stride. I had to hustle just to keep up with him. "Jimi hadn't established his image yet, but the talent, mate, it couldn't be contained. I was gobsmacked the first time he got up on the stage. I knew right then and there what I could do for him. All I had to do was introduce Jimi to the world. I knew his talent would do the rest." Chandler was deeply entrenched in the London music scene. He'd been the bassist for The Animals and had played hundreds of shows internationally before switching hats and becoming Jimi's manager.

Checking his watch, "We've got about an hour before he goes on." He rolled his eyes. "As if, right?"

"As if what?"

"As if anyone in this biz is punching a bleedin' clock. I don't think he's ever hit the stage bang on time. He's got nine songs on the set list and wants to blow the audience away."

"How could he not?"

Chandler smirked. "Right then, you tell him that because he's as nervous as a hen. He needs you to challenge him. Got it? Dueling riffs back and forth, no holds barred. He said you impressed the shit out of him and Eric back in New York. That's why I flew your guitar-picking ass out here, Sonny. Go balls to the wall with him. Crank him up real good. Otherwise, he'll get depressed, dive into a case of vodka, and won't be worth a shit for days. I wouldn't be doing my job if I let that happen."

I had my guitar case slung over my shoulder as we walked through the backstage area at the Filmore. A group of young women were huddled together, singing "Blowin' in the Wind." I didn't realize until we had passed by that one of those ladies was Grace Slick. I turned back hoping to steal another glimpse of Jefferson Airplane's lead vocalist, but she had turned the other way. I was disappointed that we hadn't made eye contact, but at the same time felt it was electrifying to be in the company of so many rock icons. It was one of the things I loved most about the music business; everyone had been so welcoming. I'd been happily accepted by everyone I'd been introduced to. It seemed we were all part of one big happy family. One day, you were pumping gas, the next, you were hanging with world-class acts. Over the course of a few months, I'd jammed with some of the greatest rock guitarists in the world and was now breathing the same rarified air as

Grace Slick. I couldn't have been more jazzed and began rolling my fingers, warming them up in anticipation of jamming with Jimi Hendrix. I couldn't help but wonder how long that tsunami of good fortune would carry me or if I'd be crushed beneath the thundering tide. "I'll give it everything I've got, Mr. Chandler."

Chandler winked at me. "That's a good lad, Sonny, but lose the Mr. Chandler shit and just call me Chas. It's a young man's business, and I can't have anyone referring to me like I'm a bleedin' codger. You handle Jimi proper and I won't forget what you did. I see a spot for you, I'll be on the phone faster than you can say Jack Robinson—build an act around you, I will. Just like I did for Jimi, putting him together with Noel Redding and Mitch Mitchell."

Along with Hendrix, Noel Redding and Mitch Mitchell made up The Jimi Hendrix Experience, a power trio fashioned in the image of Cream, a group that in less than a year had made an indelible impression on the world of rock music. Hearing that offer from Chas's mouth sent a tidal wave of electric current surging through my body. I could feel my nerves tingling.

"I think I should mention that Jimi's a little hot under the collar," Chandler sighed. "My dimwit partner signed a deal to have Jimi tour with—" He shook his head, "The Monkees, the effing boy-band-Monkees. Do you believe that shite? After all I've done to promote Jimi as a serious artist? I'm working on unwinding the deal, but Jimi was right there with me when I got the call. As you Americans say, he's not a happy camper."

Who could blame him, a cutting-edge blues rocker, like Jimi Hendrix sharing the bill with a sugary sweet pop band formed for a TV show? I couldn't think of a dumber move and didn't know what to say, so I figured it was best to focus on the mission at hand. "What's Jimi leading off with?"

We were outside Hendrix's dressing room when Chandler laughed and slashed his gaze at me. He didn't have to answer, but I knew without being told. Hendrix would lead off with Howlin' Wolf's "Killing Floor," a song most lead guitarist considered too difficult to play at a live gig. It was the same song Hendrix played when he got up on stage with Cream at the London Polytechnic in October 1966. It was his first time playing in front of a British audience, and he slayed every last patron in the house, Clapton and his bandmates included.

Chandler opened the door, and I saw Jimi standing there playing his black Strat. His fingers were racing up and down the fretboard, firing off a musical rant, an angry, hostile assault of notes that bounced off the walls of the small room like particles fired through a nuclear collider. He paused when he saw me at the door, then went right back to it.

"Like lambs to the slaughter." Chandler snickered and closed the door behind me.

Chapter Eight

Forest Hills Stadium, New York

July 16, 1967

Jimi endured six excruciating gigs, opening for the Monkees. Yes, as Chas Chandler had put it, they were "The effing boy band Monkees." They were a fictional group created by NBC Television for a sitcom. I found their existence sad and their success a travesty. But here they were, years later, one of the hottest acts of the decade.

Chandler's words looped through my mind like a proverbial broken record as I jammed with Jimi in his dressing room before the seventh show. I could feel his pain with every note he picked. He seemed miserable, and I figured it was going to take a tractor to drag him onto the stage. The multi-gig foray sat like an elephant on his chest—Jimi wasn't Jimi. It was a clusterfuck of a venture, miles outside his comfort zone, crushing the man's soul. Including the Forest Hills concert, there were still twenty-two cities left to play. I didn't believe for a second he'd make it through to the end of the tour—it'd be a miracle if he made it halfway.

He trudged through T-Bone Walker's "Stormy Monday" and cringed while he played Albert King's "Born Under a Bad Sign" with lines of anguish cutting like razors into his face. I'd never heard him sing so sad and low—the tones were guttural. He wasn't playing the blues; he was living them, feeling them. The man was in horrible pain. Jimi was an artist, but more so, an individualist, a deadly serious musician who had been forced to get up on stage and play to thousands of teenage girls and their chaperoning mothers, audiences that had never heard of the Experience and were incapable of understanding Jimi or his music. He'd fire up the amps and break out into "Purple Haze" only to be bombarded by throngs of angry young girls jeering him with, "We want Davey. Boo. Hiss. We want Davey." For a free spirit like Jimi, it was a fate worse than death. Watching him slog through the door on his way to the stage was one of the saddest sights I'd ever witnessed.

I'd stayed around the dressing room to tune some of Jimi's guitars and was about to head to the stage when I heard a knock at the door. It was Chas Chandler.

"Is Jimi about?" he asked.

I didn't answer his question but instead spoke my mind. "I can't believe you did this to him."

Chandler cocked his head to the side. "I'm always the bad one. So, what did I do now?"

He'd told me how pissed off he was at his partner for setting up the tour, but I couldn't imagine a man of Chandler's cunning and experience couldn't break the deal. "You put him together with the bubblegum Monkees, and it's killing him. Tell me you can't see it."

"You think I'm a monster, don't you? Especially after I got on my high horse and told you my business partner was a dimwit for putting Jimi together with them."

I folded my arms and glared at him as I waited for an answer.

"Young man," he continued, "Jimi's been on board with it from day one, the whole enchilada."

"He *is*?"

"Most assuredly. I know that blows your mind, but once he thought about it… Chandler sat down on the sofa and gestured for me to sit down next to him, but I declined. I couldn't believe what I was hearing.

"Touring with the Monkees is Jimi's most direct route to international success. Yes, he's a musical genius and his career is off to a magnificent start in the UK, but he's got almost no following here in the States, no traction whatsoever other than a smattering of hardcore rockers with their ears to the ground. As good as he is, I don't know how long it'll take for him to chart here in the States. He's got three top ten hits in Jolly Old, but here…nada. As crazy as it may seem, and I know it seems daft, making the rounds with The Monkees will expose Jimi to hundreds of thousands of US fans he'd never gain access to. It'll positively jumpstart his career. You know who's promoting this tour, don't you?"

Of course, I knew. Everyone following the tour knew that Dick Clark himself was the driving force behind it. I nodded.

"Dick's a wicked smart bloke. When he put it to us the way he did, it made all the sense in the world."

"Maybe it does, but it's killing him."

"A bitter pill indeed but one Jimi was willing to swallow." He patted the couch once again, offering a seat. "Now, if you're satisfied with my explanation, there's another matter I want to discuss with you."

I wasn't feeling any better about what Jimi had to do, but I was intrigued and allowed my concerns take a backseat. "What's up?" I asked and plopped down on the couch.

Chandler had an odd expression on his face. He seemed pleased with himself. "Just before I jetted off to meet the tour stateside, I had dinner with Jack Bruce."

Jack Bruce was the bass player for Cream, the hottest rock trio on the planet and Eric Clapton's bandmate. I couldn't imagine where Chandler was going with this, but I was tingling all over.

"Jack confided in me," he said with peaked eyebrows. "Sadly, he doesn't see Cream lasting much longer."

"Why? They're killing it. They've started a musical revolution."

He smiled. "That's one of the things I love about you, Sonny. You're so hopelessly naïve. There's the music and there's the musicians, and both elements have to exist in perfect harmony. Jack and Ginger Baker never really got along. You might even say they detest one another. When Clapton agreed to join them to form Cream, it was with the condition that Jack and Ginger put their feuding aside, but that hasn't happened. Jack said that

Eric's very disillusioned and he believes Clapton's talking to Steve Winwood about putting together another group."

"Steve Winwood of Traffic?

"Correct."

"That's terrible," I said. "There's never been a group like Cream. They're the best of the best."

"No, lad, it's not terrible. It's just the way things are. Think of Cream as a super nova, a star that burns hot and dies young." His smile toyed with me. "And that's where you come in, young sir."

I felt a shiver run down my neck and into my back. What did the demise of the world's hottest super group have to do with me?

"Jack's got to look out for his own career, doesn't he? And when I asked what he was thinking, he said he'd like to put together a four-piece, adding a Hammond organ to the existing guitar, bass, drums arrangement. So, I asked if he had any players in mind and asked if he'd consider you for lead guitar. You've spent so much time jamming with Eric, I assumed Jack's heard you play, at least a smidge?"

"Both Jack and Ginger were around when we jammed, but I don't know how carefully they were focused on me."

"Well, it seems he was more focused than you thought he was. Now, no promises, but he's simpatico with you giving him a call." Chandler slapped me on the knee, then stood and handed me a scrap of paper with a telephone number scribbled on it. "Give Jack a call and let me know how it goes. I'll do what I do best and put the two of you together for a get-acquainted jam session." He winked at me and was about to leave the dressing room when Noel Redding, Jimi's bassist, burst into the room, panting, eyes wild.

"Jimi just flipped off the audience, Redding said. "He fucking quit."

Chapter Nine

Cape Coral, FL

One week later

I couldn't believe it—crack of dawn, and my dad was pounding on my bedroom door. It was Saturday morning, only four hours after I'd gotten in from the west coast. I was spent, physically and mentally exhausted. I'd become an insomniac since speaking to Chandler about getting together with Jack Bruce, my mind moving at a million miles per hour and my heart keeping pace. Falling asleep in my own bed, I was finally getting a sound night's sleep, and Dad's beating on the door was the least welcoming sound in the world.

Bang. Bang. Bang. "Santiago, get up," he said. "I can't be late."

"Ah, crap," I muttered and pulled the sheet over my head. "I can't," I called out. "I'm too tired."

"I'm not asking," he said. "Your mother made coffee and sandwiches. Ten minutes. I'll wait in the truck."

Silence returned, but it did nothing for my state of well-being. There was nothing I could do but drag my butt out of bed and get ready. My dad only asked for help with the big jobs, the work he truly couldn't handle on his own. I remembered that he was scheduled to paint the exterior of a two-story house in Fort Myers. I couldn't think of anything I wanted to do less than slop paint on shingles while twenty feet in the air, with temperatures in the high eighties and humidity even higher.

The transition was intolerable. I'd gone from the top of the world to the top of an extension ladder. I'd learned so much from Hendrix in the time we'd spent together, techniques it would've taken me years to master, if ever. I never understood how Hendrix managed to keep going. The pace the man kept, playing and practicing all day and partying all night long wasn't sustainable. The few hours of sleep I'd gotten in my own bed were more than I'd gotten on any night of the tour. My parents were asleep when I got home from the West Coast. We didn't have time to talk about the trip, the people I'd met, or the experiences I'd had. Learning at the knee of the great guitarists was an otherworldly experience—it was transformative.

Aside from smoking pot, I'd avoided the other street drugs that were everywhere we went, cocaine mostly, but also LSD and pills of every size and color. And booze? I'd never seen people drink the way these people did. The artists, technicians, and fans were wasted more hours than they were sober. And yet somehow, everyone did their job—equipment arrived on time, sound checks were executed, and artists showed up almost on time for their performances…most of the time. Being a rock fan took an inordinate amount of patience. Performers almost always arrived late, and there was often an equipment problem of one kind or another, a bad cable or a dead mike, a blown amp, or what have you.

"Mijo," you didn't fall back to sleep, did you?" My mother's voice was sweet and lyrical like the song of a dove. Her tone was always soft and welcoming. I heard the door open. "Can I come in?" she asked.

Pulling up my jeans, I sat down on the edge of my bed and rubbed my eyes. "Sure, Mamá."

She sat down next to me and brushed the hair from my eyes. "I'm so sorry, Sonny. We didn't even have a chance to talk about your trip, but your father really needs your help today. You know that he can't climb the ladder with his back so bad." She squeezed my cheeks. "You look *so* tired. What did those awful musicians do to you while you were away?"

"It was great, Mamá. I learned so much. Jimi Hendrix…he's a master guitarist. The things he can do with his Stratocaster—if I can be half as good as him some day…"

She smiled ear-to-ear. "This Jimi Hendrix, he's all you ever speak about when you call us on the phone. I think he's got you under some kind of spell. I hope he's not teaching you bad things as well. I read that there are so many drugs around these days, and musicians have always been known to abuse them. You must be careful, mijo. You're such a smart boy, but I've seen so many bright futures lost to addiction. I don't want that to happen to my son. Promise me you'll be careful."

"Of course, Mamá."

"Good." She leaned over and kissed me on the forehead. "Now, get ready and don't forget to brush your teeth. Your breath is strong enough to wilt flowers."

I covered my mouth and started off for the bathroom. I was peeing when the phone rang. I had just dried my hands when Mamá knocked on the door. "It's for you, mijo."

"At this hour?" I didn't have a single friend that woke up before noon. Some of them were probably just getting to bed after a night of bar hopping.

"An Englishman," she said. "A Chas Chandler."

Chandler was still in California when I left. He'd stayed behind to make peace with Dick Clark and The Monkees after Jimi demonstrated exactly how he felt about the audience. I didn't envy Chandler's job.

"Who is he?" she asked.

"A manager, Mamá. He manages Jimi Hendrix."

"I guess these English people don't sleep?"

I shrugged and rushed into the kitchen to take the call. "Hello, Chas?"

"Rise and shine, sunshine," Chandler said. "I hope you're not lollygagging about. I'm just about ready to go to lunch."

"You're back in London?"

"I surely am, and it's pissing cats and dogs as per usual. I ought to chuck the music business and go into foul-weather gear."

"What's going on? Is Jimi unhappy with me? I did my best to keep up with him, but he's so damn good. I've got blisters on my fingers that look like caterpillars."

"Nothing of the sort, lad. This ain't about Jimi. It's about *you*. You must have a four-leaf clover in your pocket. Not only does Jack Bruce want to talk to you, but I've got an opportunity for you that only comes along once in a lifetime. How do you feel about coming over London-side? Mick Jagger and Keith Richards are in the studio recording some piece of nonsense called Their Satanic Majesties Request. The record label has an awful lot of quid invested in a pre-Christmas release, and with all the legal appearances Mick and Keith have to make after getting busted on possession, the recording schedule has gone all to hell. The Beatles are scheduled to release Magical Mystery Tour about the same time, and the Stones are trying to keep stride. Follow?"

I was hearing but not listening. The cobwebs had yet to clear. "Wait a minute. Did you say The Beatles?"

"Yes, mate, The Beatles, *and* The Stones. Keith Richards and Bryan Jones are looking for a good session guitarist, and Jimmy Page isn't available. He's busy forming a new group of his own. Pays handsomely, lad. We'll fly you over and put you up, first class. Interested, are you?"

I'm not sure if I was breathing at that moment, but thinking back, I'm pretty sure my lungs had seized. "*Am* I?"

"Yes, mate, that's my question," he said with a chuckle. "Are you?"

* * *

I was atop a ladder less than an hour later, sloshing flamingo pink paint on siding shingles near a two-story roof peak with sweat pouring off me like Niagara Falls, my athletic shirt soaked and sticking to me like a second skin.

I didn't care and didn't need the ladder—I could've walked on air. Session work with the Rolling Stones, it was unimaginable, but Chas Chandler knew everyone in the London music scene, and having been in a top band himself gave him a ton of street credit. He wasn't a modest guy, and he said my CV spoke for itself. And with Clapton, Townshend, and Hendrix as references.... He said Keith was eager to meet me and determine if everything he'd heard about my playing was true.

I'd gone through a gallon of paint and was about to head down the ladder for another. My mind was somewhere else when I heard my father call out from the ground below. "Hey, careful." He pointed to where I'd smeared the vulgar pink paint on a window sash.

"Sorry, Pops," I said, calling down to him, then cleaned away my mistake with a rag.

He waved to me. "Take a break, Santiago. You're getting sloppy."

"I was just coming down anyway. I need more paint."

Dad held the ladder steady as I went down one rung at a time. He took the empty paint can from me, and we walked to his old truck side-by-side. "Drink something and cool off. We'll break for lunch before you go back up on the ladder." He glanced at the sky. "It's getting cloudy. It'll be easier for us to work without the sun roasting us like chickens on a spit."

I watched as he used the paint brush to salvage every last drop of paint from the empty can, pushing it into a freshly opened gallon. "Waste not, want not, huh, Pops." I popped the cap off a plastic gallon-size container of water and drank until my thirst was quenched, then handed the hose-filled bottle to him."

"What they charge for paint nowadays, it's crazy," he said. "Making ends meet is tougher than it used to be. That's why you have to go to college and have a good career, become an engineer or an accountant. Make money using your head and not your hands."

I looked down at my left hand, my fingering hand, the hand with which I had emulated the playing of one of the great guitarists just days before. The caterpillar blisters were painted bright pink. "I like using my hands."

He waved his hand dismissively. "I don't want to hear it, Santiago." He put the jug to his lips and drank, then pointed to the big house we were painting. "You see this place? The man who owns this house runs a business. He works in an office, not on a ladder, and he doesn't have blisters on his hands. No. You have to get a college degree. There's no two ways about it."

"I'm talking about playing my guitar, a professional musician, Pops. These last couple of months, I've been playing with some of the best guitarists in the world, Eric Clapton, Jimi—"

Dad opened the cooler and handed me a foil-wrapped sandwich. I didn't have to open it to know what was inside: tuna salad. I knew my Mamá—it was always tuna salad, and it was always good. The way she made it, I could eat it every day, and there were times I did.

"That's a pipe dream, son," he said. "All these musicians end up dead or broke. Drugs, booze, and the road, it's no way to live, no way to raise a family. You show me any successful musician, and I'll show you a drug addict. No sir, that's not the life I want for my son."

"You haven't even asked me how my trip was or who I played with in San Francisco. Don't you even care?"

"Of course I care, my son, and you can tell me all about it after we finish painting this rich man's house, which I've been putting off until you got home. While you were playing your guitar, this guy was cursing me out because he's having a big party and wanted his house painted beforehand." He held the tips of his thumb and forefinger a quarter inch apart. "I was this close to losing the job."

I pulled my wallet from my back pocket. Holding it open, I showed my father that it was filled with twenty-dollar bills. "I got paid, padre. I made more money than I ever made before. And I learned so much."

He put his hand behind my head and stroked my hair. His eyes were soft. "I'm very proud of you, Santiago, but how long will it be before you work again? How long do you think a few hundred dollars will last? You're a man now and you'll have a family and expenses one day. How long before the phone rings again?"

"It already did."

His eyes grew wide. "It did? I'm thrilled to hear it, and you can always earn a little extra money with your guitar. But real money?" He shook his head. "Listen to your old man. I've been kicked in the teeth more often than I care to remember. And being a Latino? It's even tougher. Doors won't open for you like they will for a white man. You have to be better. Smarter. You'll have to work harder to get ahead."

"It's obvious you don't want to hear me, and right now I don't care to listen to you. I was offered session work with the Rolling Stones. Does that sound like a little extra money? They're going to fly me to London to work on their next album, all expenses paid."

"Congratulations, Sonny. I'm very happy for you. Now, please eat your sandwich and get back up on the ladder before the sun comes out again." He reached into the cooler for a banana. "Look in the glove box. You got some mail while you were away. It may be important."

I needed space, space away from my father and his rigid, my-way-or-the-highway thinking. While he made camp at the base of a shady tree, I sat down in the cab of his old truck and chomped into my sandwich. My frustration had turned to hunger, and the sandwich was gone before I knew it—I hadn't even tasted it. "I will not be an accountant," I grumbled. "And I will not work in an office." I slammed my hand on the dashboard, and the glove box popped open. A thin stack of envelopes fell to the floorboard. I quickly rifled through the envelopes, one from my high school and one from Eileen Rosado, a girl in my history class. She spelled her last name with two hearts instead of O's. She was a sweet girl with a round face and big brown eyes who told me she was going to spend the summer with her aunt in Tampa. I'd save her letter to read at home, later, when I wasn't so damn angry. The letter at the bottom of the stack stunned me and confirmed exactly what I'd just said. I would not be an accountant, and I would not work in an office. Unfortunately, I wouldn't be playing guitar alongside Keith Richards either. The letter was from the Selective Service and marked Official Business.

III

PART THREE - NAM

Chapter Ten

8th Field Hospital, Nha Trang, Vietnam

Fall 1967; Two months after the bad jump

Nurse Ray helped me back to my bed. It was a short trip down the hall from the rehab unit but one I dreaded. Private Jack Winger had passed in his sleep while lying in the bed next to mine. She wasn't surprised when the autopsy revealed that he died of a pulmonary embolism just two days post op. She said he'd been complaining about dizziness and shortness of breath, but the attending physician didn't seem concerned and attributed his symptoms to the morphine he was getting for pain. All the doctors were overworked and undertrained. That wouldn't make the death notification any easier on the twenty-one-year-old's parents or the soldier who had to deliver the dreadful news. I remember how he looked when he returned from the OR, white as a sheet, a far cry from the robust, ruddy-complected Spavinaw, Oklahoma native, who had boasted he was going to break his hometown hero's homerun record when he got home. "The Mick" was in the twilight of his career but had already belted over 500 dingers, and they weren't those skimpy just-made-it-over-the-fence home runs. He'd damn near put most all those baseballs into orbit. Winger's was a bold claim coming from a kid whose femur was just put back together with metal rods and screws. Thinking about the bed he had occupied dropped a weight on my chest so heavy it made it near impossible for me to breathe.

"Rojas, you wimped out on your workout," Ray said. "Where's your grit, Sunshine?" She always ragged on me, calling me Sunshine because I'd grown up in Florida. "It's gonna reflect badly on me if I don't get you back to jumping hurdles." Ray was as wide as she was tall and all muscle. She had no trouble moving me around from one piece of rehab equipment to another. The woman looked like she could bench-press a jeep.

The screwed-up night jump had fucked me up big time. Nurse Ray knew it. The surgeon who'd screwed me back together knew. And despite all the sunshine that Ray and all the rehab personnel blew up my ass, I knew it as well. I was still in an upper-body corset and would be for another six weeks. Judging by the letters they'd written back, I think the shock of my injury had somewhat worn off, and my folks had no choice but to go about their lives again. I couldn't even begin to think about how many novenas my mother had said since hearing about me or how many candles she'd lit at church. I never believed in the power of prayer, but I'd gladly accept any help I could get from the Almighty or anyone else.

I spent most of my days reading, napping, and writing letters home with a transistor radio by my side playing the music I missed and loved so dearly. In between, I'd chew the shit with Winger to pass the time. Injured soldiers came and went practically every day. Most soldiers returned to active duty within thirty days, but that wasn't my path. I had a full six months of rehabilitation in front of me, and the military wasn't going to keep an unproductive soldier around sucking up Uncle Sam's resources. I was headed home with an honorable discharge, home and the local VA hospital. I'd be out of the Nha Trang as soon as the doc determined I was stable enough to be flown out on a transport plane.

I had no doubt my mom, Rosa, would monopolize every moment of archangel Saint Raphael's time. Rosa Rojas would make sure that if the power of prayer was capable of healing, it would heal her son, Santiago. With all that goodwill and healing prayers directed at me, I doubt any of the other men in the hospital received any of Saint Raphael's time. That poor child of God would be totally spent and have nothing left for anyone else after babysitting Rosa's baby boy.

Nurse Ray wasn't one to mollycoddle or nurture. Leg stretches and stabilization movements started on day one and were part of every session. She had me down on the floor doing leg curls and core strengthening exercises weeks before they were called for. "One more, Sunshine," she'd command. "And another. Don't quit on me, Sunshine. You're dogging it." She had her hand on my arm as I slogged back down the hall, not to support me in any way but out of compassion. "You're feeling kind of low, ain'tcha?"

"Winger. Man, that sucks," I said. He was older than me, but still looked like a kid. He had a scraggly soul patch but couldn't raise sideburns. Big brown eyes. "How the fuck?"

"Uh-huh. How the actual fuck did that snot-nosed surgeon miss Winger's embolism? These kids put their trust in Uncle Sam, and the cold, hard truth is that he turns his back on each and every one of you. Some of these so-called doctors aren't qualified to dispense aspirin. Yet here they are administering medicine to soldiers blown half to bits."

I winced and stopped dead in my tracks.

She came around, faced me, and shored me up with her muscular arms. "Are you going into spasm, honey?"

An ache smacked me dead center in my lower back that felt as if my spine was about to topple like a pile of stacked wooden blocks. I nodded with gritted teeth.

"We're almost back. I'll get you into bed and get you something for the pain. Just a little further. Do you think you can make it or should I—"

"No," I groaned.

"Okay," she said. "Just a few more steps." She moved to my side and put her arm around me, somehow shifting my position enough to move me forward. "I'll get you settled in and get you your pain meds."

If the military was good for anything, it was handing out morphine. It was suitable for what ailed you and most other complaints a soldier had. Some took it just because. But with my level of pain, I was popping pills like they were Pez candies. We were only about ten feet from my room in one of the single-level taxpayer-structured buildings that were organized like dominoes in a seemingly haphazard arrangement. I'd just gotten through the doorway when my knees buckled, partly because of the spasm that racked me from my tailbone to the base of my neck and partly because there was someone new in Winger's bed.

Chapter Eleven

"About damn time you woke up," the soldier now residing in Winger's bed said. He was flat on his back with head turned in my direction. "I've been studying you on and off for the last two hours. You're Rojas, right? Anyone tell you that you snore loud enough to wake the dead?"

The morphine fog was slow to lift. My head hurt, but not so badly that I wasn't aware of the fire blazing along my spine. I turned my head slowly. The man in Winger's bed was a total stranger, a soldier about my age with a square jaw and sandy brown hair. "Who the hell are you?"

"What have you done for me lately, huh, Rojas? Is that the way it's gonna be?" He didn't sound glib but strained as if he too was in great discomfort.

"Sorry, man. Do I know you?" I asked.

"Roswell," he said, a moan punctuated his name. "I'm the Huey pilot who found your smashed-up ass and flew you over to the 12th Evac hospital." He tried to shift his position, grunted, and abandoned the attempt. "You're not big on gratitude, I guess."

I'd been told that a Huey pilot found me lying in the stream, but not his name. I extended my arm off the side of the bed toward him, and he did the same, giving me a light slap across the fingers, a lame-ass high-five if ever there was one. "Two gimps, I suppose it's the best we can manage." Roswell's hair was sort of long for an enlisted man. He said he was a pilot, which made him a warrant officer by rank. I guess they cut the fly boys some slack on the hair-length regs. "Thanks, man. Really. I don't know what to say."

"A nurse at the Cu Chi hospital told me you'd be moving out just as soon as you were stable enough to be transported to a fully equipped hospital. Never dreamed I'd see you here—not in the next fucking bed anyway. You were completely out of it the last time I saw you. The nurse said they had you drugged out of your mind so that you could handle the pain." He managed to laugh weakly. "I guess not much has changed. They get you patched up, okay?"

"You should see my X-rays. I've got more metal in me than a big-block V8. Have to change my oil every two thousand miles."

"No shit?"

"No shit. You take out your compass, and it'll point to me."

Roswell grinned. "I saw you hobble through the doorway. You went down like a ton of bricks. I think Nurse Ray has a soft spot in her heart for you. She hit you up with enough morphine to drop a Clydesdale."

"Don't know what I'd do without the pain meds. My back hurts something awful. Sometimes I feel like someone's yanking on a lynchpin and all my vertebrae are gonna come apart. Anyway, what are you doing in here?" I asked.

"Uncle Sam's not done with me yet. For me, it's just a quick thirty and out," he said. "Fell out of the sky and popped a couple of discs on impact. Doc shaved down the bulging discs this morning. It'll be a while before they let me fly again, but they'll find a spot for me in the command center until I'm ready to take up a helo."

"You take fire and get shot down?"

"Nah. It was someone's dumb-ass mistake. I fired on a target, and the rocket went off too soon, like a split-second after I fired it. The shockwave from the explosion knocked out my controls. I set the Huey down as best I could, but the jolt bounced me like a Spalding. Lucky for me, another helo landed and got me out of there before the enemy found the wreckage."

"Sounds like one of the munitions lackeys screwed the pooch. I guess you were flying at low altitude."

"Sometimes you've got to come down so low to take a shot that the VC fires down on you from up in the mountains. It's tense, but you can't hit shit when the Huey's way up yonder. You've got to come down real low and close. Never thought I'd fire on the enemy and blow myself out of the air. Ain't that a kick?" He winced. "I swear the doc must've sewed me up with meat hooks. Small injury like mine, he probably sliced off the bulging discs with a field knife." He ran his tongue over his lips. "So, how was it you ended up where you were? I didn't see any other chutes nearby. You jump alone?"

"I'd subsequently learned how our 700-foot night jump went wrong. There'd been a mechanical malfunction with the plane, and we were actually above 2000 feet when we left the aircraft. Unforeseen winds blew the entire team off course. We each landed separately in dense jungle, nowhere near our intended target. Many of my team members were wounded in the jump. Including myself, three of us were evacuated. Fortunately, the others escaped capture by the VC."

Roswell absorbed the report and didn't seem surprised. "So, we both got nailed by mechanical failure," Roswell said. "Weird? Bad enough, we're fighting this dumbass war in this stinking-hot jungle without soldiers getting effed-up by their own side. You got one of those million-dollar wounds?"

"Yes, sir." I'd only heard the expression since coming to the hospital in Nha Trang. It was enlisted man slang that meant I'd sustained a non-crippling wound serious enough to warrant discharge and a return ticket to the States. They'd keep me around at the Nha Trang hospital just long enough to ensure the long plane ride home wouldn't undo all the delicate work the surgeons had performed on me. They'd ship me out with a jar full of painkillers and the address of the local VA hospital. Uncle Sam was going to wash his hands of me, but I didn't feel self-pity. So many young men were going home without arms or legs. Fractured minds. Broken wills. Lying in caskets. I hadn't been deployed long enough to witness the gut-wrenching horrors of war so many others had experienced. The night jump had gone completely sideways, but at least it hadn't fucked up my hands. The doc said I might have a limp, but I didn't take the news too hard. I'd still be able to play my guitar, and I'd be damned if I wasn't going to be the best guitar picker there ever was.

Chapter Twelve

More than three weeks had passed since I'd first found John Roswell in Jack Winger's bed, barely enough time for me to get used to not seeing Winger's face first thing in the morning and certainly not long enough for his bed to be turning over again. How many would come and go before I received medical clearance to return home to the States? How long would it be before I could make it to the latrine and back under my own steam? Physical rehab wasn't going great. My pain level was still off the chart, and opioid intake had shaved my productivity down to jack shit. No one told me how badly morphine clogged up the plumbing works. I spent more time on the commode than in the therapy room, and I was dead tired all the time. Nurse Ray had to repeatedly amp up the dosage just to keep the pain at bay, and the docs didn't have time to monitor my sedative usage.

Though I missed Winger something fierce, Roswell was good company. Sure, he had some pain from his surgery, but he understood that it was nowhere as bad as mine. He did his best to distract me and did as fine a job as anyone could, telling jokes, talking sports, and what have you. He never said I owed him my life, never so much as dropped a hint. But I felt it as well as the connection that had grown between us. Turns out he was a Florida boy like me, Naples, Florida to be exact, about an hour's drive down the road from where I grew up and lived. A lot of folks from Naples had money, and I figure that was the case with John because his dad was some kind of engineer. John was down to earth. We were just two injured soldiers, chewing the shit and passing time. He told me about the nurse who gave him a penicillin shot in 12th Evacuation Hospital in Cu Chi, only he called the city Coochie Coochie because he rarely went to bed alone while he was on leave anywhere near Ho Chi Minh City. I don't think we ever had a conversation that didn't involve his sexual escapades in some way, shape, or form. Mostly shape and form.

"There was this time, Rojas, when I was hornier than a three-balled billy goat, but our CO wouldn't let us leave the base. But did that stop me? No-effing-way. I'd had a double ration of beer and was feeling no pain. Not that I knew what I was doing, but I kind of wandered off, hoping I'd get lucky, maybe meet a pretty little village girl or something. All of a sudden, I heard motorbike engines. You know the high-pitched sound those little rice burners make, like you wacked a hornet's nest and those nasty-ass things were buzzling like all get out? Well, that's what it sounded like. I jumped behind some brush, but I guess they saw me before I could duck down. I have to tell you, I was plenty nervous, but wouldn't you know it, those two motorbikes came to a stop. Two pimps with boom-boom girls riding on the back."

I cocked my head. "Hookers?"

"Portable hookers. Short skirts. Heavy makeup. They jumped off those bikes and before I knew it…"

"No shit."

"Rojas, I shit you not. I paid for the girls and bought a joint from one of the pimps." He smiled like the Cheshire cat. "We had a good old time."

"Hey," Nurse Ray shouted. I'd been so engrossed in Roswell's story I didn't realize she had come our way. She had the forearms of a longshoreman and had the back of her hand poised, ready to swat Roswell across the face. I cringed. She lunged at him but held up just short of his nose.

He held his hands up defensively. "Easy now," he said. "It's just guy talk."

"Guy talk my patootie. I can't tell you how badly I'd like to close that dirty mouth of yours, Roswell. You think you're cool, bedding all of them innocent girls what got no choice in the matter? You think they see anything other than the green in your wallet or that they'd be doing what they're doing, trudging around a stinking hot jungle night after night, having sweaty dirtbags like you lay on top of them if they didn't fear for their lives? Trust me, soldier, you're not that much of a catch."

"Geez, Nurse Ray, there's a war going on out there. Some doofus messed up my ordnance and blew me out of the fucking sky. Could you maybe cut me some slack?" Roswell said.

"No, but I will cut you loose. You're shipping out, soldier. Paperwork came through this morning."

"Already? Seriously?" he asked.

"That's right. They need your helo-flying ass back in the sky where it can do some good. All you had was an itty-bitty discectomy, you damn goldbrick. How long did you expect Uncle Sam to let you sit on your lazy ass suckling the government's teat?"

"You know what they say," Roswell began, "any teat in the storm."

Ray's hand flashed, this time grazing his cheek on the upswing. "I trust you can make it down the hall to the office for your assignment. Make yourself scarce, Roswell." She folded her arms and scowled. Roswell still moved gingerly. He put his feet down from the far side of the bed and kept his eyes glued on her until he was out of the ward.

Still peppery, she swung her gaze in my direction. "Jerks like that only talk shit because someone's dumb enough to listen. I didn't think that was you, Sunshine."

It's not. I mean— "Sorry." But what could two wounded soldiers do to fill twenty-four long hours a day but sleep, play cards, and talk shit? "We were just passing the time." Our conversation wasn't anything out of the norm, just blank-minded bullshit any two soldiers would share to kill time. I'm sure she'd overheard exactly the same harmless conversations a hundred times before. I didn't know what had gotten her so pissed off, but something had touched a nerve. She turned her back on me and walked out the door, but returned a moment later, dragging a large rectangular box.

"Here," she said, leaving it at my bedside. She placed a box cutter on my side table. "Someone must be thinking about you." She didn't wait around to see what was inside but I knew from the size and shape of the box that the treasure inside was a guitar. I hadn't touched one in months and didn't know who was capable of getting one to me, here in the middle of nowhere. My fingertips were tingling as I reached for the boxcutter and pulled the box up onto the bed. I sliced the twine and tape that bound the box. Discarding the bindings, I noticed that the shipping label was postmarked Mayfair, London. The top corner of the box was filled with red and blue stamps, each bearing a picture of the queen. I slid the clamshell case out of the box and allowed the empty cardboard box to tumble onto the floor, then popped the latches on the case. Resting within was a gorgeous yellow spruce Martin D-21 acoustic guitar. A small, folded note was laced between the strings.

Hear you're homeward bound, mate. Jimi didn't want you lying around getting rusty. Would've sent you an electric, but I didn't think you'd have any place to plug it in. Enjoy the Martin.
Godspeed,
Chas Chandler

Chapter Thirteen

Two months after discharge

Back home in Florida, I was still in bed as I reached for the amber bottle of Darvon and popped the top. This would not be a use-as-directed day. I shook two tabs into my palm, chewed, and swallowed them dry before snapping the white cap back on the cylindrical plastic bottle. Codeine was up next. Four tabs. Chewed dry. I could've called out for my mama, and she would've happily refilled my bedside glass of water, but I didn't like her seeing me first thing in the morning, stiff as a board and unable to move until the drugs worked their magic. She deserved better. It wasn't her fault I woke up every two hours, slugging water all night long. Nor was it my fault the C-130's onboard altimeter had messed up something awful on our night jump into VC territory.

Uncle Sam liked to pat himself on the back before giving his vets a boot in the ass. The support of my mom and dad aside, I was on my own. Like so many returning from Vietnam, I would never be the man I'd been. I'd returned home in one piece, one brittle piece, a flesh and blood plank of a man held erect with steel screws and rods. According to the Marines, I was a whole person, a fully functioning veteran. They wiped their hands of me, conscience clean.

Mamá would head off to work soon, stitching kids' clothing in a small factory near the pier. She'd check on me before heading out to see if I needed anything and provide a comprehensive inventory of every meal she'd prepared and left for me in the fridge. I'd greet her with one eye open, yawning, a ploy I knew that wouldn't work forever. Maybe it wasn't working now, but she hadn't complained about how late I slept. Not yet anyway. She was still overjoyed to have her son back home, alive. I didn't enjoy deceiving her and hoped I wouldn't always need to, but for now, it was the best I could come up with. Each morning, I waited until she was gone and the house was empty before attempting movement, filling the silent house with gut-wrenching grunts as I attempted to sit up in bed, sweating bullets, panting.

The Martin guitar Jimi had sent over to Vietnam had made it back to the States intact and pristine. I kept it at my bedside and took it in hand first thing every morning. It seemed to fit so perfectly, resting on my lap as the codeine's melancholy ran through my veins. We were one. My spine was rigid, but my fingers were still very much alive, my ears still keen to hear the music that resonated from the Martin's sound hole. Drowning in sleep juice and pain meds, those morning hours were the best part of my day. With pillows propping me up, I somehow managed to find a reasonably comfortable position and played until my fingers cramped. Hunger didn't kick in until mid-afternoon. My need to visit the bathroom was infrequent. The doc at the VA hospital warned me that my meds would cause constipation and something he called urinary retention, something I didn't like the sound of. Before getting drafted, I didn't so much as swallow an aspirin, and I was now wolfing down pills of every shape and color imaginable. I hated taking them but didn't have a choice. I tried to convince myself that it was only temporary, that I'd eventually be able to wean off the painkillers. Part of me hoped it was true. The bigger part of me didn't seem to give a damn.

The VA doc told me to drink a lot of water and take laxatives if needed, then handed me a stack of prescription slips to fill at the pharmacy down the hall. There was a long line of vets waiting for their prescriptions to be filled. Wounded men like me were waiting for their pain killers, and men that needed help with their brains waited for anti-depressants, anti-psychotics, and what have you. Those pharmacists were handing out so many painkillers, I figured they'd be better off with a barrel of pills and a big metal grain scooper than with their itty-bitty pill counters. I think they would've gone along with my recommendation if given the chance. The doc said we'd discuss another surgery if my discomfort didn't lessen, one to correct the mistakes the first surgical team had made. I wasn't exactly eager to go back under the knife. The field docs hadn't hit it out of the park on their first go-round. I figured I'd give it a year and see how I was at that point.

My buddy, Lorne's timing couldn't've been better. I'd miraculously managed to get on and off the commode in under thirty minutes, a feat I hadn't accomplished in weeks. I'd just washed my hands when the doorbell rang. He continued to knock while he waited for me to hobble to the front door. He wasn't impatient, just distracted. I knew he'd have an earphone stuck to the side of his head and a transistor radio in his hand. It took him a moment to react to me standing in the open doorway. Lorne was Cape Coral's answer to John Lennon, long hair, pork chop sideburns, and wire rim glasses—a cigarette dangled from his lip. The big difference was his blonde hair and sun-bronzed skin. He was like a celluloid negative of the pasty-faced Brit, light where Lennon was dark, dark where he was light. He spoke cockney English at every opportunity but was about as Scouse as short ribs and got called out on the phony accent all the time. It didn't stop him from offering what he believed to be a John Lennon-like greeting. "G'day, mate." He raised a paper grocery bag, "Fancy beans and toast?"

He must've read somewhere that beans and toast was to Brits what peanut butter and jelly was to Americans. Chas Chandler offered me a taste one morning out on the west coast, and once was more than enough. "You go too far, man," I said holding the door open for the wannabe Beatle to pass through. "Eating like John Lennon isn't going to turn you into a rock phenom," I said. Lorne walked in and straight into the kitchen. He had his grocery bag on the kitchen counter and unpacked well before I caught up with him.

"Still moving slow?" he asked. "What'd the doc say?" He began sliding kitchen drawers, open and closed. "Where do you keep the can opener?" he asked, holding up a big can of Heinz beans.

"Behind you—the drawer next to the sink."

He found what he was looking for and crimped it onto the can of beans, then turned back and saw me grimace as I struggled to sit down in one of the kitchen chairs. They were old wooden chairs with lathed spindles and unpadded seats. Getting into it was like forcing a square peg into a round hole. "So, what are they gonna do about that?"

"Just what they've been doing," I said with a long sigh, "exercise, rest, and painkillers. They said it could be a year until I'm back to normal."

"A year, huh?" He turned away from me and grabbed two plates out of the plate rack. "That's a long time to hurt so badly." A clean saucepan sat on the stove. He emptied the beans into it and lit the burner. "Think you'll want to play some after we eat?"

My fingers were still sore from playing before he arrived, but it wouldn't stop me from getting in more guitar time. Playing guitar was one of the few things left I could enjoy. "Sure." I'd let him play the Martin, and I'd play my dad's old José Fernández Spanish guitar. Dad had it forever and went a little crazy the last time Lorne used it because his belt buckle left scratches on the back. Having learned from experience, I'd have Lorne take off his big-ass Garrison belt before we jammed.

It wasn't long before he set two plates of English slop down on the table. I looked at it and my mouth dried up. I tried to force my hand to pick up the fork but couldn't make it happen. My appetite was nonexistent. I wasn't eating a ton of the delicious food my mama prepared, and this plate of unsavory goop didn't interest me at all. Meanwhile, Lorne went at his food with rabid enthusiasm. I imagined that with every bite, he was trying to channel the energy of the great British rock bands. We were in the throes of the British invasion after all and acts from the UK were dominating the rock scene. The Beatles, Cream, The Who, The Rolling Stones, The Kinks, The Yardbirds, and The Animals were some of the powerhouse bands that made up the unstoppable musical tidal wave that had swept across America.

Lorne looked up, studying me with a fork to his mouth. "Try it, would you? It's not half bad."

I picked up a bean, a solitary bean, and tasted it. I was barely able to get it down. "Maybe later." I writhed in my chair, adjusting my posture to get comfortable, but comfort was not in the cards. The pain meds took the edge off, but there was always a constant ache to deal with.

"Dude, it's hard for me to see you like this."

"Hard for you? It's not exactly a picnic for me. Finish up your Limey lunch and let's play some music."

"Soon as I'm done." He continued to scarf down his baked beans, using the toast to corral them onto his fork. He looked up when he was done, then reached into his pocket and withdrew a small glassine envelope.

"*Whoa*. Is that coke?"

"Nuh-uh, bud."

"Horse?"

He nodded. "It's good for what ails you, and are you ever ailing."

I was stunned at the ease with which he admitted to using heroin. Lorne was heavy into pot and hash, but I never knew him to use anything stronger. "How long?"

"A couple of months now. I think you ought to give it a try. It'll make your day a whole lot brighter."

"Yeah, I don't know. Maybe you ought to put that away." My mama worked too far away to stop in and check on me, but my dad was known to pop by once in a while, and he'd freak out if he saw a bag of heroin on the table. Lorne flicked the bag with his finger, enticing me to give it a try. I'd been in pain practically every day since waking up in the military hospital—something within me was crying out for relief.

"One small hit," he said as he tapped two small mounds on the table, one in front of each of us. I didn't know much about hard drugs. I thought heroin had to be injected into a vein and was surprised when he used the corner of a matchbook to shape the small piles into lines. Before I knew it, his nose was pressed to the table, hoovering the powder up his nose. I thought he'd become drowsy immediately, but he didn't seem any different to me after snorting the drug. "It's not as fast-acting as mainlining," he said. "You've got more control like this, a good ten minutes before it hits you." He looked at me expectantly. "Give yourself a break, Sonny. You look like you really need it." He let the bag sway at the end of his fingertips, hypnotizing me with it like it was a gold pocket watch. I could feel it luring me into its grasp.

IV

PART FOUR - NABBED

Chapter Fourteen

London, England

August 15, 1968

Ringo Starr walked into the Church Road recording studio after a ten-day absence. The words from the telegram he'd received from his bandmates were likely still fresh in his mind. You're the best rock 'n roll drummer in the world. Come on home. We love you.

Ringo had quit The Beatles, the most significant rock band in the world, after playing with them for almost seven years. He felt the group's magic had died, and his relationships with the others had gone sour, making him feel like an outsider. It was the endearing words on the telegram that convinced him to return to the band. It made him realize that all four members were feeling like outsiders and that his departure had brought the situation to a head.

He arrived to see his drum kit covered with flowers. After soaking in the massive gesture, he took in the rest of the studio. There were flowers everywhere.

"Do you like them?" George Harrison asked in a warm tone.

Ringo smiled tenderly. He knew without asking that the flowers were George's doing. He loved all his bandmates, but his relationship with George was special. Their roles in the band had always been subordinate to Paul's and John's. They'd always been the underdogs. Paul and John represented the band's world of songwriting talent, and it seemed that it was always George and Ringo against the world. But Ringo was feeling particularly good about himself at that moment. He felt the band had endured its crisis and emerged on the other side. He'd just returned from holiday in Sardinia and was feeling renewed. The look in his eyes conveyed a message, which he immediately put into words: "Well, are you just going to stand about, or are we getting to work?"

"We're still working on 'While My Guitar Gently Weeps,'" George said. "We've been trying to record it, but it seems to me that John and Paul are so used to cranking out their own tunes that it's difficult for them to get serious about something I wrote. I don't think they're taking it seriously, which is a shame because I think the song is pretty good."

"Sometimes I think the White Album will be the death of us all. Anything I can do to help?" Ringo asked.

"I'm not sure. The other lads are about to take off. I plan on staying late and working out the guitar bits for the song."

"I'd offer to hang around with you as well, but I know how you get when you're trying to work out your phrasing. I'm sure you prefer peace and quiet to my banging around on the kit while you're deep in concentration."

"I'm working on a particular sound I have in mind, and I don't want to use a wah-wah pedal. I'm fooling around with a reverse solo of sorts."

"Hmm, a reverse solo, you say. I'm not sure what that is, but message received. I'll leave you to it," Ringo said with a formal salute. "I'll be back in the morning." The studio door opened, and a slight young man walked in holding a Gibson Les Paul guitar. He had a hitch in his step, and his posture was askew. "Haven't seen that chap about before. Apple Records is signing so many new acts, I can hardly keep track of them all."

"Yeah, that's Sonny Rojas," George said. "He's one of Eric's friends from America. The poor bloke got cracked up badly jumping out of a helicopter in Vietnam. Eric asked me if we had any work for him, and well, I couldn't say no. He's been working on my guitar all day, getting it to play just so."

"Vietnam, huh?" Ringo said as he turned his gaze toward the lad. "Bleedin' farse that war is. Old Lyndon Baines is sending a lot of young boys to the grave." He gave George a hearty slap on the shoulder. "You've got a solid gold heart, m'boy, solid gold." He watched Rojas slowly cross the studio. "The lad looks knackered. Are you working him to death, or is Apple Records paying his wages with snowballs?"

"Who's not using these days?" George said with a shrug. "I'm not sure what he's into, but he's more than earned his keep so far. Hasn't missed a day yet, and it turns out the bloke's got a tremendous facility for playing blues guitar just like Eric said. Comes up with some clever riffs. I asked him to stay and help me work on the song tonight."

"Then I imagine we'll be ready for another go in the morning," Ringo said with his trademark bravado. "It's been a terribly long day, and I've got a hankering to drain a pint or two," he said, feigning a yawn. "I'm off."

Chapter Fifteen

January 10, 1969

George Harrison wagged his finger at me in a very un-George-like manner as he walked out the door of the monolithic studio at Twickenham. He was a gentle soul and always considered the feelings of others. Beckoning me with a hand gesture was not like him at all, but I didn't take offense. I'd witnessed firsthand his degradation during The Beatles' rehearsal of a new song they were working on.

He put his arm over my shoulder in a very fatherly manner as we left the studio. "Are you high, Sonny?"

I shook my head. "No. Is everything okay?"

"Can you drive me home?" he asked and extended his hands. He was perpetually calm, but his hands were shaking. "Did you hear what went down in there?"

I gritted my teeth. "All of it. I'm sorry you had to go through that."

"It was humiliating. I hate it when Paul's God complex rears its ugly head."

I'd worked closely with George Harrison for almost six months. Even though the man was constantly evolving, I knew him about as well as anyone could at that point in time. I perhaps knew him less well than his wife, Maddie, but certainly better than the bandmates he'd been with since 1958. They seemed to have lost their grasp of George's need to contribute and to feel valued. The genius that was George Harrison was a deep well filled with endlessly churning waters. He was quiet and introspective, always thinking about the world and his place in it. I think it was his close connection to the planet that made him such a unique guitarist and songwriter.

As I sat nearby and watched The Beatles rehearse, it came as no surprise why George reacted the way he had. The band had made an enormous commitment to perform a new album in front of a live audience and had only a few short weeks to write, arrange, and rehearse the music, putting the group under unbearable pressure. If I'd been a betting man, I could've almost predicted the moment when George would explode.

He detested the sterile soundstage environment of Twickenham Studios. To me, it was as cold as ice. The walls were stark white with towering ceilings, and it made me feel as if I was trapped inside a giant refrigerator. My guess was that it impressed George similarly.

He handed me the key to his car and walked around to the passenger side door to get in. I'd always hoofed it to the recording studio or taken public transportation, an occasional taxi when there was no other choice. I'd never driven in London and certainly had never been behind the wheel on the right side of the car.

"You look nervous," he said.

"I've never—"

He dismissed me with a wave of his hand. "I don't care. I've just got to get away from here. Can we go, please?"

I started the car and slowly pulled out into traffic, careful not to kill myself or one of the most important musicians in the world. I drove like I was playing chess, thinking three and four steps ahead at a time, when to turn, when to brake, focused intently on any car or pedestrian that might venture into our path. George was slow to call out directions, which made me even more tense.

My navigator had nothing much to say as we traveled to his home in Surrey. It was painful to see him relive those moments, and I imagine the entire morning at Twickenham was looping through his mind. Those last few minutes before the band was about to break for lunch…brutal. It had to be sheer misery for him. I could hear him in my head as we traveled the road.

George: Well, I think I'll be leaving the band now.

John Lennon: When?

George: Now. See you 'round the clubs.

And then he left with me in tow. I didn't realize it then, but my devotion to George must've irritated John, and I think he came to see me as George's spy. I felt John's irritation when I returned to Twickenham the next day. John forced his Epiphone guitar into my hand.

"Make it sing," he said with contempt in his voice, then turned away to discuss something with Paul. As I walked off, I heard him mutter, "Mir Jafar," which I later learned was a name synonymous with traitor.

George rejoined the band five days later. Though he did his best to shield me from John, the man was set in his ways. The handwriting was on the wall, as they say. It was time for me to move on.

Chapter Sixteen

I thought I had a couple of bags hidden away, but I was wrong or was too strung out to find them. The shakes had kept me up all night, so I left at first light and headed to Piccadilly, where Dr. Robert had practiced ever since I'd arrived in London. Obtaining narcotics in the UK wasn't the same as scoring drugs in New York. It wasn't regulated. Use and purchase wasn't criminalized nor had it been in the past. It was treated as a sickness and not a crime. But as Dylan sang, "The Times They Are A-Changin.'" The Brits were now passing new laws as quickly as they could think of them, and many of the penalties were harsh. I wasn't much for newspapers, but it was common knowledge they were handing out multi-month sentences for criminal possession.

To my astonishment, Dr. Robert's clinic was shackled. Not locked. Shackled, with a massive padlock on the front door. Poking around, I noticed his side window was broken, and only security bars prevented stray users from entering and scoring heroin themselves.

Strung out and off his face, a Piccadilly local I recognized was sound asleep on the sidewalk beneath said broken window. "Hey, man, what's going on here?" I asked. No movement. No response. I nudged his shoe, but the lad was too far under to hear me. I should've checked to see if he had a pulse, but I didn't. I needed to get right in a bad way. Back in front of the clinic, I figured a familiar face would show up sooner rather than later.

It was that life, you know. When you needed it, you needed it bad, and Dr. Robert was a popular destination for London users.

Three minutes and bam, a familiar face. Javier was lean with Duane Allman-like pork chop sideburns. We had chatted in the waiting room here and there. "Brother, what's going on?" I asked. Coming to a halt, his eyes were clear and his hands steady. It gave me hope—he'd recently scored.

"Sonny, right?"

I nodded.

"You haven't heard, mate? Coppers shut him down. Carted old Doc Robert away."

"Why?"

"Mate, you've got your head wedged up your bum good and proper. Robert never registered the way he should've. He's been dispensing without a valid license."

The doctor's jail time was none of my concern. I was only hearing bad news. Robert was gone. I needed a fix and didn't know where to get one. "Hook me up, brother. My back is seriously messed up, and I'm twitching like a dog trying to shit a chicken bone. I need a fix."

"You got scratch? I can help ya, but you've got to have moolah. This bloke ain't looking for junkie blowjobs, savvy? Buggery don't buy what it used to."

Thank God I hadn't descended to that depth. Reaching into my pocket, I showed him my cash. I would've handed him my savings account passbook if he'd asked to see it.

"You'll take care of me too, won'cha?" he asked.

"Sure, sure. I'll heal you, brother. How far?" Turning in every direction, I hurt so badly I hoped I could see the supplier from where I stood.

He motioned with a turn of his head. "Five-minute walk. This way." He had long legs and took off like a shot.

The back injury had rendered me a notoriously slow walker, but I somehow found another gear and motored after the Duane Allman lookalike. Getting well was calling to me, a siren's voice luring me to my demise.

Chapter Seventeen

I didn't know where I was when I woke up but felt sure that Piccadilly was in the rearview mirror. My head hurt something awful and pounded nonstop. The cobwebs cleared slowly, and I remembered my last moments of consciousness. Javier's guy explained how Dr. Robert's patients had cleaned him out, and he didn't have any pure heroine, only Karachi, a mixture of heroine, phenobarbital, and methaqualone. I sat down on his couch, fixed, and got knocked on my ass. Coming around, my head spun and didn't feel as if it would stop, but my hands were steady. I had completely forgotten that I had a spine constructed from potato chip crumbs.

On the downside, I was handcuffed and sitting on a bench in an official-looking building. There was no doubt in my mind—I'd been arrested and was awaiting arraignment in Old Bailey, the Central Criminal Court of England and Wales. Shit!

To date, I'd only seen it from the outside and learned it had been in use since 1902. It was a massive structure attached to a prison. Back in the days of barbarism, sentences like hanging and being drawn and quartered were handed out for severe crimes. Thank God those days were no more.

It felt as if I was shackled to that bench for hours before a bald gent approached me wearing an official robe of the court. "Santiago Rojas, I am Lester Ledger, I'll be serving as your solicitor, or as you yanks call it, your lawyer."

"Why do I need a lawyer?" I asked. "All I did was—"

"You're not a citizen of the crown, Mr. Rojas. You are here as a guest, and you've abused that privilege by engaging in an illegal activity."

"Since when is drug use a crime in England?"

"Since 1967, m'boy. The year the Dangerous Drugs Act was passed. It empowers the police to search and detain any person suspected of committing an offense under drug laws."

"Dr. Robert has been treating me with heroin for almost two years. What's changed?"

I don't know this Dr. Robert, but if he's like a lot of old-time physicians, he hasn't paid attention to or has ignored changes in the law, just hoping he won't get caught. The police are coming down hard on these junkie doctors who fail to keep prescription registers. I surmise time ran out on this Dr. Robert of yours, and as I said, penalties can be very harsh. Last year, a journalist was sentenced to nine months just for buying a small bit of marijuana."

I felt a cold sweat break out on the back of my neck. I wasn't sure if I needed more dope or if my nerves were shot. "So what happens to me now? I'm late for work and don't want to lose my gig."

"Gig? You're a musician?"

"I play guitar."

Ledger's eyes became dull. His throat sounded dry when he spoke. "My boy William played tenor saxophone. I lost him to drugs about a year ago."

"I'm sorry. The music biz is no walk in the park."

"Why do so many of you turn to drugs? Is there no other way?"

"I use because I got injured in Vietnam. Field docs turned my spine into chop suey. I think most of us are trying to reach a higher level of consciousness. I've played with Jimi Hendrix, and I'm sure that's why he used so often. Me, I'm just trying to make it through each day."

"You played with Jimi Hendrix?"

"I did. These days, I play with George Harrison."

"*The* George Harrison?"

"Far as I know, there's only one."

He placed a finger on his chin. "I might be able to pull a few strings with the magistrate if George is willing to acknowledge your employment. The judiciary has been under scrutiny ever since the arrest of Keith Richards and Mick Jagger on minor drug charges. The calamity was not viewed kindly in the court of public opinion. Do you think George would be willing to do that?"

"I'll say a prayer."

"Yes, young man, prayers would be appropriate."

Chapter Eighteen

Heathrow Airport, London, England

August 1969

I wanted to do a bump in the taxi on the way to the airport but couldn't find it in my backpack. I'd packed in such a hurry. Everything was a mess, and I couldn't remember if I'd put it in my backpack or my suitcase. The flight from London to New York is a long ride, and I didn't want to chance getting strung out flying over the Atlantic. I wasn't sure how I was going to make it, needing a fix all that while or if I even could. My heroin addiction had gotten heavy, couldn't-live-without-it heavy.

Lorne had introduced me to the drug back in Florida before I was invited to do session work at Apple Studios with George Harrison. He said I couldn't get addicted to it unless I injected it, which I never did, but he was wrong, dead wrong. Heroin imparted a euphoric feeling I hadn't felt since before getting injured in Vietnam. The pain meds the VA docs prescribed were light duty compared with heroin. Darvon and Codeine lessened my awareness of pain, but it was always there, threatening, nagging, reminding me it had the power to snatch away every iota of joy. Heroin was a completely different animal. Heroin made life palatable. It made everything easy breezy.

I was on my way to meet Chas Chandler in the lounge of the Post House Hotel near the airport. It was one of those places you never forget, painted bright red with a black and red polka dot carpet. I was hoping to get there before him and duck into the men's loo to find my stash.

No such luck.

"There's my boy." Chandler greeted me with open arms. His big cheekbones practically hit the ceiling. "It's been a dog's age."

"It's good to see you, too."

"Busy as hell, lad. Busy as hell. They keeping you busy down in Westminster?"

"George used me a lot when he was trying to get his song on the White Album but not nearly as much since then. But there are a lot of new faces every day, so I'm always doing session work."

Chandler's expression piqued. "Anyone I might've heard of?"

"James Taylor, Billy Preston."

"I know Billy. He's quite a talented bloke. Never heard of the Taylor fella. What's he like?"

"Folksy music. Blues. He's amazing and has a beautifully melodic voice."

"Any bands being developed?"

"Badfinger. Paul and George are writing songs for them."

"They are, huh?" Chandler didn't seem to take the news in stride. "Guess that's one way of guaranteeing a new band's success—stacking the deck as it were."

I felt the shakes coming on and peered past Chandler to the loo, hoping he'd give me the chance to duck into it.

"You alright, Sonny? You seem a bit on edge."

"Just nerves. I've been abroad more than a year. Haven't seen my folks and long-distance calls aren't the same."

"That is true, lad. That is very true. So, here's the deal I have for you. Like I told you on the telephone, The Experience is done. Jimi busted it up."

The news was hard to accept. Jimi's power trio had dropped three smash albums, and the world was aching for more. "Why?"

"Things get stale, son. That's just the way it is. Clapton walked away from Cream. The artistic lot, always trying to create something fresh. Jimi's playing with some old acquaintances now, a band he's calling Gypsy Suns and Rainbows. Players he met in Nashville years back. Now, these new bandmates, Billy Cox and Larry Lee, they're top-notch musicians, but they've been rehearsing for this festival in upstate New York and—"

"Woodstock?" I asked excitedly.

"Yeah, that's it. Woodstock is what they're calling it. If you ask me, it's gonna be one gigantic shitshow. All the promoters have got is a big patch of farmland and good intentions, but they've signed several headliners, and Jimi's gonna be the featured act. He's gonna be the last one to take the stage, and they're paying a royal sum for him to do it." He paused. It seemed as if he'd forgotten his point. "Oh yeah. So, this new lineup Jimi's put together is all black players, a tribute to the Chitlin Circuit. And like I said, they're all gifted musicians but…" He shook his head. "The rehearsals are crap. They did a run-through at some hole in the wall called the Tinker Street Cinema, and Jimi was so disappointed he got me on the line the minute he walked offstage." Chandler put his enormous paw on my shoulder. "That's why you're here, lad. Why, Jimi thinks you can help pull the act together is well beyond me, but he's always had a soft spot in his heart for you, as you well know." He checked his watch. "Shit. We better get you over to Heathrow and checked in. There'll be a car waiting for you at JFK to drive you directly to the house Jimi's staying and rehearsing at." He put his hand behind me and ushered me toward the door.

I got so nervous, I pulled away and barked at him. "*Chas*, I have to use the loo."

"Rubbish," he said, once again guiding me forward. "Surely you can hold your water until you're at the bloody departure gate."

Chas held up his end of the bargain. He got me on the plane and on my way to New York, but I never made it to the car that was waiting to drive me to where Jimi was staying in Bethel, New York. JFK was as close as I would get to Woodstock. A beagle sniffed out my stash as I walked through customs.

V

PART FIVE - SLAMMED

Chapter Nineteen

The detention area at JFK was small and cramped, a nothing-by-nothing room with white walls, and barely enough space for pacing back and forth to prevent my back from stiffening. Several hours had passed, or I imagined they had. I didn't wear a watch, and there wasn't a clock in view. No light filtered in from the outside world, but I knew it had to be evening. No one came by, and no one checked on me. There was no activity in the immediate area save an occasional passerby. I hadn't been told anything and hadn't yet been charged with a crime. All I knew was that the guy with the beagle made a call on his radio after finding my stash, and three uniforms swooped in to drag me off. They weren't gentle about it. They sort of grabbed me by the scruff of the neck and muscled me through a steel door into the bowels of the airport. With every fleeting moment, I realized that any chance of getting to Woodstock was going down the drain. Jimi would have no idea what had become of me, and Chandler wouldn't be able to shed any light. And I really had to pee. I hadn't hit the john since before boarding the flight in London. All told, I was holding a good half a day's worth of water. Far worse, it had been eons since my last bump. I was jittery and drenched in sweat. There was an air vent in the ceiling that blew bitterly cold air on me. The room was so small that I couldn't escape the draft but kept moving so that the polar blast would hit me on different parts of my body, allowing selected spots to warm slightly.

I called out repeatedly, then discouragement growing, with less frequency. No one responded. No one wasted enough energy to shoot me a nasty stare.

Jimi was supposed to take the Woodstock stage around midnight. At least that's what I'd been told. I was supposed to arrive scant hours before his performance and go balls to the wall until he and Gypsy Suns and Rainbows grooved as smooth as butter. The best laid plans of a musical genius and his manager had gone to shit, soured in a sterile cubbyhole in Queens, New York.

Footsteps. Finally. What a goddamn relief.

Two officers. Two different uniforms. The guy who locked me up and a blue shirt, an NYPD cop.

"Bathroom?" the arresting officer said after unlocking the door and pushing it open. His gaze was directed at the floor as I moved past him. No eye contact, none whatsoever. He made me feel like trash. Vermin, which was the way I felt, a contemptible, sick, emotionally faltering, and on-the-verge-of-losing-my-shit piece of human filth. I was starving, dying of thirst, and in terrible need of a fix. The way the uniform spoke to me was dehumanizing. "Forward. Door on the left. Make it quick."

The blue shirt cop said nothing. He seemed to take it all in stride. No doubt he'd been there before, seen it a thousand times. I'm sure he'd dealt with much worse. Me, a strung-out musician with a stash of heroin dime bags. I was small-time, a walk in the park for a New York City cop. He was probably thinking about where he'd go on his meal break.

They both followed me into the bathroom. I didn't care. I stepped up to the urinal and enjoyed the best piss I'd taken in recent memory. It was such a strong release it bordered on sexual arousal. I washed my hands, and that was the end of the arresting officer. The cop took me by the arm and escorted me down a lengthy corridor.

"Where are we going?"

No answer from the street-hardened cop. He was tough-nosed and really didn't give a shit about me. My question rolled off him like water off a goose's back. The guy was Teflon.

"Can you please tell me what's going on? Please? I've never been in trouble before."

He stopped and squinted at me, then shook his head sorrowfully. "You mean you've never been caught before."

He ushered me forward once more, down another long corridor and out a door. We were now outside the airport. It was dark. Late. Quiet. A police car was parked just outside where a second officer was lounging against the front fender. He pushed off the car, meandered aft, and opened the back door. "You read him yet?"

"Not yet. Not without a witness," the first dickhead said and got straight to it, "You have the right…"

Dickhead number two helped me into the back seat while my rights were read. After ignoring me for hours, they were now wasting no time. They'd probably take me to the local precinct, book me, and move on. I guess their biological clocks were attuned to when a fresh batch of donuts was coming out of the fryer at the local coffee shop. They'd wash their hands of me just as the donuts were coming out of the hot oil.

"I'll take him," someone said.

"Huh?" Dickhead One said just as Dickhead Two closed me inside the vehicle. Dickhead Two was rotund, and his backside obscured my view as his partner walked back toward the terminal. There was a discussion taking place, but I couldn't hear what was being said. The back door opened, and I was let out. I felt someone take me by the arm, but Dickheads One and Two stayed with the car. It wasn't until I'd taken a step that I turned to see who I was tethered to.

"Hello, Sunshine," he said. "Remember me?"

Chapter Twenty

"VIP Room," John Roswell said as we entered an interrogation room somewhere in the terminal's maze of corridors and offices. The last time I'd seen him, he was battlefield lean, his skin perpetually gleaming with sweat. He'd changed considerably since leaving the 8th Field Hospital in Nha Trang. His dark hair was no longer untamed, but now dense and well-groomed. His face was fuller. Cleanly shaven. He looked good in his nylon FBI jacket, his tailored slacks, and cordovan penny loafers. He looked comfortable as he slid into the chair across the table. His smile hadn't changed—he still looked like the soldier who recovered from back surgery in the bed next to mine. He still looked like a friend. Was he a friend I could count on?

Like the holding room I'd occupied, this space was painted pure white but was far larger. Celotex ceiling tiles were stained with plumbing leaks. It was every bit as cold and impersonal as the first closet they'd locked me in. The room reeked from decades of cigarette smoke that was embedded in the carpet and permeated the paint. Ordinarily, cigarette smoke didn't bother me, but the air in this room made me want to retch. I suppose many who'd occupied the hot seat before me had felt exactly the same.

An immense conference room table took up most of the space. It was old, chipped, and covered with water stains and cigarette burns. It had been abused and neglected, like the detainees airport security and the police taunted all hours of the day and night. I suppose I should've been honored. This big room housed twenty swivel chairs, and we were just two lowly Vietnam vets. A paper plate with a cellophane-wrapped sandwich waited halfway down the mammoth table. It looked like tuna. Maybe chicken salad. Either would do. Alongside the sandwich stood a can of Coke. I was starving and as dry as a bone. Still, as appealing as the beggar's banquet was, I would've traded it all for a bump of heroin. Half a bump. A little dust to rub on my gums.

"Don't stand on ceremony," he said, gesturing toward the sustenance that waited for me on the conference room table. "You must be starving."

"Amen, brother. It won't bother you if I eat?"

"It's not filet mignon, Sonny. I'm not jealous."

"Guess not." I gawked at the food, then snatched it and unwrapped it. It tasted something like tuna, but nothing like the tuna my mother made, which I always wolfed down with gusto. It was probably made in the airport cafeteria twelve hours earlier. The fish had turned brown where the air had gotten to it—the lettuce was wilted. It smelled like that rotting fish concoction I'd smelled in bleak Vietnam villages. I consumed the fermented crap quickly so I wouldn't barf and prayed it would stay down. The Coke was warm, but it was still Coke, sweet and fizzy. It killed the decaying fish taste in my mouth. I churned it over in my mouth like mouthwash before swallowing it. Belching, I gazed across the table at Roswell, wondering what the hell was going on. "What are we doing here?"

He grinned. His cheeks were fleshier than I remembered, his dimples deeper. "Why, isn't this our reunion?" he began, "Nurse Ray will be along any minute."

"I don't suppose she's packing any morphine."

I heard air whistle up his nostrils as he shook his head. "Not likely. I guess you're in a bad way."

"At least I'm not hungry anymore."

"I'm glad you've still got a sense of humor." He scooched his chair up close to the table and locked his fingers. "Narcotics possession. I'm glad they nabbed you here and not overseas. Poor Florida boy like you could be in for a world of hurt in a foreign country."

"I was in London, not Istanbul."

"Trust me, Sonny, just because the Brits sashay around in tailored suits and wear bowler hats doesn't mean a magistrate with a hard-on for an American spic won't stick his umbrella up your ass. In all your time in London, you never got a glimpse of Old Bailey? Has a great history that courthouse. Way back when they'd sentence a man to the pillory for stealing a loaf of bread."

"What's a pillory?"

Roswell hung his arms in the air and elongated his neck downward.

"The stocks?"

Roswell dropped his hands and straightened his head before nodding. "Serious crimes, lynching, beheading. Very civilized, those Brits. Want me to stick you back on a plane to Heathrow?"

"I've seen the inside of Old Bailey. They must've torn out the stocks along with the privies." I pressed my back into the chair and felt my vertebrae pop. "It was just a bunch of dime bags, John. What in the world is going on here?"

Roswell blinked his eyes into billiard balls. "Dime bags? Did you say dime bags?"

And that's when I saw it for the first time, the man Roswell had become. The soldier who'd spent weeks with me rehabilitating from a war wound and bragging about all the notches in his belt was salivating, hungry to own me. He was going to take my liberty and do with it whatever he wished. A shiver ran through me because there wasn't a damn thing I could do about it.

Chapter Twenty-One

Back in Vietnam, I'd spent weeks with John Roswell under unimaginably difficult circumstances and enjoyed his company every moment we were together. But confined with him in the same sedan made my skin crawl. Who was John Roswell now, alien John Roswell? What planet had he come from? What could've happened to my friend to turn him into this cold-blooded thing? Had he been replicated in a pod and replaced in the middle of the night? It almost seemed plausible.

He drove south along I-95 as if he owned the interstate at eighty miles per hour. Ninety. He'd been pulled over twice, and each time a flash of his ID allowed us to continue on our way practically unimpeded. We were on our way from New York to Florida, and Roswell was hell-bent on breaking a speed record. "Why Florida? I never asked for a ride home." I certainly didn't think I was free to go and getting door-to-door limousine service.

A third speed trap. He blew by it doing a steady eighty miles per hour, the big Mercury gobbling blacktop with ease. The drone of the big American-built V-8 was hypnotic. He yawned while cranking down the window. Roswell flashed his FBI credentials one more time. This trooper was chatty. Maybe he'd never met a fed before. Maybe it gave him a thrill. Roswell obliged with some innocuous banter before spitting gravel as he peeled back onto the interstate.

"I'll get to that," was all he'd say each time I asked what he wanted with me, what he wanted me to do. What was I agreeing to? Was it worse than standing trial for possession of illegal drugs?

And all the while, Johnny boy was glib and happy, acting as if there was no tension between us, as if I had not been duped into some god-awful deal I couldn't escape from. Yes, he'd kept me from going to an arraignment and a possible prison sentence, but what did I owe the man in exchange? Why was he acting as if nothing had happened? As if this thing, this chit, was such a minor ask as to be inconsequential. In light of all he'd done for me. For what?

"It's not like they nabbed you with a half-smoked blunt," Roswell said while we were still in the JFK interrogation room, six hundred miles north of where we were now. "They grabbed you with heroin, Capital H. Congress just passed The Controlled Substances Act, and heroin is on Schedule I, defined by the federal government as a drug with no accepted medical use, and high potential for abuse. First offense for possession of heroin is two years minimum, five to ten for repeat offenders."

"It was just some dime bags. Some dime-fucking-bags."

"Was it?" Roswell had said, hammering nails into my coffin. He didn't bat an eyelash as he bent the truth to serve his purpose. "The arrest record didn't note the amount of narcotics recovered. Could've been dime bags. Could've been several grams. I guess we'll sort that out later." He reached into his shirt pocket, pulled out a pack of Juicy Fruit gum, then popped a stick into his mouth before flicking the yellow wrapper over his shoulder onto the conference room floor, where the smoke-saturated carpet would mask the fruity aroma with its dark tar and nicotine spirit. "Want one?" he asked.

I was too nauseous to think about putting anything in my mouth. The SOB was going to take my soul.

The putrid tuna sandwich I'd gobbled down at JFK was now bubbling up my throat and gasping for air. I had to suppress a smirk—at that moment, hurling in Roswell's face seemed like a Jim-dandy idea. I was having difficulty accepting what was happening to me and who was doing it. Johnny Boy and I were supposed to be brothers. Then again, Cain slaughtered his brother. Was I John Roswell's Abel? Is that who sat behind the steering wheel?

We'd just crossed the border from North to South Carolina. I would've known where we were without seeing the welcome state sign because my aunt and uncle lived in Manning, South Carolina. I remembered visiting them years back and being unimpressed with how little there was to do and how much nothing there was in every direction. Cape Coral, Florida, wasn't exactly Paris, but Manning, SC, seemed like the end of the earth, just one field after another, none of it particularly impressive. Lots of caterpillar-ravaged trees. Dead gray bark. Gnarled, ashen-colored limbs like old arthritic fingers bent downward, facing the ground. It was all so depressing to look at. Maybe that's why no one ever wanted to do anything with the land, make it better. Bring in an amusement park or something.

One thing the South had plenty of was Waffle Houses. There seemed to be one everywhere you turned. Worse still, there were almost never any other restaurants near them. My parents and I ate our way from one Waffle House to another on that trip to Manning. I could smell them before I saw them, the bleach water they used to mop the dirty ketchup-stained floors. Roswell pulled off the interstate. I could smell bleach the minute he cut the wheel.

"You're going to feed me, too? Gee, how lucky can a war veteran get? When are you going to tell me what's going on, man? It's not like you're going to give me a choice." Sure as shit I saw the yellow Waffle House sign with the black letters and a parking lot packed with pickup trucks. "I'd rather starve."

He ignored me and piloted the sedan into a spot, then threw the gearshift into park. Before cracking the door, he reached into his jacket pocket and tossed me a bag of dope. "Shove this up your nose, then meet me inside." He got out and slammed the door. Roswell was a savvy fucker—he had me by the balls, and he knew it. He'd given me a taste when we left New York, just enough to steady my nerves. I guess he figured I'd go anywhere he wanted as long as he kept feeding me smack. He wasn't wrong.

After fortifying myself, I found him at the very last table, next to the supply closet with a bucket and mop in front of it. The hell dust he'd supplied me with was pure, even better than the stuff they'd taken from me at JFK. I felt a bit more together as I made my way to the table. He was already sipping black coffee, but the color of the liquid was light, transparent enough to see the stains around the inside of the coffee mug.

"I ordered for you," he said. "I didn't get you any burnt swill. You're welcome." His nose wrinkled with the next sip. "I swear someone must've pissed in the coffee pot."

One thing about Waffle Houses, they were greased-lightning fast. A gal as wide as the counter lumbered over to us and dropped two platters on the table in quick succession, making a thunking sound like a drummer playing a flam. "Anything else?" She dropped the bill on the table and turned to walk off before getting an answer.

I was hungry as a horse, but the eggs were tasteless, and the bacon swam in grease. I covered everything with artificial syrup and began slogging it down. "Only the best on J. Edgar's dime, huh?"

"Beats prison chow," Roswell said, oozing sarcasm. He was more judicious with his use of syrup than I was, using it sparingly on his butter-slathered pancakes, making sure it didn't encroach onto his eggs. "What am I saying? A rock star like you, I should've taken you for lobster."

"I'm no rock star."

He motioned to my plate. "That ain't no lobster." He put down his fork. If he found the meal as unappealing as I did, he probably lacked the will to hold the fork aloft and shovel the food into his mouth. "What happened to you, Sonny? Was it the surgery or the music, the pain or the fantasy?"

"You wouldn't understand."

"Of course not. Because, being an FBI field agent, I've never dealt with drug addicts before. And musicians, hell, heroin is like their catnip." He attempted to lift his fork, then dropped it. "I'm asking again, was it the back surgery or are you one of those hallucinating artists who believe the drugs lift you to a higher level of consciousness?"

I told him straight and didn't know why I felt the need to be honest with him, but I was. "It keeps me from screaming like a banshee in the middle of the night." I pulled the slide back on the syrup pitcher and once again showered my plate with amber goo. "I'm almost a whole person in between bumps. It's as good as it gets for me, John. It's not pretty, but that's my life.

Uncle Sam gave me a drug habit and a boot in the hind parts. You don't hear me bitchin' about it, do you?"

"What about Hendrix? What about The Beatles? We're not talking wedding bands here. That has to be a pretty good life."

Was he digging for details, or was he simply envious? His career afforded him a power trip, but glamour? The G-man's job was barely a rung above Waffle House waitress. "I'm always happy when I have a guitar in my hands. Ecstatic. It's what I live for, but I'm not an act. I'm not the face on an album cover. I'm a session player. It's not fancy. It pays the bills, the important ones anyway, rent, food. One day maybe…yeah, it could happen, but right now it's all about the exposure. You play with the best, and you get better. You learn from talented artists and feed off their genius. If you're lucky, something clicks. God points his finger at you and says, 'You, it's your turn.'" There was a night when I helped George Harrison work out the bones of a guitar solo for "While My Guitar Gently Weeps", and for a moment I thought he might ask me to play when the group recorded the next morning. It didn't happen. George arrived at the studio with Eric Clapton, who played the lead and killed it. His haunting melody on the guitar was better than anything I could have ever come up with. It differed completely from what I had imagined. The man was in a class by himself, but disappointment crushed me all the same. I thought I was about to get my shot. "Not too many musicians ever see God point at them. But you're fingering me for something. So, what the hell do you want from me, John?"

Something sizzled. Sputtered. Popped. Bacon on the griddle? A lump of cold lard on the scorching steel? It hit my nose a moment later. Definitely bacon. Nothing smells quite like it, the intoxicating aroma given off when sugar and fat break down at a high temperature. Sheer heaven. Roswell didn't answer right away. I think he was savoring the airborne ecstasy just as I was. The bacon's tang refused to be ignored.

"Two years," he said, directing his eyes at me. His mind had been somewhere else. Maybe salivating over the thought of a BLT.

He wanted two years from me, the same sentence I'd get if convicted on a first offense of heroin possession. Two years doing what? "Maybe I'll take my chances in court."

He cut a wedge in his stack of pancakes. "I suppose that's a choice." He spread more butter on the wedge, then chewed it. "But that'll be two years lost, two years living like an animal. In filth. Getting beaten. Maybe worse. And when you get out you'll be scum. An ex-con. Unhirable. You'll be back out on the street. Using again. Is that the life you want? How about your mom and dad? Think they'll be proud of you?"

He worked on his food, letting his words sink in. His pitch was coming. I said nothing and waited for it to arrive.

"Here's what we can offer you."

"We?"

"US of A, Sonny. The same Uncle Sam you claim turned his back on you."

I had nothing to lose by hearing him out, and the restroom was nearby in case that tuna sandwich decided to pole vault the tasteless flapjacks and make a move for Roswell's kisser. I could only hope.

He grimaced as if something was stuck in his throat, but I didn't think it was his meal. "You check all the boxes."

"What boxes are those?"

"You're Spanish-speaking, and you're a rock star. Well, not really a rock star but close enough to fake it."

Full stop. Anger fused the circuits in my mind. The food I chewed turned to granite in my throat. The fork fell from my hand and clattered onto the Formica tabletop. "What the hell are you talking about, man?"

He blew out a long, labored breath. His eyes flicked back and forth before reaching into his pocket, then he tossed a wallet-sized photo on the table. It looked as if the photo had been taken with a telephoto lens. It was grainy, and the image was unclear: a young man with dark hair caught hustling down a set of stone steps outside an immense villa. "Gage Serna," he said. "Thirty years old. Harvard-educated. Wannabe rocker. *Serious* wannabe rocker."

"He plays guitar?"

"Yes."

"This is about guitar lessons? That can't be it."

Roswell shook his head. "Trust me. It's not. Gage Serna is the reigning head of the Serna Oil out of Colombia, one of the country's largest oil exporters. Their biggest customer, the good old US of A. Gage's father, Andres Serna, met with an untimely passing about two years ago." He mimed a gun with his hand and placed it to his temple. His hand bucked.

"Oil people do that sort of thing? Esso? Texaco? They shoot people in the head?"

Roswell used his fork to scrape the rest of the bacon off his plate while glancing up at me. "Think out of the box, Sonny. All those ships moving back and forth across the Caribbean—how hard do you think it would be to cram freight pallets of cocaine into the hold of one of those supertankers?"

"I see. So, this isn't about gas prices."

"Not even close. Gage now wears the crown, and as they say, heavy is the head."

"I've got a bad feeling about where this is going, and I don't want any part of it. I'm a musician, not a spy."

"You're combat trained, you were a paratrooper, and you've got an established cover. You're better suited to the task than you think."

I heard the floor creak behind me, preempting my response. "Pay at the counter," the waitress said, implying that she'd completed her obligation as our server and wouldn't be stopping back. She topped off Roswell's mug with piss-thin coffee and departed.

The story was in Roswell's eyes, what he wanted me to do. The mission: prove Serna was smuggling cocaine. And then what, kill him? Use him? Roswell was FB-fucking-I. A slap on the wrist wasn't in their playbook. "I've got a back that's ready to snap like an overbaked breadstick and a serious-as-shit drug habit. I'm 4-fucking-F, John. The army wouldn't take me the way I am now. I served my country. Honorably discharged. Or did you forget?"

"You were caught smuggling narcotics into the United States." He picked up the creamer and lightened his coffee. "Or did *you* forget?"

I didn't need a reminder. I hadn't forgotten that I'd been pinched at the airport. Nor had I forgotten Roswell's threat. A small stash of smack was going to be reported as several grams of heroin if I didn't do as he asked.

"This is bullshit, man. Some real bullshit. I play guitar. I'm not some kind of undercover operative."

Roswell took a final sip of coffee and grabbed the check. "You gonna follow me to the car or do I need to take you out in cuffs? We're halfway between New York and Florida. We can continue south or I can turn around and bring you back for your arraignment. It's your choice, Sonny. Think it over." He stood and walked over to the cashier.

Chapter Twenty-Two

The combination of bad nerves and rotten food made a merciless combination. We'd barely made it back onto the interstate when my stomach began to churn. Another taste of smack would've smoothed the waves, but Roswell didn't offer, and I didn't ask. We were once again heading south, and I was up shit's proverbial creek without a paddle. Somehow, my senses were still keen. I could taste day-old fish with every belch.

"I can't throw you bags of dope forever, but we'll get you on methadone," Roswell said. "Either that or you can man up and go cold turkey. As for your back, I've got a doc who'll write you all the scrips your heart desires. When you're done… there's the Hospital For Special Surgery in Manhattan. We'll get you the best neurosurgeon in New York to fix the mess the army doctors made with a pocketknife in a Quonset hut hospital."

The promises he made went in one ear and out the other. "When I'm done? Done with what? John, could you just stop jerking my chain long enough to give me specifics?"

"I was hoping to put that off until we got to Miami, but since you won't shut the fuck up—" With a rattle of his head and a blast out his nostrils he swung the wheel, crossing two lanes and cutting off everyone in his wake. As he pulled off onto the shoulder, the horns of enraged motorists blared. Tires screeched. Middle fingers rocketed through open windows. "Is this who the hell you are, Sonny? I thought you were a goddamn Marine, not some whiny pain in the ass. Believe it or not, I'm doing you a favor."

I forced myself to turn and make eye contact, my gaze slicing into him.

"Yeah, John, it really looks that way. What kind of favor exactly should I be thankful for, trumped-up drug charges or abduction? Right now, all you're giving me is the shaft. How the hell did it work out that you just happened to show up when I got arrested? It's not like we keep in touch."

Guilt averted his eyes. He glanced out the driver's side window and the endless procession of cars whizzing past close enough to shear paint off the big sedan. "You've been on my radar. I've known where you were, what you were doing, and that you were using narcotics for some time now," he admitted, finally flashing his eyes in my direction. "Lights went off when you booked a flight to New York." This thing we need you to do, it's very specific. I was in New York for a briefing, and when the call came in that Santiago Rojas had been detained…I jumped in a car."

"How was it they knew to call you?"

"As I said, I've been watching. Your name is on a list."

"What list?"

"What does it matter? There are a lot of lists, people the government has taken an interest in. You're on one of them. An FBI list. My list."

"This is about this Serna guy?"

His head bobbed quickly, almost imperceptibly. "He's the guy. Young, rich, and ruthless. But the one thing he really wants, he can't buy, steal, or kill for."

What, I wondered, *could that be?* Suddenly, I knew. What did every young guy want growing up, to be an astronaut, to be Mickey Mantle, or Elvis? What was it that everyone wanted? Fame. To be idolized. "Serna wants to be a goddamn rock star?"

"A guitar hero, to be specific. He idolizes guitar players. And you…I don't have to spell it out, do I?"

Roswell's insult banged around in my head, growing bigger and bigger until it became an 800-pound gorilla pressing against the inside of my skull. "You're Spanish, and you're a rock star," he'd said not thirty minutes earlier. "Well, not really, but close enough to fake it." Did he want me to get close enough to Serna to spy on him? Kill him? What? I was to impress the shit out of a drug czar with my flimsy connection to Hendrix, Clapton, and The

Beatles. Serna could buy anything he wanted except celebrity. Not that kind of celebrity.

"You want me to risk my life? You want me to go undercover in a drug cartel?"

"Wouldn't be the first time you put it all on the line, Sonny. Night jumping behind enemy lines into the jungle wasn't without risk. You're a Marine. You've got balls. That's why I set down my chopper and dragged your broken ass to safety. Seeing you lying in the jungle, I knew you had what it takes. I knew you had balls. The fucked-up altimeter on that C-130 screwed the crap out of your mission, and some good men got badly hurt because of it. Not everyone gets the chance to go back and make things right. But you do. You've got the opportunity to be a hero again."

"And do what, exactly? After I buddy up to the kingpin. What then?"

"That's the beauty part, my friend. All you have to do is take a leap of faith," he said with a seal-the-deal smile. "You can do the courageous thing and help your government, or you can be a convict." He waited a beat, giving his comment weight. "So, which is it, Sonny? Are we headed to Florida or back to New York?"

I felt my pulse pounding in my ears, thudding, growing more rapid. A chill shuddered through me, and I broke out in a cold sweat. Then, before I knew it, I had day-old tuna on my shoes.

Chapter Twenty-Three

Cartagena, Colombia

Mid-November 1969

Señor Whisky Bar was an homage to 60s hodgepodge. The walls were covered with old license plates and beer posters, featuring half-naked girls and bare-chested cowboys. It was all-American advertising stuff, brands like Winston cigarettes, Pepsi Cola, and Schlitz beer. Anything that could be nailed or taped to a solid surface found a home on the walls of Señor Whisky Bar. The floor was covered with sawdust and didn't look as if it had been swept out since President Guillermo Muñoz left office back in '66. Buried in the sawdust were peanut shells, beer bottle caps, rat turds, cigarette butts, and small change. Coins. Pesos. The place didn't smell bad as long as you didn't park yourself too close to the bathrooms. In the month since I'd moved to Cartagena, I'd learned to hug the trees out behind the parking lot when I'd had more to drink than I could hold. Señor Whisky Bar's *el trono* wasn't fit for a #2, and you were risking life and limb attempting a #1. All manner of transactions took place within el baño. The secluded location was home to every manner of fluid exchange, and I mean every. All things considered, though, the place was magnetic. Señor Whisky Bar drew a diverse clientele, a mix of locals and elite, almost every night of the week. By elite, I meant drug bosses, *droguistas*, men with plenty of money to throw around. The overabundance of chicas was the big draw.

Some were gold diggers looking for sugar daddies, a wealthy *droguista* to lavish them with gifts. Mostly, the women liked to drink, dance, shake their asses, and have fun. I enjoyed having fun. I had no complaints about the Colombian women. They were curvy, flirtatious, and didn't beat around the bush. No guilt, just good times. A man could learn to love that kind of attitude in a woman.

Roswell had just arrived and was staying for a few days, just enough time to make sure the mission was moving in the right direction before heading back home to the States. So far, he'd been true to his word. They (the FBI) supplied me with enough cash to get by plus a little extra to make a splash when I needed to, buy drinks, and make friends. I was subtly making connections and spreading word about my celebrity rock and roll connections. Until now, it had all been talk. I hadn't plugged into an amp for anyone yet, but that was all about to change.

We were looking for a local called Cachumbo, a sweaty mess of a man with a mop of unkempt curly hair. His face glistened, reflecting light like a hundred tiny mirrors. Thick cheeks. Stubble rising into profuse sideburns. Pushing forty. Pushing it so hard he'd be damn lucky to see fifty. He was a big man, a planet. And like a planet, his gravity drew people to him like a magnet.

"He knows everyone," Roswell said, carrying my guitar case into the bar, making sure he was seen with it. "You think this will draw the groupies?" he asked, giving the long, hard-sided case a rattle. "I look a little like Keith Richards, don't I? *Think the birds will dig me*?" he said, adding a British accent.

"First of all, before you can have groupies, you need a group." I pointed to where four kids were setting up their equipment. "What we have here is a garage band gigging for maybe the first time. I hope to God they're not terrible. There's only so much I can do without decent players backing me up." This was no Murray the K spectacular. It was a bare bones audition. These kids were probably working for the pocket change that got tossed into the tip jar. If the patrons drank, they'd be asked back. If not, it was hasta la vista, muchachos. You're out, and the kids with the sexy chica vocalist are in. Of course, I could've been wrong, very wrong. The four kids setting up their equipment had that unmistakable novice look about them. Who knows? They might be prodigies, guitar shredding, drumkit pounding terrors that will leave me and everyone else in the bar annihilated.

Roswell might've been a fed, but he was first and foremost a dyed-in-the-wool pussy hound. He held fast to the case handle and scanned the bar for talent. "But if you want to lug that case around for me…suit yourself," I said.

Cachumbo had scored me one hell of a sweet instrument, a Fender Jaguar. It was a '64 and unlike most I'd seen, this one had a semi-translucent blond finish over ash wood and a natural finish peg head. The tremolo arm was original, a little bent, but no biggie. I don't know what kind of condition it was in when the stout man originally found it, but he'd had it restored by a local craftsman, and man, it played like a dream. The action was wheel-smoking fast and the tone velvety rich. The Jaguar was a great sounding guitar but played through a rookie amp setup and over the screams of a bar full of drunken hombres, I wasn't sure anyone would hear how good it was. Or how good *I* was. I'd have to leave it all out on the stage and hope the drummer and bass player could keep up with me.

Cachumbo had arranged to have me sit in with the kid band and spread the legend of the bona fide rocker now living in the local town, the one Roswell and I were trying to spread. The big man didn't work for the FBI. He worked for Do-Re-Mi. The feds were greasing his already oily palms, and believe me, those hands were the size of catcher's mitts. He stood. The arms of his wooden chair clung to his hips only to fall free a moment later. "Over here," Cachumbo said in a deep baritone voice, waving us over to his table. He wasn't drinking alone. The table was littered with dead soldiers, empty bottles of Costeña. More than a dozen. A quick count tallied seventeen. Cachumbo was a large, sweaty man giving his all to stay hydrated. "Sit. Sit," he said. A snap of his fingers and a barmaid hurried over with a gray plastic tub to whisk the fallen heroes off the table.

She wiped down the table with a stained rag. Stained red. It made me wonder how many brawls the place saw. I pushed the thought from my mind. "Cervezas?" she asked.

"Si," Cachumbo said. "Tres cervezas." He was quick to notice Roswell salivating over the barmaid. She was skinny. Top-heavy. Heading off, her butt rolled in and out like a conductor's wand. Cachumbo's cheeks rose. "*Esta vieja está buena. Si?*"

Spanish is Spanish, but every county has its own proprietary dialects and slang expressions. It wasn't hard to figure out what the big man was saying. "Si," I said, laughing. "Buena."

"What did he say?" Roswell asked impatiently.

"He said, 'She's hot,' genius. You should've been able to figure it out on your own."

"Speak English, damn it," Roswell said, eyes pressed shut. He opened them just in time to see the beer served.

The waitress held all three bottles in her right hand, the bottle necks between her fingers. She placed all three on the table at once, depositing them like a pinsetter, then cut her eyes at Roswell, taunting him, gazing down as if she could sense how badly he lusted for her, then spun and abruptly left.

"Christ, I want her," Roswell said. He swigged his beer and smacked the bottle back on the table.

"Easy, *perro*," Cachumbo said with a chortle. "You don't know anything about her. That look she gave you, she's setting a trap. She's got two little niñas at home, no man and no money. A rich gringo like you…you're just what the doctor ordered."

"*Perro?*" Roswell asked with a cocked eyebrow.

I smirked. "He called you a horn dog." Roswell seemed more like the man I'd met during the war, the swaggering, tail-chasing helo pilot I'd bonded with in a field hospital. He was no longer the man I knew but a calculating federal agent. Still, I preferred him this way.

"Funny," Roswell said once again, grabbing the bottle and swigging down a gulp. "Let's get down to business."

"Yes, I agree," Cachumbo said. "Let's." He leaned forward and was about to speak when a panhandler stopped by the table.

"*Lucas,*" the bum said with an open hand in Cachumbo's face. "*Présteme dos lucas para irme a casa.*" The beggar had a piss stain on his jeans and a fly buzzing around his head. He combed the knots out of his ponytail with his fingers while waiting to see if he'd found an agreeable mark.

Cachumbo's upper lip rose on one side, exposing a chipped canine tooth. *"Qué seba de man."* I didn't understand what the big man said but supposed it was something like "Take a hike." He snatched his beer off the table and stood, his chair once again clamped to his hips. *"Vámonos,"* he said, motioning to the front door. He rapped on the wooden tabletop with two downward-facing knuckles, then tucked some cash into the waitress's back pocket. With a twist of his torso, the narrow chair fell free, this time falling over, sending a mouse scurrying for cover. We grabbed our beers and followed Cachumbo outside. I grabbed the guitar and moved on. Looking back, I saw the scrounger with his hands held high, saluting us with both of his middle fingers before moving off to apply his trade at another table.

Cachumbo pounded the ground with his motorcycle boots as he strode across the dirt parking lot, kicking up muck. He stopped alongside a black pickup truck. "Crowded tonight," he said as he rested his backside against a dust-covered fender. He chugged his beer and looked at Roswell. "The parking lot is better suited for talking business."

"You expect Serna to swing by tonight?" Roswell asked.

"Tonight?" Cachumbo's shoulders rose. He pursed his lips. "Hard to say, Jefe." He sucked saliva from between his teeth and hacked at the ground. "Tonight. Tomorrow. Your guess is as good as mine."

"I expect better intel for my money," Roswell said.

"Take it easy," the big man said. "This place, he comes. Once, twice a month. Sometimes more. I don't make his schedule. Meanwhile, go to the beach. Lots of pretty girls there. Cheap beer. Cartagena is not such a bad place to spend a couple of days. Cabrera says Sonny can play anytime he likes. Sooner or later, Serna will make the scene, and I'll be here when he does."

"Cabrera? He own the bar?" Roswell asked.

"Si. Sonny and Cabrera have already been introduced." He emptied the bottle and set the empty down on the floor of the cargo box. "That's where the money goes, Roswell. Got to grease the wheels."

"Thanks for the economics lesson," Roswell said.

"It'll be okay," I said. "Rome wasn't—"

"Please don't, Sonny," Roswell said with a dour expression and a hand in my face. He turned to Cachumbo. "Fine. We'll play the long game...for now."

Cachumbo rubbed his palms together eagerly. "*Excelente.* Let's go back inside. Maybe Serna comes by. Maybe not. The night is young. Sonny can charm the chicas with his fancy guitar playing, and for you, Jefe," he laid his massive paw on Roswell's shoulder, "Let's see what we can do to put a smile on your sour puss. I know a chica that will make your eyes roll back into your head."

Chapter Twenty-Four

Thanksgiving 1969

A new album had landed that was blowing up the charts. Thirty-seven minutes of pure Latin rock ecstasy led by a Mexican-born guitarist out of San Francisco named Carlos Santana. The critics said it was shit, denouncing the album as "Fast, pounding, frantic music with no actual content." But I knew better. All the rockers did. Santana's music was unique and played to an audience that had never been acknowledged before, people like me, people of Latin blood. It touched me. It touched all of us. The proof was in album sales. Copies of the nine-song compilation were flying out the door of record shops, and the collection was cruising toward the number one position on Billboard's Pop Album Chart.

I was pissed because I would've heard Santana's band live if I hadn't gotten busted at JFK and missed Woodstock. Rumor had it that Santana was high when he performed and that Jerry Garcia of The Grateful Dead gave him something that had him hallucinating within moments of taking it. Miraculously, he somehow managed to stay on time and in tempo during the performance.

Santana's style was similar to my own, with sustained notes and trills. His timing was so close to my own that I could practically feel the notes before he played them. In and around the fabulous guitar were percussion instruments rarely heard by American rock audiences that included timbales and congas. Their sound was absolutely unique, and I couldn't get enough of it. FM radio played tons of live recordings from Woodstock, and Santana got plenty of airplay, airplay that made it all the way down to Cartagena, Colombia.

It turned out that the wet-behind-the-ears house band at Señor Whisky Bar had some chops after all. I'd played with them just one time before their guitarist realized he was seriously outgunned and split. I didn't feel good about driving him off, but he was definitely the weak link in the chain, and the others were ecstatic about me stepping in. What was initially called Acción was now named Sonny Cielos, a play on words for Sunny Skies. We weren't Cream or The Jimi Hendrix Experience, but we were packing the house night after night, covering Santana and playing the ever-loving shit out of every track. After just a couple of weeks, we were drawing a big-money crowd, bankers, government officials, and most importantly, high-level *droguistas*, players from the Cali and Medellin cartels, and independent dealers from all over Colombia. My guitar licks, tantalizing their ears, would most definitely spread the word.

But Gage Serna was not among those who'd come to hear us play.

Cachumbo said he was a regular, but it made sense that there was nothing regular about a man like Gage Serna. A guy with all the money in the world could spend his time however he saw fit. My job was to get close to him, to buddy up to him, and somehow worm my way into the workings of his drug operation. But there was no way for me to get close to him unless he came to hear me play. I had to sit around and wait and hope he'd show up and like what he heard, the riffs and the story—I was the Latino kid who'd jammed with rock gods. "Push the story," I'd been told. Push it far and wide, then push it some more. I was told that if I spun the dial long enough, eventually the tumblers would fall into place, like the dial on the safe I imagined was in Cabrera's office.

Dario Cabrera *was* Señor Whisky, the bar's proprietor. One thing I'd learned about Cabrera in the short time I'd been in Cartagena was that no one knew anything about him, not really. Not where he came from or where he lived. His office door was always locked, and he came and went from the establishment whenever it suited him. I never saw him get into a car, not his own or a taxi. He simply walked down the street and faded into the crowd.

He never met with anyone at the bar, not suppliers or city officials, and he rarely talked to the patrons. He did so only if he absolutely had to—he'd permit a quick exchange and immediately get back to business. He walked through the bar with his permanently pissed-off expression, keeping an eye on the bartenders and staff to make sure no one had their hands in the till. He'd bark at them. Snarl occasionally. Threaten them if he needed to. It was his place, and he ran it the way he wanted to. If you didn't like it...well, that was too fucking bad.

He didn't cut the liquor and didn't talk out of school. I learned that if I stayed out of his way, he'd stay out of mine. He let the band use the bar to rehearse during the day and paid us when we were supposed to get paid. The cash went from his hands to ours, no middleman. No accountant. No one who might have sticky fingers. He'd pluck the take from the register and disappear behind his locked office door. I never saw him walk out with a briefcase or a bag or anything that could be used to transport pesos. I mused that he had a secret passageway in his office that led straight to the bank vault. Either that or one of those vacuum tube setups that sucks cylindrical canisters through a maze of plastic piping culminating in the bank safe.

Telefónica Colombia, the country's equivalent of Ma Bell, was a screaming hot mess. Getting anyone on the line was a crapshoot, and most times that roll of the dice came up snake eyes. There was always chatter on the line. You never knew who was listening, only that someone was. Conversations with Roswell were infrequent. We spoke in improvised code. He knew what I meant, and it was obvious that he was unhappy about our lack of progress. Short of waving Merlin's wand, there wasn't a damn thing I could do beyond what I was already doing to draw Serna into the club. He'd usually hang up first. As bad as the sound quality was, there was no mistaking the sound of him slamming the phone onto the receiver. I guess my report of no news precipitated him getting a healthy ass chewing from his superiors, and the slamming phone was his way of letting me know what he had in store.

The band was sounding...not bad. Jalen was a maraca-shaking maniac with a scratchy voice reminiscent of Rod Stewart. He was our front man and always performed bare chested. I don't think he did it to sex up the girls. I truly believed he didn't own a decent shirt. His abs were carved up pretty good, so no one complained about him being half-dressed during performances.

Fargo had a shirt, one. It was a long-sleeved white crew. I don't know how he kept it on while playing drums because the bar was always so damn hot. He sweated like an animal, shedding so much moisture he could launder the shirt in his own perspiration. He didn't have a lot of experience but was eager to learn. Every musician has sat behind the drum kit at one time or another. I taught him what I could, how to count and emphasize the beat. He was no Ginger Baker, but who was? His saving grace was that he had a reliable sense of rhythm.

The bass player went by the name Pescado, which meant fish. It could've been his surname, but I didn't think so. I think it was a nickname that just stuck. He didn't look like a fish, no big lips or bulging eyes. He was like a lot of bass players I'd played with, nothing fancy—he never extended himself nor attempted to solo, but he stayed in the right key.

As far as I was concerned, my bandmates were perfect if you took perfect with a grain of salt. They provided a solid foundation for my leads. They didn't get much of the attention, but they didn't complain. They shared the stage with an evolving local legend. True, it was a legend I'd created but one I had no difficulty peddling, one the locals eagerly bought into.

Rehearsals were long, not because I was such a tough taskmaster but because it was fun, and I found it gratifying to watch the others grow as artists. Our jam sessions got longer and smoother. Transitions were executed with precision. We learned each other's styles and musical voices.

The Stones had just released a new album, *Let It Bleed*. We'd already worked out "Midnight Rambler" and had it down pat. Next up was "Gimme Shelter," which was much more challenging but doable instrumentally. The rub was that the song sounded hollow without a second vocalist challenging Jalen's lead in the way Merry Clayton's rebellious rants competed with Jagger's for dominance. The song was about war, murder, and rape, but our rendition lacked the fierce tension so pronounced on the Stones' recorded track. I tried to create an aggressive counterpoint with the guitar, but it wasn't the same, and the audience at the bar liked their music to mirror the polished recordings they heard on the radio. We couldn't give it to them, not on this one. What the song really needed was a strong female co-lead. I was stymied, ready to scrap our cover and move on to another song when the distinctive creak of Cabrera's door drew our attention. And then a slender chica walked out, holding a compact, fixing her lipstick. Cabrera came through the door right behind her, adjusting his belt. He moseyed toward us, his permanent scowl in place, his eyes cutting a groove in the sawdust-covered floor. He took her by the arm and escorted her toward us.

"She's in the band now," he said without asking our consent. His eyelids sat just above his lower lashes, squinting like opaque window shades expelling a thin sliver of sunlight. It almost seemed as if he didn't have eyes. He was faceless. Expressionless. An enigma. A blank wall resolved to shun one and all. As he returned to the seclusion of his cave, the young chica popped a stick of gum into her mouth. She smiled at me, her eyes perky and full of life. "I sing, yes?" she asked, but didn't ask. It wasn't a question but more a declaration, optimistic, perhaps swollen with promise, but a declaration all the same. Cabrera had ordained it. She dropped her small purse on the floor, then bounced excitedly on her toes. "What I sing?"

I was dumbfounded. Despite being astonished by Cabrera's insolence I found myself musing, *Maybe she can belt it out like Merry Clayton.* "You know The Rolling Stones?" I asked.

Her eyes lit up. "Sì, Mick Jagger. I know. I know."

"Bien." I turned to the band. "'Gimme Shelter,' once more from the top."

Chapter Twenty-Five

December 1969

Senior Special Agent Petraglia, Roswell's New York-based commanding officer, had gotten pressure from the Miami field office. The vast majority of illegal drugs entering the country were coming through Florida. Though the mission had been greenlit by New York, Miami wanted in on the action, and their share of credit should any credit be forthcoming. Dotted line reporting had been added to the organizational chart—Roswell now had a new clown to report to. His name was Cutter.

Flights from New York to Florida were abundant, seats aboard aircraft for last-minute bookings, not so much. Roswell got a seat in the smoking section on a late-night flight, which was equivalent to being crammed into an iron lung with nicotine and tar rammed through your nostrils and down your airway. The intensity and duration of inhaling the airborne toxins made him sick to his stomach. He awoke the next morning still coughing from lung irritation. He was the one pale-skinned agent in the Miami field office filled with deeply tanned Floridians

Roswell was biding his time in an empty office cubicle when Cutter approached. He wore a white short-sleeve shirt that made the deep color of his suntanned arms seem all the more striking. "When was the last time you were on the beach?" Cutter said. "If you don't catch some rays, I'll have to call you Paleface."

"Haven't been getting a lot of R&R. Bureau jobs don't afford a lot of play time."

"Nature of the beast I guess. Let's get busy." He signaled with a wave of the arm. Roswell got to his feet and followed him into his office. It was located in the corner of a one-level structure. Full-windowed exposure. Palm trees in the foreground. Translucent shades drawn to reduce the intensity of the unbearable Florida sun. "Always lived in New York?"

"Except for my tour in Nam," Roswell said. "Almost as delightful down here as it was over there. Tell me, what do you people do for air?"

"No one told you to wear a suit and a tie."

"And no one told me not to. Nor was I told I'd have to report to two offices when I accepted this post, but here I am talking to CO Number Two. What would you like to know?"

"You're not very subtle, Roswell. Anyone ever tell you that?"

"My ex-wife wasn't a fan."

"How long were you married?"

"Just briefly enough to squeak in under the annulment wire. No muss, no fuss, no alimony."

Cutter leaned back in his chair and crossed his legs. "I guess we can cross pleasantries off the list." He picked up a bound folder, weighed it in his hand, then let if fall lightly onto his desk. "Your field report, it's kind of light. When do you expect to have something of substance to report?"

"I'll be in Cartagena tonight and meet with Sonny Rojas tomorrow. I'll know better after we talk."

"Rojas, that the aspiring Elvis Presley you put in play. He any good?"

"I don't know. He's no James Bond, but he's smart and doesn't want to go to jail. I think he's up to the task."

"He'd better be."

"And why's that, Cutter? Is there a clock ticking on your next promotion?"

Cutter slammed a palm on his desk. "You're out of line, Roswell."

"And you horned in on an operation I've been working on for months. You're the one who summoned me down to this sub-Saharan sweat box. Petraglia and I are in lockstep on this one. So, maybe *you're* the one who's out of line." Roswell pinned him with an angry glance. "Are we done here?"

"Good and goddamn done. Don't let the door hit you on the ass on the way out." Cutter said and dismissed him with a wave of his hand.

Chapter Twenty-Six

The next day

Roswell's follow-up trip to Cartagena was a hush-hush meeting on the other side of the city. I knew the visit was coming. It was long overdue. He waited for us at a rotted wooden picnic table near a children's playground when we pulled up in Cachumbo's shiny blue Renault. How the big man wedged himself into the clown car without a gorilla-sized shoehorn was beyond me. Watching him enter the tiny automobile was an eye-opening spectacle. After opening the door, he stood with his back to the doorway, then fell backwards into the seat, somehow managing not to smack the back of his head on the doorframe. He then swung his legs ninety degrees, wedging them under the steering wheel. The car sat so low with him in it that when he got out, I could almost hear the Renault's springs sighing with relief.

Roswell had a cigarette in his hand, the smoke trailing away in the breeze. He looked pale from a distance, but closer up, I saw it was just his natural coloring, washed out by intense sunlight. Everyone in Cartagena was brown, brown skin, brown hair, brown eyes. He stood out like a cue ball against the dark green felt of a pool table. The playground was an ideal meeting spot, a place where we wouldn't be spotted together. Now that I was a known entity at the club, there was no way I could be seen with a gringo like Roswell, a man who reeked of G-man tang. It was early morning—kids were in school, the swings and slides unused. A bum was stretched out across one of the benches, shoeless with his shirt pulled over his head to keep the sun out of his eyes.

"Never too early," Cachumbo said as he set a six-pack of beer on the picnic table. A brown paper bag saturated with grease stains contained breakfast grub, tamales, and cheese-filled Arepas Boyacenses. It was an obscene amount of breakfast food for the three of us, but Cachumbo ate like a horse, two or three portions at a sitting. Food was cheap, and Cachumbo's appetite robust. I didn't anticipate leftovers.

Roswell looked somber. Gone were the days of chewing the fat in adjoining hospital beds, complaining about the war, the Army, the Marines, the lousy food, sparrow-sized mosquitoes, and sweltering heat. Not to mention stories of his female conquests. The FBI had stripped all the color out of him, removed it like bleach extracts ink from a white shirt. He was blunt and to the point, businesslike to the nth degree. He seemed to be under pressure or putting pressure on himself. The trouble was, he didn't wear it well. He seemed frazzled, almost angry about having traveled to South America and to be meeting with us in this bird-dropping paradise of a playground.

Cachumbo tore the soggy paper bag from the top edge to the bottom, and a pile of wax paper-wrapped grub cascaded onto the bird shit-encrusted table. In Vietnam, they warned us about disease-carrying birds, about psittacosis and histoplasmosis, nasty diseases our feathered friends passed out like strip club handouts in Times Square. I covered the guano with an ample amount of wax paper, hoping it would protect me from the bird turd and any germs contained within, much in the same way a condom prevents against spreading the clap.

Cachumbo exposed the top halves of a tamale and an Arepa Boyacense. They filled his massive hands as he alternated taking bites from the right and left. Roswell passed on the grub. "You're not hungry, boss? Cachumbo asked.

"I don't eat breakfast," he replied. "I don't want anything interfering with the octane in my coffee."

"Coffee on any empty stomach is a bad idea, jefe," Cachumbo said in between mouthfuls. "The acid will eat you alive. Especially Colombian coffee." He tried handing him an Arepa Boyacense. "Check it out. Run it through your gringo gut and see if it toots."

Roswell chuckled in spite of himself, in spite of his grumpiness, but waved him off. "Maybe later. I'm more worried about my ass getting chewed out than ulcers." He took a puff of his cigarette, which was burned most of the way to the filter. "We've got to speed things up. I'm getting my head handed to me over the lack of progress. So, we're gonna sit here until we come up with a more aggressive plan." He looked from me to Cachumbo, making it clear that responsibility fell on both of us. "Start spit-balling."

"What do you want us to do, jefe?" Cachumbo's shoulders rose into his steampipe neck. "I know Serna comes to the bar. He just hasn't come in a while."

"A while? A while is a week or two," Roswell said as he flicked away the smoldering butt. "We're more than a month into this operation. It's time to make something happen, and I mean pronto."

I was deep in thought as I nibbled on the tamale's outer crust. I knew this confrontation was coming. Roswell wasn't long on patience. He hadn't verbalized a threat, but I knew there was always one waiting in the wings. Get it done, or our deal is off the table. He'd fly me back to the states and wring me through the legal system. I'd been having a good time, almost like a vacation, using methadone to get clean and playing a hell of a lot of music. The weather was warm, and hot ladies were plentiful. Inexplicably, bedhopping seemed to agree with my lousy back. In the time since meeting Cachumbo, I'd learned that he was as laid back as they came and not one to push the envelope. I knew I was the one who had to come up with a plan, and I did. Not so much a plan as an idea, something to throw against the wall. It was hardly a stroke of genius, and I wasn't sure it would stick, so I threw out a hook to see if anyone would bite. "Serna's not going to the bar, so where is he going? We should be able to find out that much. Let's get a line on where he's hanging out these days and show up there."

I turned to Cachumbo. He'd stopped eating mid-bite. Gravy dripped from his hand onto the bird shit-covered table as he slowly ground food between molars large enough to crush a beer can. It looked like the gears in his head were turning. He had pulverized meat in his mouth as he spoke. His eyes large, he seemed charged up at the prospect of a new course of action. He raised each of three fingers like flags for each of the venues he ticked off. "Café Getsemani. Club Bazurto. El Discoteca."

"That's where he hangs?" I asked.

Cachumbo's jaw was once again operating at full speed as he nodded. "Yes. Sometimes. The chica he's dating…one of them, anyway. I heard she likes these flashy places."

"Can you get us in there?"

"El Discoteca, no. It doesn't pay—they don't play live music there. The other two…" He mulled it over in between bites. "Maybe. I can try. But the owner of Club Bazurto…" he gestured with the partially eaten tamale in his hand, "He's, how you say…a pain in the ass. Thinks his shit doesn't stink. I'm not sure your band is ready for a place like that."

"Sell the story and get Sonny in there. That's your job," Roswell said, eyebrows peaked, revealing a demanding glare. "Latin guitar god. Jammed with Hendrix. Clapton. The Beatles. Lay it on thick and make sure this guy bites. Get Sonny in front of him. Whatever it takes."

The big man gritted his teeth, his expression suggesting that getting the band into these clubs was a tall order. Maybe insurmountable. "I will do my best, jefe. You know me, right? I give it my best shot." The weight of added responsibility didn't deter him from polishing off his food and licking the gravy from his giant sausage fingers. "I start with Café Getsemani first. The owner hates Cabrera. Maybe I can use that to my advantage."

"Just get us an audition, and I'll do the rest," I said. "The band has gotten pretty tight and with Willow sharing lead vocals with Jalen…it gives our sound a lot more depth."

"Who's Willow?" Roswell asked, searching our eyes.

Cachumbo wasn't exactly a mover and shaker, but he was a survivor and smart enough to keep tabs on the band's goings on, smart enough to ensure he stayed an integral part of the plan and on Roswell's payroll. He hadn't been surprised when Cabrera's latest conquest was thrust upon the band.

Not that Cabrera had a reputation because he didn't. He was an enigma, a money-grubbing puzzle with no history and no personal life that we knew of. But as Cachumbo had put it, "He's a man, no?" The implication being obvious. The upside of having a new addition to the band was that Willow was sexy as all get out and had one hell of a sultry voice. It never gave out and never got thin. It was bold with enough grit to front for a first-rate rock band. Jalen didn't have her chops, but their harmonies bordered on magical in the way Paul Simon and Art Garfunkel complemented each other rhythmically. "She's new with the band," Cachumbo said. "Voice of an angel. Tits so perky they spit in God's eye."

"No one mentioned it," Roswell said.

"You haven't been around much, John," I said. "It never came up, and I didn't think you'd be interested."

He exhaled hollowly. "You're not wrong. I really don't care. Would've been nice if you mentioned her perky tits though." He lamented, "This job's killing me. Can't remember the last time I got any."

The admission took Cachumbo by surprise. It almost seemed as if he choked on his second tamale. "I can take care of that, jefe. Straight up," he boasted. "What's your type? You like big butts or tight little buns? Laid back or savage like a wildcat? I fix you up, bro."

Color slowly returned to Roswell's face. His cheekbones rose. "No reason this trip should be a total loss, I suppose."

That sounded more like the man I knew, the John Roswell I remembered and loved. My brother in arms. The G-man business had worn down his veneer, but deep down, the old Roswell was still alive and well. All it took was the prospect of getting a hot piece of tail to draw him out.

The vagrant who'd been sleeping on the playground bench stirred, sat up, and tugged on his shirt, uncovering his head. I could see him squinting to blot out the intense oncoming sunlight. He was bony. Looked neglected.

Full of himself, Cachumbo reached for more food to fill his empty hand. I snatched it away before he could snare it with his bear-sized paw. "He needs this more than you do," I said, motioning toward the homeless dude. I added an Arepa Boyacense to the collection of sandwiches and paid my new friend a visit.

Chapter Twenty-Seven

The following week

As it turned out, Cachumbo's information was dead on. Ramón Uribe, the owner of Café Getsemani, was not a fan of competition and Dario Cabrera in particular. He jumped at the chance to steal us away from Señor Whisky Bar. He wasn't so much stealing us as wooing us. Having heard rumblings of a hot rock group at Cabrera's place, he detested losing business to his enemy.

We played five nights a week for Cabrera and had two days off. Granted, our days off were the slowest nights of the week, but that didn't seem to matter to Uribe. As best Cachumbo could determine, there was bad blood between the two club owners, and Uribe was thrilled to take something valuable away from Cabrera. Let's face it, Cabrera was less than likable, bordering on hostile. On his best day, he treated his staff with indifference. And with Gage Serna nowhere to be found, Cabrera's appeal was wearing thinner by the day.

It was time to move on.

Uribe knew how Cabrera managed his club, and that's probably why he treated us so nicely when we showed up for our first gig.

Uribe's club wasn't flashy in the way Cachumbo had described it, but it was head and shoulders nicer than Señor Whisky Bar. It wasn't chrome and glitz but more old-world appealing, just shy of classy. The staff was well-trained and supervised. They were dressed crisp and clean. No ripped jeans. No bottom-of-the-hamper shirts. No body odor. No shit on the shoes. No attitude. The floors were scrubbed, and the mirrored shelves behind the bar were dust-free. Liquor bottles were full and lined up like soldiers. And Uribe knew how to smile with a mouthful of pearly whites so large his teeth resembled the keyboard on a piano. He had long, wavy hair and a neatly trimmed mustache.

He welcomed us with a bottle of rum and a fistful of shot glasses. "Amigos!" he announced energetically. He opened his hand, somehow managing to keep all the shot glasses upright on his flat palm and extended it toward us. He'd only met us once but remembered everyone's name without hesitation. "Jalen, Pescado, Fargo, grab a glass." We each took a shot glass, and Uribe poured. "Here's to your first show at Café Getsemani. Make it a night to remember." The man had personality, miles of it, and was warm and engaging. Two minutes with him made me realize how completely antisocial Cabrera was. We clinked glasses and drank. He refilled our glasses the moment they were empty, then corked the bottle and set it down. I saw him looking around. "Where's the chica?" he asked.

"Willow? She should be here any minute now," I said, glancing at my watch. Willow was hard to figure out. She was quirky, and I liked quirky, but she was also a bit of a headcase, and I never knew from one day to the next what kind of mood she'd be in. One day, she'd be so into the performance I couldn't drag her away from the mic. The next day, it was like pulling teeth. She'd be solemn and moody, unwilling to put real effort into her performance. And being on time…never. It wasn't a question of her being late but more of degree, ten minutes or an hour, Johnny on the spot or a no-show. I didn't care if she was late as long as she arrived before we went on. We'd completed the soundchecks with Jalen at the mic. As far as I was concerned, she could simply show up and sing. I just hoped she brought her A game. Cachumbo had made it clear to us that Uribe expected nothing less.

"I don't have to worry, do I?" Uribe asked. I saw his smile fade, and in that short pause saw that he was capable of anger. It lingered in his eyes for only a moment, but it was nonetheless present and palpable. Unnerving.

"She was pretty nervous about playing here tonight," I said. "Probably took her two hours to pick out the right pair of shoes."

"Women, you know?" he said as his grin slowly overshadowed his darker side. "Men aren't supposed to understand."

"Si," I replied with large eyes and a thoughtful nod.

"I talked you up to all my friends," he said. "I know you won't disappoint me." He slapped me on the arm, then pointed a finger in my face that said there'd be consequences if we missed the mark, but it wasn't his sinister side speaking; it was the affable one, the one he presented to glad-hand me.

He was about to turn away when the clattering sound of women's heels traveled across the nightclub floor and came to a stop behind us. Willow was overdressed, decked out for a sold-out performance at the Copa Cabana in a sequined minidress that looked as if it had come straight out of Marilyn Monroe's closet. Jalen's mouth dropped because he knew no one would be looking at him tonight, not bare-chested, not even if he sang like Elvis. Dressed as she was, she was going to suck all the air out of the room. Her appearance had already extracted the life out of Jalen. Pescado and Fargo were reeling as well, whispering to each other.

"Look at you," Uribe said, his eyes wide, beaming delight. He took her hand and kissed it. "You've already stolen the show."

"I'm sorry I'm late," she said, sweet as pie in her thick accent. "I had nothing to wear, so I went to my friend's place, and she loaned me this dress."

"Well, it looks lovely on you," Uribe said. "You look beautiful."

Willow blushed three shades of red: scarlet, ruby, and flame-red. There was a lot about her I didn't understand, but what I did know was that she knew how to sell it. She was playing up to the boss. Her motive? Anyone's guess. I was too worried about the others losing their shit to care about what she was playing at.

Uribe tapped his watch. "Light the place up," he said and walked off.

"Nice getup," I said as I turned to Willow, barely able to hold back a scowl. "Who's your friend, Zsa Zsa Gabor?"

"It's a fancy club, no?" she asked innocently. "The lead singer's not supposed to be a Plain Jane."

I didn't buy what she was selling, the innocent girl routine. She knew all too well that she was attempting to upstage the rest of the band. There wasn't time for a fight. We had a job to do, and I wasn't going to let her long legs get in the way of our gig. "You'd better sing for all your worth," I said.

"Of course," she replied, her inflection shouting certainty. She took her spot at the center mic and adjusted the height on the stand. I had to admit she looked hot as hell standing center stage, fronting the band. She exuded sex appeal, which was exactly what she was supposed to do.

We started out with "Come Together." It was obvious from the first verse that Jalen and Willow were going to crush it. Their harmonies on the choruses soared, filling the room with competing octaves. I was proud of Jalen. Instead of cowering, he stepped up and delivered powerful vocals, challenging Willow on every lyric. It was a steadily paced song and gave the band time to get in sync, to find our groove.

And once we did…

We kicked it up tenfold, launching into "All Along the Watchtower." No one played Dylan's tune like Jimi, and no one played Jimi like me. I'd spent so many hours jamming with the man that I knew his riffs as well as he did and could play them note-for-note with the same feeling the left-handed master was famous for. I could picture him standing in front of me, wailing on his reverse-strung right-handed Strat, duking it out with me note for note. Then his image disappeared from my mind, and my guitar became a lightning rod, ripping electricity out of thin air. I could feel the power blazing from the neck of the guitar into my fingers. Incendiary licks. Blazing chords. Feedback reverberating off the amps. It was out of control. The audience responded with everything they had. They left their tables and crowded in front of the band, singing along, dancing, and grooving to the tunes. I saw Uribe smiling, nodding with approval. The dollar signs in his eyes teased a long-term contract. He wanted to tie us up for as long as he could. He wanted to rip us away from Cabrera. And from the way he was ogling, the dress off Willow's back as well.

Chapter Twenty-Eight

Mid-December 1969

It was only a couple of weeks before word of our betrayal got back to Cabrera. Señor Whisky Bar was practically empty when I arrived for rehearsal early in the afternoon, and I was stunned to see Cabrera out of his office. He sat alone at a table with a cigar, a glass of whisky, and a half-empty bottle of Jack. The smoke rolling off the lit end of his cigar formed a lazy S chain pattern as it rose toward the ceiling. He took a puff and waved me over. "Sit," he said without making eye contact. "Que Pása?"

What's going on? It was the closest thing to a conversation we'd had since I came aboard. Cabrera didn't speak to the hired help other than to order someone around. Bus the table. Take out the trash. That sort of thing. He never asked how we were or took any interest in our lives. We were only cogs in his wheel. To hear him broach a conversation… I was unprepared.

"Nothing, Señor Cabrera. I came in to rehearse."

"For me, or Pretty Boy Uribe?"

Breath caught in my throat. I'm sure he saw the color drain from my face.

"It's alright," he said. "Sit. I don't talk much, but I don't bite either." He grabbed an empty glass, poured two fingers, and slid it across the table to me. "Liquid courage, *sì?*"

He lifted his glass, and I joined him. The Jack burned like fire going down. My cheeks flushed as a wave of warmth washed over me.

"Have anything to say for yourself?"

"Apologies. You didn't seem like the kind of man who was open to conversation."

"Normally, no. You're right about that." He swirled the whiskey in his glass. "Still, you didn't have to go behind my back to that slimy bastard, Uribe. Had you gone to any other club owner, I would've looked the other way." He sighed, and air whistled through his nostrils. "But not him. Not Uribe."

There'd been talk about bad blood between Cabrera and Uribe, but Cachumbo had never gotten into specifics. Either he didn't know the details or figured it wasn't important to pass them along. Regardless, Cabrera had me at a disadvantage. "You're right. We should've been upfront about playing for Uribe. That's on me."

"He's not who you think he is," Cabrera said.

"I'm not sure what you mean."

I heard his neck crack when he shrugged. "You'll have to figure that out on your own. I'm a businessman, not a babysitter." He motioned to the door. "Anyway, you're not under contract. You can leave whenever you want to. Just give me reasonable notice."

I told a half-lie. "We didn't plan to quit." We'd have been happy to move on if the opportunity materialized, but for the time being, Uribe was good about having us two nights a week. I kept my mouth shut and waited to hear how Cabrera would respond. He took his sweet-ass time. I expected anger, but he seemed at ease.

"You can work every bar from here to Playa Blanca. Serna rarely goes clubbing anymore—he doesn't have the time."

I wasn't sure if he could see that I had stopped breathing, but I could feel the skin around my orbits stretching as my eyes widened. How did he know that I was interested in Serna? How did he know anything? What game was he playing at?

"Don't look so surprised," he said, his normally emotionless expression giving up a slight smile. "If Uribe told you Serna is hanging out at his club, he's full of shit. He doesn't go there anymore. He doesn't go to Club Bazurto, and he doesn't go to El Discoteca. Cachumbo's full of shit and is only interested in peddling horseshit and stretching out American paychecks as far as they'll go. The Americanos are stupid, but they're not brain-dead. He knows he won't be able to reach into the FBI's pocket forever." He tapped ash off his cigar, and it drifted lightly into a stamped metal ashtray. The front door opened. Pescado walked in with his bass guitar slung over his shoulder. Cabrera leaned forward and slapped me on the leg. "*Guitarrista*, close your mouth. I saw a jumping spider in here just before. You wouldn't want one to hop in."

Chapter Twenty-Nine

Later that day

The vibes of blues players past and present were nowhere to be found as we rehearsed the next day. I couldn't channel anything, nothing I'd heard or practiced, and nothing I remembered. The guitar was dead in my hands, nothing more than a slab of wood with strings that refused to resonate. I couldn't put my usual combinations together and when I did, the tone sounded thin, as if I was playing through a cheap transistor radio and not a Marshall amp.

Cabrera sat at his table and watched me the whole time. He was pokerfaced on the outside but must've been laughing on the inside. He knew he'd messed with my head. The others didn't know what was wrong, only that I was playing like shit, off tempo with boring repetitive notes. My sound was about as fresh as a fish left out to rot in the sun.

"Dude, what's up?" Jalen asked when we took a break. "Late night or what?" He glanced at Cabrera. "You've got to forget he's here. I've never seen you so stressed before."

My music can be loud, but my mind needs to be quiet when I play, and the clamoring in my head was unbearable, like the frenzied, unending explosions from a series of exploding mortar shells. So many thoughts were surfacing at once. I couldn't focus on any of them. And playing, well…forget about it. I just couldn't.

"You're very tense today," Willow said. She gave me a peck on the cheek.

"Cool out, muchacho. It's just music, right?" She danced off and started hamming it up with Jalen. The two vocalists had begun to gravitate toward each other since the night Willow showed up at Uribe's place in her go-go dress. Jalen showed everyone that he wasn't going to wimp out, that he was willing to go balls to the wall with her, and the effect of his newly-found machismo on her was obvious; their transformed chemistry was palpable.

Cachumbo never told us that Serna would appear at Café Getsemani. He only suggested that if we widen our net and play at other clubs, Serna might be likely to visit one of them. But Cabrera had spoken with such confidence. He seemed certain we wouldn't find Serna at Getsemani or anywhere else. How did he know what we were up to? Had Cachumbo blabbed? Was he, as Cabrera said, full of shit? Was he doing whatever it took to suck Roswell's coffers dry?

Cabrera reached into his shirt pocket and pulled out a cigar. Standing up, he used his free hand to gesture to me. I followed him outside. The midday heat was brutal. Sweat ran over me in a torrent.

"Are you sure you're cut out for this kind of work?" he said as he bit the tip off his cigar and spit it into the gutter. "Look at you, our little conversation has you going to pieces." I didn't know what to say and waited patiently for him to speak again. He used a wooden match to light his cigar and puffed on the end until the tip glowed red and the brown tobacco turned to whitish ash. "Go back inside. Apologize to your band for not having it today and pack up your guitar. I'm taking you on a field trip. I'll prove my worth."

"Where are we going?"

"Never mind. You'll see when we get there. Now do as I say and grab a bottle of Jack on your way out. You need to get your head on straight." He drew heavily on the cigar before expelling the smoke into the air. "You're not moving, and you should be. You want to stay out of prison, don't you?"

Cabrera was obviously more than he'd let on to be. He knew that Roswell was using prison time as leverage for my participation. What else did he know? Who was he working for? I walked into the bar and packed my guitar. I was not a spy and never suggested I was. I knew I wasn't. Roswell knew it better. Still, he put me in this game, and I was floundering.

* * *

We were in a car a solid forty-five minutes, traveling down the coast to the port city of Mamonal. Driving along the waterway, we passed several docked ships of every size and description, everything from modestly sized fishing boats to huge container ships. Cabrera tapped the window on my side of the car. Looking out, I saw a massive oil barge. The markings on the side of the ship read Serna Oil.

My eyes were still wide as I turned to him. "Is this why we're here?"

He laughed a deep, rumbly laugh. "Yes, that's why I instructed you to bring your electric guitar. We're going to serenade the ships moored at the pier."

The taxi continued on past the port, then turned inland. Within a few minutes, we stopped in front of a paneled building. The wood plank exterior was gray with wear from the sun and salt air. It didn't look like much of anything, no more than a dilapidated hovel tucked away at the end of a road surrounded by tall thickets.

"Where are we?" I asked.

Cabrera handed cash to the driver and gave him instructions to wait for us.

I got out of the cramped compact car and took my guitar case out of the trunk, then Cabrera handed me the bottle of Jack. "Settle your nerves before we go inside," he said.

I shook my head. "No, I'm okay."

He shoved the bottle into my hands and insisted. "Take a short one," he said, "a quick snort."

I took a swig and left the bottle in the cab before we went inside. I heard music coming through the rickety old structure as we approached. Once inside, a short hallway stood before us. Cabrera rapped softly on one of the doors and opened it without waiting for a reply. It led to a small recording studio sound room. There was no one at the mixing desk, but through the glass panel that separated the control room from the live studio, I saw a band rehearsing, two guitarists, a bass player, and a drummer. One guitarist seemed to be demonstrating a fingering position, but I couldn't see his hands on the neck.

The other guitarist had his back to us. With the control room monitors switched off, I couldn't clearly hear what they were playing.

Once again, Cabrera tapped on the glass, drawing my attention to the guitarist facing away from us. He was completely blasé as words came out of his mouth, "As promised, I prove my worth. Finally, you will meet *Serna*."

Chapter Thirty

Two days later

The Cartagena Del Mar was a one-star hotel in a half-star area with a hooker-to-tourist ratio of nearly three-to-one. Mere days before Christmas, there was no sense of the forthcoming holiday except for a small, decorated tree in the corner of the lobby and Bing Crosby's "White Christmas," looping endlessly from overhead speakers.

The lobby-floor saloon was dark and shabby. Dim light provided reasonable anonymity to male tourists hoping to get acquainted with the local *prostitutas* without garnering attention from crooked cops. The hotel manager paid off the local *policia* to keep the establishment sting and bust free. It was money well spent.

Roswell didn't go to many of the band's gigs because he didn't want anyone to connect the G-man with the band. He'd told Sonny he wouldn't make it to their evening performance and was glad he had. His sensitive digestion and the local cuisine were a hit-and-miss proposition, and he was still feeling queasy from lunching on fried mojarra fish. The bartender told him alcohol would kill the bacteria in his stomach and poured him two fingers of cheapo swill.

"You like our music, yes?" Willow said as she took a seat next to the American at the bar. "You don't come around a lot, but I see you even though you try not to be seen."

John Roswell had turned down solicitations from tawdry women all night long. He was no choirboy but had grown fond of peeing without setting the commode on fire with bacteria-infected pee. He'd indulged working girls frequently during his tour in Vietnam and couldn't shake the memory of all the penicillin needles he'd taken in the butt. He heard that they stop working after a while and worried he'd pick up a strain the doctors couldn't cure.

Sitting face-forward, he was reluctant to turn his head and make eye contact with the prostitute, but he thought her pickup line interesting; the relentless sound of Bing Crosby's voice was driving him mad. Turning toward her, he recognized the band's singer immediately, in particular the form-fitting go-go minidress she'd worn at Café Getsemani the last time he'd looked in on Sonny's band. He placed his glass on the bar and eyed her coolly. Knowing that the singing gig paid peanuts, he wasn't surprised that she had a side hustle. She seemed out of place amongst the other five-bucks-a-blow denizens working the bar. She was young and pretty without the telltale signs the other girls carried, their testimonials to endurance and need, their makeup-covered bruises and torn stockings. Willow's eyes weren't dead like the others.

"Aren't you supposed to be at the club with Sonny and the band?"

She shrugged. "I needed a night off," she said and rubbed her throat. "My vocal cords needed a rest, and Jalen can handle things very well on his own."

"I see." He took a sip of the painfully bad hooch. "This isn't a good idea," he said.

"And I recognize you," she bubbled, then picked up his tumbler and gulped the last of his whiskey. She grimaced. "How can you drink this? It's *teh-rree-bleh.*"

"Beggars can't be choosers, and I still think this is a bad idea."

"I've seen you in the audience here and there, at Café Getsemani and also at Señor Whisky Bar. You're a fan, yes?"

"Something like that." He hailed the bartender and ordered two beers. "It's shitty beer, but it's better than the shitty hooch. One drink and then you go." He bumped his eyebrows to convey his seriousness, then peeled off a twenty and handed it to her. "Here. You can take the night off. You're not coming up to my room."

"I'm not a hooker."

"Then, what are you doing here?" he asked. The beers were placed on the bar. They clinked bottles and drank. "This isn't exactly the classiest part of town," he said.

"Yet, you're here."

"I'm writing a book. It's called *Colombia On Five Dollars A Day*."

"You're full of shit," she said in a playful manner, then swigged her beer. "I see through you."

"Obvious, am I?"

"Uh-huh. Our band is good, but not so good that tourists follow us from bar to bar in Cartagena. It has to be something else." She put her hand on top of his. "Admit it. You like me. Let's go upstairs together."

"I thought you said you're not a hooker."

"I'm not." She picked up the twenty and stuffed it in his shirt pocket. "See."

"I'm no slouch, but you're a very pretty girl, and nothing in life is that easy. You showing up at my hotel is not a coincidence," he said. "What's the catch?"

She nuzzled his earlobe. "Take me upstairs, and I'll tell you."

Chapter Thirty-One

It was an hour later when Willow rolled off of Roswell, pulled a cigarette out of the pack, and lit it. Staring at the revolving ceiling fan, she inhaled deeply and exhaled a perfect smoke ring that rose no more than a few inches before the breeze from the fan scattered it. As she'd expected, the hotel room wasn't much, drab and unremarkable with chipped paint and monstrous spider webs, but it was exactly the type of lodging she'd become acquainted with since arriving in Cartagena. There were two very diverse socioeconomic classes in the city, the drug-dealing trade living high on the hog and everyone else, a populous barely scraping by.

She pulled the sheet up from the foot of the bed, leaving her naked from the waist up, her nipples erect and pointing straight up.

"You've got the most spectacular tits I've ever seen," Roswell said.

She glanced at him briefly, her lips curling upward at the corners. "Not too big and not too small. I think they're just right."

"And so do I." He took the cigarette out of her hand and took a long, satisfying drag. "Now that the festivities are out of the way, should we get down to business?"

"Really, two pops and out? That's all you've got?"

"No, I've got pops galore, but I'd like to understand what we're doing here before I get so giddy on hot, sweaty sex that I lose my ability to reason."

"What's the rush? We're having a good time, aren't we?"

"Sure, but you know why you're here, and I don't."

"You're a party pooper. This is the sixties. Haven't you heard about free love?"

"Heard about it and sampled it heavily, but nothing is truly free. Everything comes at a cost." He turned to her with an expression that showed he was all business. "What's yours?"

"Okay, be like that." She slipped a thin leather wallet out of her small clutch bag. Opening it, she presented her credentials.

He read the letters slowly, "I.C.P.O.? What the hell is this, the International Crime Police Organization? This is bullshit, right? Something you had made at a local print shop?"

"Yeah, of course," she began curtly, "because America is the only country with an intelligence network."

He studied her identification once more, this time more carefully. "Cayetana Blanco. That's you?" She nodded demonstratively. "No shit, you're a cop?"

"What did you think? All I could do was sing and shake my ass?"

"Don't sell yourself short, Honey. Anyone can be a spy, but a pretty woman with mad vocal chops isn't easy to come by. Sonny was lucky as hell to find you."

She peaked an eyebrow. "He didn't find me. I found him. Did he tell you how we got together?"

"Sonny said Cabrera followed you out of his office with his fly open and he figured that you…" Roswell's eyes flashed, then he smiled. "You cunning little bitch. You engineered the whole thing, didn't you?" A moment passed. "Is Cabrera working with you?"

"Yes. We know all about Sonny Rojas and why he's in Cartagena. Correction, why the FBI set him up here in Cartagena, the Serna empire, and how it's smuggling narcotics into your country. You Americans think the entire fucking world revolves around you and you alone, but most of the narcotics coming out of Colombia don't land in the United States. They're smuggled into Europe. The combined population of the European countries is three times the population of the United States." She glimpsed his lessening erection and grinned. "I see that news comes as quite a blow to your ego."

He grabbed the sheet and covered himself. "And the I.C.P.O.?"

"We're based out of Spain, and our sole focus is to stem the flow of narcotics into the European Union."

Roswell snorted as his head fell back onto his pillow. "You sure had me going. Jesus, you don't sound anything like you do when you're around the boys. You're like a Latina Dr. Jekyll and Mrs. Hyde."

Her eyes twinkled. "It's all part of the package, Roswell. I hope you're impressed?"

"Impressed? Honey, I'm fucking floored." He laughed quietly for a moment, reveling in the simple pleasure of being outdone before turning the other cheek. "So, what is it you want from the FBI and what's it going to cost?"

"What makes you think it's going to cost anything?"

"Because you high-on-the-hog Europeans don't have two nickels to rub together from having Hitler run amuck across your storied land all the way from the tip of Norway down to bottom of Greece. Besides, you wouldn't have led off with a roll in the sheets if you didn't want something from me. For all its purported grandeur, Europe is still on the balls of its ass."

"Here's something that's very, very American," she said as she sprang from the bed and gave him the finger. "Read your history books, asshole. Spain wasn't attacked in World War II. We're thriving. But you are right about one thing: I slept with you because I wanted something, your cooperation. And one more thing, despite all the bravado, you're just a mediocre lay."

VI

PART SIX - WHAM

Chapter Thirty-Two

1970

Señor Whisky Bar had just undergone a state-mandated extermination to get rid of the rodents that were as hopelessly addicted to food scraps as the stoners were to pot and coke. El ratas were a big problem in the city, and the government was enforcing pest controls to cut down on the spread of disease. The bar reeked of pesticide. I mean it outright stunk. I figured it was the reason Willow was a no-show for the evening's gig.

I hadn't told anyone that I'd met Gage Serna, not Roswell and not Cachumbo. I didn't know how to communicate that Cabrera had set up the meeting. Not so much a meeting but an introduction. He'd arranged to have me work with Serna and his instructor, a talented local musician far more proficient at classical guitar than rock and blues.

All the nervousness that had plagued me earlier in the day had disappeared when Cabrera and I got to the makeshift recording studio. I wailed on the guitar, impressing the hell out of Serna. It wasn't long before he asked about my background. I laid it out as modestly as my ego would allow, my time playing with Townshend and Clapton in New York, playing with Hendrix in California, and Harrison in London. It didn't matter how much I played it down. The look in his eyes told me he was astounded, and an instantaneous bond between us had been formed.

Once back at Señor Whisky Bar, we laid down a great session, and Jalen didn't seem to mind having the mic to himself. He'd been feeling full of himself, and his confidence fronting the band was impressive to see. He was like a bird who'd escaped its cage.

I put my hand on his shoulder. "You kicked ass tonight," I said.

Jalen smiled, ear-to-ear, blushing an intense shade of crimson. "Gracias, hombre." We pounded fists, and he boogied over to Pescado and Fargo for a round of well-deserved high-fives.

We were going to play at Cabrera's bar again the next night, so there was no need to break down our equipment. A serious-looking guy waited for me when I left for the evening. I looked at him and said nothing. He turned and pointed to a glistening, black Lincoln convertible. It stood out like a diamond amongst the drab hues of discarded litter and mud puddles on the Cartagena street. Gage Serna waved to me from the Lincoln's back seat and called me over.

He was dressed down in a white shirt and jeans, but it didn't take a practiced eye to see that he was a wealthy man. There was the expensive haircut and the understated elegance of the way he put an outfit together. He spoke with practically no accent at all, which wasn't surprising. I had been extensively briefed on his background and his family's as well. The Serna family had a plan for succession that was laid out in concrete as rigidly as the succession of Queen Elizabeth of England by the heir apparent at the time of her death. Serna had known from a very young age that the family business would be his to run when his father passed away. Just as his younger brother Thiago would succeed Gage when he died.

"Yo, Sonny," he boomed. "What's with this place? I wanted to listen to your band, but the place stinks like shit."

"Sorry, man," I said. "Rat problem."

"Too bad." His eyes lit up. "Hey, you want to grab a beer?"

I couldn't believe that after all this time, Roswell's plan was actually falling into place. I was so excited I forgot to answer.

"Well?" he asked.

"Yeah, okay." I got in, and the guy who'd met me outside the bar got behind the wheel. "Where to?" I asked.

"Don't worry. I've got a place." He tapped the driver on the shoulder. "Jacobo," he said in a joyful tone, "to the pier."

* * *

We made a lot of small talk on the way to the harbor, all the items I'd been schooled on by Roswell, the cover story I'd memorized. Serna asked about where I was born and where I'd learned to play guitar, all items I responded to truthfully and without the need to invent lies. Roswell told me the less I invested, the less chance there would be of getting caught up in a lie. I passed it along exactly as it had happened, raised in Cape Coral, Florida, living at home with my folks, and the bold move, hitching to New York, where I met Townshend, Clapton, and Hendrix. He was curious about my encounters with the guitar gods—again, I laid it out exactly as it transpired. The only thing I had to lie about was what I was doing in Colombia, my cover story. It had run through my mind so many times it actually felt like the truth. Deep down, though, I knew it was pure bullshit, a lie that might result in my death, especially since the story involved Cachumbo. I now suspected that he was playing all sides and was only interested in milking revenue from Roswell. "Cachumbo's a friend of the family. He invited me down and set me up with the gig at Señor Whisky Bar.

"You must be having second thoughts," Serna said with peaked eyebrows. "One day you're working out riffs with George Harrison and the next you're playing to winos and stoners in the low-rent district of Cartagena. I'm sure it's not what you expected."

"Definitely not, but it's given me a chance to work on my music without the influence of rockers I feel the need to impress. These big names, they've got definite ideas about the way things should be done, and it doesn't always align with what I want to do. Don't get me wrong, Cartagena is not a forever thing for me. It's just a bus stop. I've got some new stuff I've been working on and figured I'd head back to New York when it's perfected."

He slapped me on the back. "Then I'm glad we met when we did. Mejia, the instructor I've been working with, I thought he had a lot to teach me until you showed up. Now I know how limited he is."

"Mejia's a talented musician, but he's no rocker."

Being naïve about Serna's wealth made it easy for me to play dumb. Especially when we arrived at the dock. I outright gasped when I got my first glimpse of his pleasure yacht. It had to be one hundred feet long and was lit up from the bow to the stern, the lights twinkling brightly before a velvety black sea with crisp stars burning in the heavens above. It was surreal.

"What do you do?" I asked like an amazed child, once again telling the truth. "I've never seen anything like this."

"My family is in the oil business," Serna said matter-of-factly as we got out of the Lincoln and made our way along the gangway. The name stenciled across the stern of the yacht was Liquid Gold. "I'm very fortunate."

"There's oil down here in Colombia?"

"Oh, yes, Sonny," he said with a chuckle. "There is indeed. It's the country's largest export, and my family is one of the largest holders of fuel oil. We export all over the world."

I was tongue-tied, a wide-eyed kid in a candy store with confections wrapped in gold paper. "Wow," I said, repeatedly. The only thing preventing me from being absolutely giddy was the voice in the back of my head. The only reason I was on Gage Serna's pleasure boat was to ingratiate myself and investigate his ties to the narcotics market.

We boarded and entered the saloon. It was immense and decorated in ivory and blue, the walls paneled in expensive wood veneers. A steward appeared from below deck and offered us champagne. Serna handed me a flute. "To rock and roll," he toasted. We clinked glasses and drank.

"This is a far cry from the stuff they pour at Señor Whisky Bar," I said. The bottle on the steward's serving tray had an orange label and read Veuve Clicquot. I knew little about champagne, but I'd often seen the orange-labeled bottles in rock stars' dressing rooms.

"Enjoy!" he said. "Drink up, and I'll show you around afterward." He sat down on one of the sofas and crossed his legs. "I love the sound of the electric guitar. Especially Clapton's so-called woman tone. I was crushed when Cream announced they were breaking up."

"Yeah, well, Jack Bruce and Ginger Baker never really got along. They were always going at it, ridiculing each other and making life a pain in the ass. Eric had had enough of the drama and decided to move on."

"That's a real shame. They were so good, so fucking good. One of a kind. Do you know how Eric does it, the so-called woman tone, that is?"

"Well, yeah. Eric's pretty forthcoming about that stuff. You turn the bass all the way down, the volume all the way up, and play over the neck pickup, but what makes the sound so unique are the combinations he puts together. I mean, he comes up with groupings and patterns no one's thought of. Don't get me wrong, it all has its roots in American southern blues, but he makes it his own if you know what I mean."

Serna seemed enthralled. "I do. I've a large collection of blues albums. But Clapton…the man is a genius. For a minute there, I thought you were going to tell me that duplicating his sound was going to be easy, a simple adjustment of the volume and tone controls, but I have the sense that's not so."

"Gage, nothing that sounds that good is that easy. If it was, every guitarist from London to San Francisco would be doing it, and as far as I know, no one's been quite able to duplicate the sound."

"Does it have anything to do with the guitar? I know he played many of his performances with the Gibson model SG."

"That's true. Eric toured with the SG, but he told me he recorded most of the album tracks on *Disraeli Gears* with a Les Paul he bought off Andy Summers."

"I don't know who that is," Serna said.

"Andy's a great guitarist, Gage. Do you know that long solo on Traffic's 'Coloured Rain'?"

"Yes, sure. It's fantastic."

"That's Summers."

The rich man's jaw flapped open, and his eyes grew large. He was eating up the rock star inside scoop. "I'm angry that I know so little about the music I love," Serna said. "I should've known who played on that track."

"Eric's artistry aside, I think the key is the Les Paul's double humbucker setup played through a Marshall one-hundred-watt Epi."

He set down his glass. "It just so happens I've got a Les Paul and a Marshall amp set up in one of the state rooms below. Can we give it a try?"

Why not? I thought. *The man wants woman tone, I'll give him woman tone up the wazoo.* Of late, I'd been keener on playing brighter music with more of a Latin vibe than playing psychedelic rock, but I'd devoured my Cream albums in the past and had copied many of Eric's riffs note for note. Would I sound as good as Clapton? Not quite. But would it be good enough to impress Serna? No sweat.

"Come on," he said as he stood. "You know, I've had a thought—what do you think about giving me private lessons? You probably make chump change working at the bar. I'm quite sure I can make it worth your while."

It almost seemed too easy, as if Roswell knew exactly how the scenario would unfold. If I said yes, I'd have the opportunity to see Serna on a regular basis and get close to him. It was exactly what I was supposed to accomplish. "Let's talk about it," I said, doing my best to keep my eagerness in check. "Now, where's that Les Paul?"

Chapter Thirty-Three

Serna was a different person after the guitars were plugged in and the amplifiers cranked. He was a voracious student, and though he didn't pick up new techniques quickly, he practiced until he got them right. He was a knowledge sponge, willing to soak up anything I laid down. I fed him a pretty heavy dose of new material and passed out aboard his yacht about four in the morning. I didn't rise until late the next morning. The mattress in my stateroom was super thick and incredibly comfy. I got the best night's sleep I'd gotten in ages and woke up without a severe backache for the first time since arriving in Cartagena.

Serna was already gone when I got up, but the steward prepared a delicious breakfast, affording me a brief glimpse at what it felt like to be rich. Looking out at the Caribbean Sea while I drank strong coffee, the evening of guitar jamming was still resonating through my brain. It was the closest I'd been to heaven, but sadly, I felt in my gut that it was the closest I'd ever come to it again. I'd finally connected with Serna, and though it was the objective I had set out to accomplish, I knew I was heading down a dangerous path, one that might cost me my life.

I was driven to the bar in a different car and by a different driver, a stately Mercedes sedan. Rapping against the side window, they seemed so thick I figured they were bulletproof. I couldn't hear road noise or the children begging for money as we drove past. Was that why the big Benz was in Serna's fleet, or was it because the glass was bulletproof? Rather than reveling in the luxury of the immense sedan, I was stricken by the fact that Serna needed a car with bulletproof glass, that he must've had a slew of enemies who wanted him dead. Was it merely because of his extraordinary wealth, or was it because of the drugs? How many enemies did a man like Gage Serna have? *Too many*, I reasoned.

Serna was enamored with me at the moment, but how would he react if he discovered my true motive or that I was working with the FBI? The question was redundant. Roswell would send me to prison if I quit my assignment, but betraying Serna would result in my death.

Chapter Thirty-Four

I was mulling over the impossible decision when I spotted Roswell waiting for me down the road from the bar, sunglasses, head down. The words *I quit* formed in my mind but hadn't yet made it to my lips. I needed more time to think, to try to be rational. Was there a way to make a deal with Roswell for the time I'd already worked? For the efforts I'd made? Roswell had a strange expression on his face, one I found hard to read.

"Did you eat?" he asked as I approached him after the big Benz disappeared from view.

Did I? Like a king. Like a robber baron. Like a drug lord. I didn't want my lavish breakfast to be my last meal. In my heart, I knew it was time to get out. Those two words, I quit, were now formed and on my lips, ready to be set free when Roswell threw me a Sandy Koufax curveball.

"How's Serna?"

"What?" How did he know? What did he know? I grabbed him by the arm and dragged him further down the block.

"Easy," he said as he pulled free. "Don't sweat it, Sonny. I'm in the intelligence community. Remember? You shouldn't be so surprised?"

"I'm surprised because for the last several months and probably longer, you didn't know anything about Serna's whereabouts. He was a ghost. A goddamn ghost. I jammed with him last night, and all of a sudden, you're all-knowing? Do you want to tell me what's going on? Did you know Serna's car has bulletproof glass? What does that tell you?"

"That he doesn't like bullets?" he said with a sly grin.

"I'm not laughing, John. This is my life we're playing with." We continued to walk down the street, through the midday crowd. The street was teeming with workers grabbing quick lunches and locals doing their food shopping. "I'm waiting, John."

"Willow," he began, "she's not who we thought she was."

I knew there was a side to Cabrera I really didn't understand, but I never suspected Willow of being anything other than the woman she presented herself to be, a local Cartagena girl with great vocal chops and fabulous tatas. "Willow? What do you mean?"

"She's a plant, Sonny. She's working for Spanish intelligence."

"How'd you find out?"

Roswell was not one to mince words. "She fucked my brains out, then asked for my cooperation."

I was astounded by the news. Not about the two of them going at it, but because she was a spy. I never saw it coming.

She and Cabrera work as a team. "Remember what you told me the first time you met her? That it looked like she'd just put out for Cabrera to get a spot with the band?" Eyes closed, I nodded. "That was one hell of a con job. They made you think what they wanted you to think. Pretty clever, if you ask me."

"I know about Cabrera. I mean, I didn't know who he was working for, but that he knew far too much to be a simple club owner. He's the one who set me up with Serna and his guitar instructor."

"They work for some organization called the ICPO. They've got huge drug problems in Europe, apparently, many times greater than the problem we have with illegal drugs coming into the States. They want to cooperate and share information. Introducing you to Serna was their way of showing good faith. An olive branch."

"Shit."

"What's the matter now?"

"I'm out of my depth, John. I had no idea we were being snowed by Cabrera and Willow." A lump formed in my throat. "It's the kind of stupidity that can get a man killed. A man like me. I'm going home."

"You mean you're going to prison."

"Better than dying. Way better. I didn't understand the stakes. Now I know and they're too high. Way too high. I still don't fully understand, but I'm starting to get the picture."

The afternoon heat and humidity were brutal. We stopped at a street vendor's cart, and Roswell bought a couple of cold sodas. "I think you're overreacting, Sonny. How does more help and more information relate to the situation getting worse? After all this time, you're finally in a position to get close to Serna. You want to pull the plug now?"

I took a swig of soda. "Yeah. I'm smart enough to know that I'm in over my head."

Roswell sighed and rolled the cold glass bottle across his forehead. "Sonny, you can't just up and leave. Serna's not stupid. He'll put two and two together, close ranks, and make himself completely untouchable. Don't do that to me. You owe me, man. You owe me your goddamn life."

"Shit!" I repeated with disgust as a cold, hard memory rocked me. I was only alive, only breathing because he'd pulled me out of the Vietnamese jungle and flew me to safety. Had it not been for Roswell, I would've died in the same spot where I'd smacked down in the rocky riverbed.

"Sonny, I hear you. Just give me some time to put together Plan B. A few weeks, alright?"

I felt my chest tightening. Coupled with the heat and humidity, my nerves made it difficult to breathe. "I don't know, John. I need time to think about it."

"Fine. Let me make it easier for you. Just do what you've been doing. Teach Serna the guitar and stay close to him with no additional strings attached. Just keep the connection alive until I can figure a workaround. Do that and I'll let you walk, no prison time, no nothing. Can you hang in there a little longer?"

Roswell made it seem so easy and by extension, so hard to say no. It was all coming at me so fast. I was a musician, not a spy, and I was playing a game I didn't understand, one that might mean the end of life as I knew it. "I don't know, John. I just don't know." I shrugged, shook my head, and walked off.

Chapter Thirty-Five

September 18, 1970

Serna sent his car for me every Tuesday and Thursday. It picked me up in front of the Carmen Church, in the old town of Cartagena on Tuesdays and by the San Pedro Claver Church on Thursdays. Serna never said the alternating locations were picked for my safety. He didn't have to. I'd begun waiting for his driver, Jacobo, inside the church, and I made it a practice to arrive a few minutes early so that I had time to say a prayer. I prayed not only for my own safety but for the well-being of my parents back in Florida, and for my close relatives and friends. In Colombia, I was cut off from everyone I knew. The telephone service in Colombia was terrible, but I reached out to my parents whenever I had time to tell them that I was alright, even though, in my heart, I felt my safety was no more than an illusion. I gave them lots of assurances, more than necessary, and I could hear greater concern in my parents' voices with every new phone call. The bulletproof car and armed chauffeur were meant to instill a sense of well-being, but they had the opposite effect. I cringed every time I saw the tank-like Benz waiting for me outside one of the churches because I knew I might lose my life at any time.

Sometimes Serna would be on his yacht. Other times, we met at one of his residences. I'd been to three of his lavish homes and had the sense there were more. He had instruments and equipment in each of them, tens of thousands of dollars of equipment, all top-end stuff, the best money could buy.

I taught him songs, not music. He had no interest in the mechanics of musical composition. He simply wanted to emulate everything he loved: the chords, the riffs, and the solos. He wanted to copy the records note for note, effect for effect, distortion for distortion. In time, it became one big bore. Copying Clapton didn't make you Clapton. Mimicking Keith Richards didn't make you a Rolling Stone. Sure, I was no stranger to simulating the music I loved, but I'd traveled that road ages ago and was now only interested in learning and creating, not imitating. I'd taken what I learned and changed it into something original, something I could call my own. Perhaps Serna would get to that point one day, but I doubted I'd be around to see it. He wasn't a musician; he was a hobbyist. Music was his diversion—for me, it was my life.

We were about two hours into a practice session. I'd have to leave for the evening's gig within the hour. We broke for dinner. I knew it would be a treat because Serna was a generous host. The dinner table was always set up buffet style with a large assortment of meats, shellfish, and sides. Booze flowed, not the cheapo brands they poured at Cabrera's bar but top-shelf stuff. I had to admit that I looked forward to our meals together. We'd hang out, talk, and drink to excess. Jacobo would drive me to the club afterward. It felt as if I was punching out at work only to head to a second job.

"Is Southeast Asia as bad as I've heard?" he asked as he picked at fruit and cheeses.

"Vietnam was bad, Gage. It was fucking awful." I set my fork down and sat back in my chair. "I was lucky to get out as quickly as I did. And in one piece. My back's a jigsaw puzzle, but I've learned to live with it. So many soldiers got shipped home in body bags that..." My stomach tightened. "In a way, I was lucky to get injured and discharged. Chances are I wouldn't have made it out alive otherwise."

"But I see the way you move around. You're in constant pain, no?"

I shrugged. "Yes, but at least I came home with my arms and legs. I wasn't there long enough to get a full dose of the shit show. I didn't have to trudge through the mud on my belly, praying not to get shot. Or worse, captured by the VC, imprisoned, and tortured. I didn't come home with my mind frayed like pulled pork." I picked up my fork and speared a cut of steak. "I'm here eating like a king. Trust me, I was lucky, effed-up spine and all."

"You have a good attitude, *mi parcero*. No crying in your beer, right?"

"I let my guitar do all the crying for me."

"Yes, you do and very well." He savored a mouthful of wine. "So, tell me about the skydiving. Did you learn that in the service or before you were drafted?"

"Fort Benning, Georgia. Military jump school."

"So, what went wrong? Did they not give you adequate training?"

"No. It was a mechanical error. We were told we were making a low-altitude jump, but the plane's instruments went haywire. We jumped from a much higher altitude, and the wind carried us way off course. Some of the men in my platoon got seriously hurt, but none died, thank God." A lump formed in my throat. "Like I said, I was lucky."

"And now I'm lucky." Serna reached over and slapped me on the shoulder. "Fate brought us together. Do you think you might ever skydive again? My younger brother Thiago has tried a few times. He's a thrill seeker, but I don't think he's into it enough to become good at it. To tell you the truth, my heart is in my mouth every time he straps on a parachute."

"Is your brother here in Cartagena?"

"No, he goes to school in the States. At this moment, he's in Florida working on something for me." He rested his fork on his plate and looked me in the eye. "So, what about it, would you jump again?

"I don't know, Gage. There'd have to be one hell of a goddamn good reason for it. I really screwed up my back making a night jump over Vietnam. The military docs put me back together with spit and chewing gum. It's a huge problem for me and might always be."

"I have access to some excellent doctors in the States. I'd be happy to—"

The sound of Jacobo's heavy feet interrupted us. He walked purposefully into the dining room, eyes serious, deadly serious. "*Boss*, you have a call," he said.

"No," Serna said with a shake of the head. "You see I'm busy."

"It's Guzman," he said. Serna's expression became somber as Jacobo leaned over and whispered in his ear. Somehow, I managed to hear a bit of what Jacobo said, "Guzman doesn't sound happy."

Checking my watch. "I have to get back anyway—don't want to keep the band waiting."

"Give me a few minutes," Serna said as he stood up. "I'll take the drive back with you." He picked up the remote control and turned on the TV in the large den. "I have a special antenna and get all the US stations. You'll wait for me, Sonny?"

As if I had a choice. "Sure."

"Good. Make yourself comfortable."

As Serna walked briskly from the room, I refilled my glass with bourbon and made my way over to the sofa in front of the TV. ABC evening news was on. It had been such a long time since I watched TV that I was mesmerized by the coverage of the Vietnam War. The damn stupid war was still part of me and probably always would be. The news anchor reported that we were just past the halfway point in the month and already more than two hundred American soldiers had lost their lives. There were still close to half a million US troops deployed, and though there had been talk of American withdrawal in the near future, Nixon was slow to make things happen. Sure, he talked the talk, but I didn't see American boys boarding transports and heading home. As usual, Tricky Dick was full of shit.

Serna was not his bubbly, effervescent self when he returned. It looked as if he had something on his mind, but he remained quiet. He sat down on the sofa next to me while war coverage continued.

"You okay?" I asked.

He shrugged. "Business, you know? Never a dull moment." Pointing to the TV screen, "I see that the war is still very close to your heart."

"Those soldiers and me, we are one." Looking at the time again, "I really have to get going."

"Jacobo," he called out. "Bring the car around." We both stood. "Sonny, something has come up, and I'm afraid I can't ride back to the bar with you."

"Not a problem, Gage. Thanks for dinner. It was delicious. I'll see you—"

Fresh news coverage had begun. The first words out of the reporter's mouth stole my breath. "The Experience is over." I fell back onto the sofa, stricken as the report continued. "The rock and roll musician died in a London hospital today, apparently from an overdose of drugs." It felt as if my heart had been crushed, as if an anvil had fallen on it. "During his brief career, Hendrix flailed his electric guitar into some of the most unusual sounds of music. A report now from ABC's Gregory Jackson."

Serna read the grief on my face, sat down, and put his arm over my shoulder. "I'm so sorry, Sonny. I know how much Jimi meant to you. What can I do to help?"

I knew that Serna's intention was sincere, but his timing was lousy. All of my fears walloped me like a thunderclap to the chest. Then, two sedans pulled up in front of his house, and armed men poured from the cars.

Chapter Thirty-Six

Straight from Serna's home, Jacobo drove me back to my apartment instead of the bar. I pulled out my backpack and stuffed it with clothes. Laundry day had come and gone—there wasn't a lot that was clean. It didn't matter. Everything went into my backpack, regardless of when it was last laundered. I pulled my desk chair into the closet. Standing on it, I reached up inside to where I'd cut a wedge in the sheetrock, reached in, and removed my passport and any cash I'd squirreled away. I'd just stepped off the chair when someone knocked on the door.

I was still feeling numb after watching the assault team pull up in front of Serna's home. Those men could've been sent to kill him, but they weren't. They were his men, which was just as bad and just as terrifying. I didn't know who Guzman was, but the phone call Serna received set off alarm bells and prompted him to call for protection. Yes, thank God, they were his men and not an adversary's kill squad, but could the arrival of assassins be far off? I didn't think so.

I went to the door and cracked it without exercising caution. I didn't think anyone was after me specifically. That conclusion didn't add up. Roswell was waiting outside with his gaze pinned to the floor. "What's up?" I asked.

He lifted his eyes. "Can I come in? I just came from the bar. Everyone's waiting for you." He tried to move beyond me, but I held my ground. Looking past me, he noticed my backpack and all my clothes strewn across the bed. "What's going on, Sonny?"

"I'm taking a trip."

"Where?"

"Anywhere but here. Seattle, I think."

He tried to get past me again. This time, I stepped aside and let him in. "Talk to me, Sonny. What's happened?"

"What happened? I was at Serna's place, and he got a call from someone named Guzman. Ten minutes later, two cars filled with armed men screeched to a halt outside his front door. I thought they were going to wipe out everyone in the house."

"I see," he said with concern as he came to rest leaning against the dresser. "So then, they were Serna's men." He rubbed his chin. "I'm glad you're alright."

"The point is those men could've been killers sent for Serna. I doubt assassins leave witnesses. I'm out there on my own with no protection. It's over for me. Do you hear me? It's over! You asked for some time to put a contingency plan together, and I gave it to you, but that was ages ago. I've been cozying up to Serna just like you asked me to. Honor our deal and cut me loose."

"I hear you, Sonny, but I'm still trying to stitch together a backup plan. It's not as easy as you might think."

I went back to packing. "I don't think you're trying hard enough. You have allies now. Have Willow throw on a micro dress and a pair of fuck-me pumps and sic her on Serna. I doubt he'll toss her aside."

"She's not a guitar idol like you, Sonny, and that's all that Serna's interested in. Do you really think a guy like him has any trouble getting laid? Of course not. I've got agents working on some of the best studio musicians in New York and California, but without leverage…" He shook his head dejectedly.

"No leverage? You mean you haven't tripped up any of them going through customs with dope in their pockets like me? That was a really shitty thing you did, John, and you know it."

"I thought we were past that."

"Yeah, I'm sure you did." I truly didn't know what I'd thrown into my pack, but I couldn't find anything else I thought I might've needed. I zipped it closed.

"Look, Sonny, it's okay for you to disappear for a few days to blow off steam, but you've got to come back. You've got to finish this."

"That's not what we agreed to. You asked for time. I gave you time. Way more than I should've."

"What's in Seattle anyway?"

My head dropped, and my throat tightened. When I looked up, my eyes were glassy. "Jimi died."

He gasped. "Jimi Hendrix? No shit?"

"Came over the news about an hour ago."

"Jesus, I'm sorry. I know how you idolized the guy. How'd it happen?"

"They didn't say much, only that it might've been caused by a drug overdose."

He gritted his teeth. "Shit. That really sucks. Not that a rich guy like Hendrix can't get whatever he wants, but that's why we do this job, so you don't hear about tragedies like this. They're going to bury him in Seattle?"

"That's where he's from, so I figure, yeah, that's where they'll bury him. That's where his family lives. When I get back to the States I'll try to get ahold of Chas Chandler. He's not Jimi's manager anymore, but I'm sure he'll know the details."

Roswell propped himself up and paced back and forth in front of the window. "Let me take care of the travel. I'll arrange for you to get where you're going and back. I know you're upset, but I'd hope we can agree on that much?"

"I don't know. I'm on my way to the airport. I'll hop on the first flight heading to the US."

"Are you sure you want to do that? Núñez Airport isn't exactly JFK. You could be there for days until you find a flight to take you where you want to go. Let me hook it up for you."

I shook my head. My mind was made up. It might not have been the smartest plan, but I was determined to see it through. I picked up my backpack and slung it over my shoulder.

"What about the band?" he asked.

"Fuck the band, John. I don't give a rat's ass." I left him where he stood.

Chapter Thirty-Seven

Roswell wasn't the type to give up without a fight. He followed me to the street and shadowed me while I looked for a cab to take me to the airport.

"You're being impulsive, Sonny," he said. "Take a deep breath and follow the plan."

"Whose plan? Yours or mine?"

He gestured strangely, a shrug that progressed into a shake of the head. He was clearly frustrated. I clearly didn't care. No way did drug possession equate to indentured servitude with the possibility of losing my life. As far as I was concerned, he could follow through on his threat of incarceration and throw me in jail. It was hollow intimidation, and he must've known it because he was no longer beating me over the head with that threat.

"Sonny, please, you've heard the saying, let cooler heads prevail. It's good advice.

A cab finally appeared in the distance. I stepped into the street and flagged it way before I thought the cabbie could see me. I wasn't taking the chance that it might drive by, but Roswell grabbed my arm and pulled it down.

"A cup of coffee—that's all I ask. You can go to the airport afterward if you still want to. I won't say a word."

The taxi was now just a few car lengths away. I flagged it down, then raced toward it, got in and slammed the door. "Aeropuerto, por favor." I aimed my gaze straight ahead and didn't make eye contact with Roswell as the taxi moved off.

Traffic was light but moved slowly, which wasn't unusual for Cartagena.

What should've taken fifteen minutes took almost thirty. We passed two accidents along the way, which I considered par for the course. I grabbed my pack and entered the terminal, searching for the signs for the international destinations counter. I'd just located what I was looking for when Jacobo appeared out of nowhere.

"Sr. Serna has seen to your travel arrangements," he said.

I shook my head, dumbfounded. "What?"

"Please come with me," he said insistently. "He's waiting for you in his car."

"No thanks. I'll take care of myself. Offer my thanks and let him know I won't be around for a while." I walked away, but he quickly raced to catch up and got in front of me.

"I'm afraid I must insist," the big man said, planting his feet squarely on the concourse floor.

"Gage doesn't even know where I'm going."

"It doesn't matter. His pilot will take you wherever you like." He pushed aside his jacket, exposing a sidearm tucked into the waistband of his slacks.

"Ah shit. Why the gun? I thought Sr. Serna and I were friends."

He gestured for me to exit the terminal—I saw the black Mercedes tank as soon as I hit the warm air. The windows were darkly tinted—I couldn't tell if Serna was waiting for me inside. Jacobo said he was, and his gun wasn't giving me much of a choice. I sighed deeply, then did as instructed.

Chapter Thirty-Eight

Serna was indeed waiting for me inside the Benz. He had changed into a white linen suit and was sporting his piano keys smile. He had a glass of whiskey in his hand, which he set into a cup holder when I got in.

"Sonny," he cheered. "Thanks for joining me."

The door closed behind me as I settled in. "Jacobo didn't give me much of a choice."

"Yes, he's an excellent employee, and he doesn't like to disappoint his boss."

Serna was doing his best to appear congenial, but I sensed that something had changed. Despite the smile, there was something in his demeanor that seemed decidedly more businesslike, harder, edgier.

I didn't know how he knew I was planning to leave the country and could only assume that he'd been having me watched. I wasn't going to ask if that was the case. "What's going on, Gage?"

"You were very upset when you left my home, and I was worried about you. Where are you going, Sonny?"

I knew the truth would satisfy him, so I told him straight out. "I think Jimi's going to be buried in Seattle. He was a good friend. So…"

"You want to pay your respects. Very admirable, Sonny. This airport is a nightmare—you won't have much success getting there on your own. Serna Oil has a pilot and a Gulfstream Jet hangared at our private terminal. They are at your disposal, my friend."

"I can't ask you to do that, Gage. It's too much."

His eyes brightened. "Ah, but you didn't ask. I offered, and I insist. It's the least I can do for a dear friend."

Were we friends? I wasn't sure if that was the case or if, like Jacobo, he considered me an employee. Calling me a friend didn't make me one. I had the sense that the favor he was about to provide would come with strings attached. More like tentacles than strings.

"Honor Jimi Hendrix, the guitar virtuoso, and take the time you need to grieve. I'll send the pilot to collect you when you're ready to return."

I didn't want to show my emotion, but I gritted my teeth. "About that, Gage, I'm not sure how soon I'll be returning to Cartagena."

"That sounds permanent," he said as his forehead creased. He picked up his scotch and took a sip. "That's not what I was hoping to hear." All cordiality disappeared from his voice. He snapped his fingers, and Jacobo handed him a photograph. "You're a damn fine guitarist, but I'm in need of your help in another area. You see, Sonny, the nature of our relationship needs to change."

"Change?" I asked. "To what?" He was holding the photo so that I couldn't see it. "What are you holding?"

"This photograph," he began, "is what I call leverage."

I hated the word he used, *leverage*. It was Roswell's leverage over me that put me in this position in the first place. If a man like Gage Serna needed leverage, he wasn't going to ask for help trimming the estate hedges. What he was going to ask me to do would be something I'd never contemplate doing under normal circumstances. It had to be something dangerous. Something illegal. In the time I'd known him, he'd only ever spoken about his role as the CEO of Serna Oil. He'd never mentioned narcotics in any way, shape, or form. I had the sense that it was all about to change. He tossed the photo onto my lap, a photograph of me and my parents, standing in front of our home in Florida.

Chapter Thirty-Nine

Sonny's mother and father, Rosa and Luca, hadn't been harmed, or abused, roughed up, or mistreated in any physical sense. But rarely had anyone spoken to them, and that was a true torture, a torture of the mind. They'd been taken from their home in the middle of the night. Blindfolded, they'd been transported from their house. To where? Why? They didn't know if their son was dead or alive but felt in their hearts that his life was in jeopardy. Was theirs as well?

The cottage in which they were kept was clean and well-maintained, but it was small, and they were confined within for days at a time without the opportunity to go out for fresh air. When they were allowed out, it was only into the small backyard bordered by a tall fence and were continually supervised by an armed guard. Luca tried to befriend the guard, but the man would have no part of it. He was unfriendly and only interested in the burning cigarette that hung from his mouth. When their allotted time outdoors was up, he hurried them back into the house with barely a word, directing them with a wave of his pistol. He once said *Vámanos,* but only once. More often than not, a grunt would accompany the movement of his weapon.

A maid visited to clean and take out the trash every few days, but she didn't speak with them either. She had kind eyes and was not the hardened soldier the armed guard appeared to be. They hoped she'd be more willing to communicate and tried to engage her in conversation, but the look in her eyes explained that she couldn't, that she was afraid to. More likely than not, she knew nothing about their predicament.

There was nothing in the kitchen except paper plates and cups and plastic utensils. Meals were brought in three times a day. They were not asked what they wanted to eat and understood they had to sustain themselves on whatever the captors offered.

Standing in the kitchen, Rosa was in a daze. There was nothing for her to do there. Accustomed to spending hours in the kitchen each day, her frustration grew to a new level whenever she entered.

"Why are you standing there?" her husband asked. There were no pots or pans, no provisions, no spices, no nothing. It was an empty sarcophagus in which food was meant to be prepared. Uselessness unnerved her.

"I'm going crazy, Luca. I just can't stand it." She walked to the oven and turned on the burners. "No gas—I can't even kill myself."

Luca put his arms around her and wiped tears from her cheeks. "Be strong, my love. They can't keep us here forever," he said. "I'm sure Sonny is working to get us out of this prison."

A torrent of tears welled in her eyes when she looked up. "Is he? I know he would if he could but he's in Colombia. He may not even know what's happened to us. When was the last time we heard from him? When? All we know is that he's on some kind of mission for the government. He said he couldn't tell us more than that. What does our government want with a guitar player?"

"It sounds crazy, I know, but think about it, *mi vida*. Why would anyone kidnap us? We have no money. Believe me, I think about this until my head hurts, day and night. Someone is pressuring Sonny to do something he doesn't want to do. We are what they call leverage."

"Leverage for what, Luca? What do they want from our boy?"

"Nothing good, I'm afraid. That much, my love, is for sure."

Chapter Forty

I spent nearly two weeks in Seattle. Jimi died in London on September 18, 1970, and wasn't buried until October 1. In my days playing with Jimi, he often talked about his family, his dad, Al, his stepmother, June, and his brother and sister. Arriving in Seattle so far ahead of the funeral was a blessing. I met Jimi's family and learned about the many sides of a complicated man he never spoke about. I learned about him growing up in Seattle and his stint in the army. Like me, Jimi had been a paratrooper but received an honorable medical discharge and was exempted from service in Vietnam. Had things been different, we might've served side-by-side in Southeast Asia.

Jimi's dad was absolutely at wits' end coordinating funeral arrangements long distance with Jimi's new manager, Michael Jaffey. I helped him out with some of the phone calls, and he seemed genuinely grateful for my assistance.

The trip also afforded me the opportunity to meet some of the musical legends that had been Jimi's heroes, giants like Miles Davis and Buddy Miles. I also met Al Aronowitz, who wrote the Pop Scene column for the New York Post. I was blown away when he told me that Jimi had mentioned me more than once. He asked what I was doing, and I said that I was experimenting with Latin influences down in Colombia. He gave me his business card and told me to get in touch when I was ready to go out on my own. I also got to play alongside Jimi's Experience bandmates, Noel Redding and Mitch Mitchell, in a musical tribute held in the Food Circus Building at the Seattle Center. We played many of Jimi's well-known hits. It felt good to be counted among those who were part of Jimi's posthumous family.

It was a great trip for a terrible reason.

And then I went back, back to Cartagena and the life that was choking me like a python's stranglehold around the throat. Serna had made it clear what would happen if I attempted to disappear, the swift death my parents would face if I didn't play ball. He no longer wanted me to instruct him on the guitar. He had other plans for me, plans I wanted no part of, plans involving a drug called Sublimaze, a substance I'd never heard of but quickly learned about from Roswell. Working with Roswell again was not something I was happy about, but given the change of circumstances, I had no choice. Sublimaze was a synthetic opioid with a street value worth one hundred times more than heroin and was insanely addictive. The twenty kilos I'd be bringing into the States was worth many millions once cut up to dilute heroin. The weight of seeing my dear friend laid to rest was awful, but it was nothing compared to the weight I'd have strapped to my back when we made shore in Florida. It wasn't the physical weight, mind you, but the heaviness of the undertaking that I found oppressive, the perfect storm of all the terrible things I dreaded all rolled into one.

Stripped down to the fuselage with the two aft seats replaced with auxiliary fuel tanks, the Cessna 172 H had a maximum range of close to 700 nautical miles, enough to get me, the pilot, and our precious cargo from Colombia to Montego Bay, Jamaica where we'd stop over for refueling before continuing on to the drop zone over Cape Coral in Lee County, Florida, close to my hometown. It was the kind of homecoming I wouldn't wish on my worst enemy.

The pilot's name was Lando. He wasn't much of a talker, and I wasn't in the mood to chat. He mentioned the name Guzman, presumably, it was the same Guzman who'd called Serna shortly before all hell broke loose at his home. Roswell had gotten a line on the man. He was a powerful drug distributor headquartered in Florida. Apparently, Sublimaze was his very top priority because it took so very little to earn so very much. Traditional drugs were cumbersome. They had to be shipped in large quantities that were slow to transport and easy game for the feds to track down. It eliminated the need to smuggle pallets of heroin within the hold of Serna's oil tankers. This new drug, on the other hand, a mere duffle bag equated to a ton of wealth and could be transported aboard a small aircraft like the Cessna. Guzman and Serna were eager to develop widespread distribution.

We were approaching the west coastline of Florida when I spotted a pair of single-engine prop planes coming toward us at roughly the same altitude. I pointed them out to Lando, who acknowledged the sighting but barely twitched. "Coast Guard?" I asked. He nodded but didn't seem to give a damn. I guess he'd been in spots like this before.

The Coast Guard planes split and began to loop in divergent directions. My guess was that they were spreading out and would swing around on both sides of us, flying off our wingtips. It didn't take long until I was able to make out the distinctive blue and white US Coast Guard markings on the fuselages. I turned and glanced at Lando. He was still as cool as a cucumber when the two planes leveled off on both sides of our Cessna, and a voice boomed through our headsets. "This is the United States Coast Guard off your left and right doors. You are in violation of the air defense identification zone. We are ordering you to turn around and will escort you away from restricted airspace. Acknowledge."

"What now?" I asked.

"Nothing," he said with a nonchalant shrug. "They have no guns. They can do nothing."

Of course, he wasn't worried. I was the one who'd be jumping out of the plane with a duffle bag filled with Sublimaze. He, on the other hand, would land with a drug-free plane. The Coast Guard pilots would radio the police with the coordinates of my jump, and police cruisers would be on my tail within minutes of having my boots on the ground. "Turn around, Lando," I said. "I'm not going to jail."

"Relax, my friend. I've got you covered."

"Covered? Covered how?"

He didn't respond but edged the throttle forward and continued to the planned drop zone over Cape Coral, Florida.

"Hey! I don't think you heard me. Turn the fuck around!"

"Or what? Can you fly the plane? If I were you, I'd wait until we were over land before jumping. That duffle bag will take on water, and you'll sink like a stone."

"Bullshit. I'll—"

He pulled a gun. "Get ready to jump. We're almost in position."

That's when the massive tidal wave engulfed me. I hadn't jumped since Nam, and that last attempt had ended in disaster. How my troublesome back would handle the landing was still a question mark. I might hit the ground and be crippled for life. All that and the probable risk of arrest sucked the air out of my lungs. I was frozen. Paralyzed.

He nudged me with the gun. "I told you to get ready. Strap on your gear."

"They'll see me jump. They'll radio my position, and I'll be done. Fucking done. Turn around, and we'll try again tomorrow."

"There's not enough fuel for us to turn around, and Sr. Guzman is expecting his product today." The sky grew dark as he raised the gun and pointed it at my temple. "Now," he said, pulling back the hammer.

"You won't shoot me. You can't—"

"I can and I will." He pressed the gun against my leg. I won't kill you, but shoot you? Without hesitation."

I reluctantly reached for my gear, strapped on the parachute, and secured the drug-filled duffle bag.

The Coast Guard pilot repeated his warning. "I say again, this is the United States Coast Guard. You are in violation of United States airspace. Turn around at once. Acknowledge!"

We were now flying over land. Lando seemed very focused, intent on piloting the plane. "We're here," he said. "If you follow my instructions, they won't see you jump. Put your hand on the door handle and get ready to jump." Without warning, he slammed the yoke forward, pushing the Cessna into a steep dive. I just made out the images of the two Coast Guard planes streaking by and disappearing into the darkness as we plummeted downward. Then he hauled back on the yoke, straining and fighting inertia as we leveled off. "Now!" he screamed. "Before they can turn back."

I was in shock. Frozen and unable to move. He read the expression on my face. His eyes flashed as he released both of our seat harnesses, then leaned past me, opened my door, and shoved me out.

Chapter Forty-One

Earlier that day

Deputy Butch Drake's day began quietly. Lee County skies were blanketed with clouds. The searing West Coast Florida sun was conspicuously absent in the sky. No complaints. He was born and raised in Valdosta, GA, and didn't feel comfortable unless the back of his neck was soaked with sweat. It wasn't until half past ten in the morning that he received his first call on the radio. A Desert Beige Plymouth Valiant was missing from Sanford Clay's used car lot. Not exactly a SWAT raid, but something to break the monotony of pulling over speeders and issuing traffic violations. He was happy to take the call.

"Just about the last car I'd expect someone to steal," Clay said when Drake arrived at his car lot. Clay was a young man, but his paunch and receding hairline made him look older than his thirty-eight years. His was a blue-collar car lot with a large inventory of sedans and wagons, nothing flashy, just cheap. "So damn plain and boring, customers yawned every time I tried to sell the damn thing. Maybe it's best you don't bother reporting it. Insurance will cover the loss, and Lord knows it'll be easier than trying to sell it."

"Don't want it back?" Drake said with a smirk. He knew Clay on and away from the job, but his demeanor was always cut and dried. Ten years chasing lawbreakers through the swamp will do that to a man. "You're making my job too easy."

"Maybe I ought to buy flashier cars. Make things more interesting."

"That would be a start," Drake said. "A Corvette or XKE would be nice. Something to give me a run for my money on the interstate."

"You'd like that, wouldn't you?"

"Sure as shit I would."

"Me too. I'd drive through town and maybe pick up some of that spring break talent. I swear, Butch, I've never seen so much bare skin. Those college gals don't know the meaning of the word modesty. Why, if my daughter ever dressed like one of those tarts, I'd—"

"Same thing I'd do to *my* offspring, handcuff her to a pipe and tell my wife to homeschool her." He pulled a memo pad out of his shirt pocket. "Now, about the Plymouth. You said it was beige?"

Clay nodded. "Vomit beige. Puke beige. You get the picture."

Drake noted the color, repeating Clay's description matter-of-factly. "Two doors or four?"

"Four-door sedan, whitewall tires. Trust me, Butch, you don't want to break a sweat looking for that snoozemobile. If that rolling pigpen were to drive right past us, it would put you to sleep faster than Sominex. You'd wake up later on and swear you'd been dreaming. Wouldn't even know you saw it."

"Four-door sedan, whitewall tires," Drake repeated, noting the subsequent details on his pad. "I'll report it."

"You do that, and I'll keep my fingers crossed that it's already out of the county. I'm only reporting it so that the insurance company doesn't get the wrong idea. You get me?"

"Got it, look, but not too hard." He leaned against the fender of an Impala and rolled his neck. "Say, you wouldn't be above bribing an officer of the law with a tall glass of iced tea, would you? My thermos leaked. Picked the damn thing up and it was bone dry. As I am just about now."

"Sure thing, Deputy. I've got a full pitcher in the fridge. Follow me inside." The sales office was just big enough for Clay's desk and a pair of chairs, but the air conditioner blew strong. The office windows were covered with condensation. Clay settled in behind his desk. A plaid sports coat was draped over the back of his chair. Drake fell into one of the chairs facing him and crossed his legs.

"How's business?" Drake asked as he sipped his tea.

"Spotty. Just when sales get a little brisk, they die off. I think it's because the economy stinks. Folks are driving their clunkers until the wheels fall off." He opened the desk drawer, took out a tin of gingersnaps, and pried off the lid. 'Help yourself, Butch, or I'll end up eating every one of 'em, and my doc told me I'd better shed a few."

Drake took a cookie and snapped off a bite. "Thank you kindly."

"How's your case-close percentage, Butch?"

Drake shook his head slowly. "If you're asking about rescuing cats out of trees, it's one-hundred percent. On drug dealings? Not so good. A twin-engine plane crash-landed on Diplomat Parkway on Tuesday last. When we found it, the dang thing was completely empty. Our crime scene guys did their due diligence and found marijuana residue."

"But no product?" Clay asked.

"Not so much as a burned-down spliff. A few months back, a Convair 240 was abandoned on the Jacaranda Parkway."

Clay's jaw dropped. "Smack dab on the parkway?"

"Yes indeed."

"And the cargo?"

"Hasta la vista, muchacho. Once again, the plane was empty," he said with a wave of the wrist. "Based on the plane's load capacity, we figure close to ten tons of marijuana made it into the country." The roads in the treeless and uninhabited northwestern sections of Cape Coral were drawing airborne drug smugglers like moths to a flame. By night, abandoned and lightly traveled roads welcomed an endless stream of small incoming aircraft, guided by the headlamps of transport vehicles.

"Shit, Butch, ain't you figured out their MO by now? I mean, how many roads are there to keep an eye on? You just stake 'em all out and watch the skies for the banditos to show up." He scratched the back of his neck. "Near as I can figure."

"You'd think so, wouldn't you? But we'd damn near have to be sitting at the end of the landing strip waiting for them when the plane came down. You can't believe how many shit-kicking little roads we have out here." He took a last swig of iced tea, then shook an ice cube into his mouth and crunched it between his molars. "We don't have the men or the money to watch them all. Hell, I'm not saying we don't make a dent. We've confiscated millions worth of planes, boats, cars, and what have you, trucks, vans, swamp buggies, and semis." He shook the glass and finessed a last sliver of ice into his mouth. "You name it, and we've impounded it. And we nab some product from time to time as well. It's just that the lion's share is getting through."

"But no smugglers?"

"Not hardly. I tell you what, it's getting so that drug running is becoming Florida's most lucrative industry."

Clay reached for another cookie. "I don't believe that. Right here in sleepy little Cape Coral?"

"Yessir. The FBI claims that as much as eighty percent of the cocaine and marijuana smuggled into the country touches down somewhere along the southwest Florida coastline."

"Where's all this shit coming from, Butch?"

"Columbia mostly."

"She-it, seems like I'm in the wrong line of work."

"Guess we both are. You fixing to take up a new endeavor?" He winked at Clay, then set his empty glass on the desktop. "See you around." He tugged his hat into place and sauntered out the door.

The sun never came out that day, and the humidity never left, and it was dank as hell. Butch kept the engine running and the windows open so that he could get a drop on fast-approaching headlights and tag them with his radar gun. His uniform shirt was soaked through and through, his disposition snarly.

It was early evening, and the sun was already down. Drake set up on the side of the road, figuring that between the darkness and low-level fog that speeders would be easy prey for the radar gun. He'd already nabbed two offenders and would've ticketed one more, but the young woman he had just pulled over had recently gotten her license, and he could see that she was scared shitless. He let her go with a warning, knowing that she was on probation and a speeder would've put the kibosh on her future as a motorist. As miserable as he was feeling, he hoped to write several additional tickets before ending his shift.

He was walking back to his cruiser when something caught his eye. It was a slight hum, but he knew from his time in the field that it wasn't a natural noise like the din of katydids and crickets. It was different enough to draw him into the thicket even though he hated the brush and all the creepy crawlies that dwelled within it. The area was rampant with snakes and bats and laden with marshy wetlands that were home to gators. And gators, they eat all the time. They sun themselves during the day but often lie awake in muddy dens at night just waiting for a dumbass deputy to lumber by. He pulled his searchlight and checked the terrain carefully. The footing was dry enough for him to venture deeper in. He was about one hundred feet in when he detected the smell of brackish water. A map appeared in his mind, and it occurred to him just how close he was to the ocean. He'd be surrounded by narrow inlets if he went any further. The dominant reptile species in those parts was the crocodile, and they were aggressive, far nastier than alligators. The bugs went quiet for a moment, and he was able to discern the noise that had aroused his curiosity. Automobile engines. Running engines. He switched off his searchlight, but didn't see any headlights, just heard the soft burble of multiple exhausts, which was unmistakable. He knew in that instant what he had. Through the brush, he could see the burning tip of a cigarette. Straining his eyes, he could see a few men mulling about. A low trail of chatter filtered through to Drake's ears.

He checked the terrain once more and proceeded further. He was maybe thirty feet away from the running cars when his foot landed in a bog, and he sank knee-deep into the mud. Water wicked up his pant leg. He heard movement as he dragged his foot out of the sludge. His heart hammered quickly as he cast the searchlight beam over the wetland area. "Motherfucker," he muttered. A drug bust was close enough to touch if he could just make it across the damn swamp.

Overhead, the drone of a small aircraft filtered down to him. He could hear it but couldn't see it and knew that it was flying dark to avoid detection. He switched on his searchlight and leaned against the trunk of a pond cypress tree while he surveyed the area, careful to keep the beam from being detected. He saw that he'd be able to leapfrog the narrow inlet by hoisting himself up on a cypress limb and swinging across. Stowing the searchlight, he prepared himself for the maneuver.

No sooner had he landed, when an array of headlamp beams exploded, saturating the bog with light. He drew his sidearm and hurried forward as the cars quickly backed down the road, all save one. Clearing the brush, he came upon an unoccupied car. "Shit!" The area evacuated, he couldn't determine the make or model, but the searchlight beam revealed the chrome insignia badge on the front fender just behind the tire well. It was a Valiant, a Plymouth Valiant.

Anguish ate at his gut. He kicked up a spray of loose sand just as a scream rang out, followed by a cacophony of snapping tree limbs, then a muted thud. The noise had come from the inlet he'd just traversed. The noises had startled him, but they couldn't possibly have been caused by a plunging airplane, no matter how small the size. Adrenaline surged. *It's a drop*, he reasoned, and once more called on his searchlight to illuminate a path in the direction the noise had come from. He hurried, somewhat recklessly to where he thought the noise had originated, certain he'd find a duffle filled with narcotics. He bounded through the bog he had circumnavigated minutes before. Hip high through the muck, he came to a dead stop. Something was in the water in front of him, flailing weakly. He gasped and felt his limbs go numb. *A croc.* A tremor rolled through him, paralyzing him. He stood frozen, breathing shallowly, his skin crawling.

He heard moaning, human moaning, and couldn't have been more shocked or relieved. Forcing himself forward, the first thing he saw was a collapsed parachute caught on an outstretched tree limb. Following the searchlight beam downward, he saw a man flat on his back, writhing and gasping for air, but the paratrooper was still by the time he reached him. He took in the fallen skydiver and intuited that the man had missed his drop zone. As he knelt to assist him, he wasn't sure if he was unconscious or dead. Ear to the fallen man's chest, he listened for the sound of life, the beating of a heart as blood coursed through its chambers. His two hands centered over the man's chest, he initiated chest compressions, steadily, metronomically. He counted to thirty, compressing the chest a solid two inches with his elbows locked and his shoulders directly over his hands. "Twelve, thirteen." He continued to count as he studied the lifeless face, covered in swamp mud. "Fourteen. Come on, man, come on." He wiped the mud from the stricken man's face, then grimaced as he tilted his head back and was about to administer breaths when the jumper gasped, and air wheezed into his lungs.

Chapter Forty-Two

Lee Memorial Hospital, Cape Coral, FL

The following day

Run! *Get up and run. Escape.* I jerked my right arm and found it shackled at the wrist. My eyes filling with light, I woke up with a thud. Not on my chest but from within, a knock like a wrecking ball against the inside of my ribcage. I looked around frantically. *The hell? Where am I?*

As my head cleared, I saw that I was not in a Viet Cong prison but in a hospital, but what hospital? It sure as hell wasn't the 8th Field Hospital in Nha Trang. That was for damn sure. I wasn't sweating, and my skin wasn't clammy. The first sensation I felt was cool air blowing on my face from a vent in the ceiling. Vietnam had always been deadly hot, damp, dank, and steamy. Even indoors, musty dense air was ever present, sticky like slime on your skin. Every breath you drew, heavy, too warm and moist to oxygenate your blood, making you feel as if you were dragging all the time. There was real weight to it. It was oppressive and made breathing difficult, near impossible, as if you caught one of the dozens of flu bugs the enlisted men were always passing around, viruses that filled your chest with heavy mucus. Turning to the window, I saw that I was in a room several floors up. The 8th Field Hospital had been a one-level structure, not much more than a series of small, interconnected cottages.

But how? How was it possible?

The last thing I remembered was the glare of a flashlight beam stinging my eyes as I lay face up in water. I was disoriented and confused. For an instant, I thought I was back in Nam on the night I had smacked down in the riverbed. I could barely make out the individual kneeling alongside me, but I sensed that it was not a soldier and certainly not the VC. The person administering chest compressions wore a pointed bronze star. Somewhere in the atrophied crevices of my mind, I seemed to recall where I'd seen that kind of shield before. *Of course*, I thought. *Shit*! It all came back: being forced out of the plane and the bad fall into the swamp, the cop that brought me around, and the ambulance ride. The ER docs hit me up with a syringe during the examination. I must've been out since then.

I half-expected to see Nurse Ray, the old Nam army nurse, standing over me when I opened my eyes, but I was dead wrong. A young male nurse was in the room when I came to, checking the bag of fluids on the IV hook. He was tall and ungodly thin with bleached blonde hair and sculpted eyebrows, a far cry from the squat Latina who cared for me when I was recovering from back surgery in Vietnam. Ray was short for Raymona, and she had been my ray of light, watching over me all the while I was in the military hospital.

"Welcome back," the nurse said, turning toward me. A smiley face button was pinned to his white shirt that read: Hi! I'm Ted. His features appeared delicate as he leaned over and placed his hand on my forehead. "You took quite a nap, sky jumper. Doc gave you enough tranq to drop a Clydesdale."

"Where am—?" I wasn't quick enough. He had a thermometer under my tongue before I could finish the question. It didn't stop him from answering.

"You're at Lee Memorial Hospital, Cape Coral, Florida. I'll provide specifics in case you don't know where on God's earth you landed. They brought you in around three in the morning. As I understand it you fell from the sky right into the swamp. You would've become a gator's late-night snack if Deputy Drake hadn't been right there when you smacked down." He crossed himself. "Praise Jesus. The good Lord was surely smiling down on you last night. Falling in a muddy bog like you did might be the only reason you're alive. And oh, by the way, your wrist isn't broken. That's a very sturdy stainless-steel handcuff you feel ratcheted snugly around it. Not that you're in any condition to walk out the door," Ted continued, then pulled the thermometer out of my mouth, checked it, and wiped it down with an alcohol-moistened cotton ball. He shook down the mercury so it would be ready for the next patient and tucked it into his shirt pocket. "Normal," he said. "As I was saying, a Cape Coral deputy found you flat on your back, resuscitated you, threw you over his shoulder, and hauled you out of the swamp. You wouldn't be alive if he hadn't saved your life. The man's a dang hero."

What? How? My mind was overloaded, wild with the conflicting information I'd just heard. I felt a tremor building. It began at the back of my neck and ate into my chest, then into my bones. I heard the bleeping of the heart monitor accelerate, climbing quickly. *Breathe, Sonny, breathe*, I told myself. I couldn't inhale but somehow managed to expel air through my nostrils, then felt my chest rise. Once, then again, and again. It took a few moments, but the pieces gradually fell into place. I must've relived my night jump over Vietnam while I was passed out in the Florida swamp. I believed I'd come to in the Vietnam jungle. It was the only scenario that made any sense at all. Only this time I wasn't 10,000 miles from home. I was in my own backyard. I gave the wrist restraint a light tug—things were beginning to make sense. I wriggled my fingers. All of my picking and fingering digits moved freely and without pain. Thank God, my life as a musician still held promise. One day I'd hold a guitar again, but I was damn sure it wouldn't be anytime soon. I turned my head and looked out the window. The sun was past peak intensity. It felt as if the time was somewhere in the waning hours of afternoon. Not far away, I imagined my father would be heading home from a long day of physical labor. If only Serna hadn't taken them and they were home. *Mucho trabajo, poco dinero*, as he would say as he walked through the door. He didn't have an easy life. My mother would greet him, arms open, sadness in her eyes. Sadness, I put there. The son she never saw, no longer understood, and worried about endlessly.

I wondered if Roswell had made good on his promise to locate them and place them somewhere safe. I crossed myself with my free hand. A prayer ran through my mind as I begged for assistance, *O Holy Spirit…*

I blew out a heavy sigh. As the tremor ebbed away, my eyes settled on the nurse. "I guess I'm two for two. When I woke up just now, I thought I was back in Nam, having fallen through the dark into a jungle stream. I guess all swamps look the same in the dark."

I assumed I was expressing a thought, but once again, I was wrong. It was the second night jump gone bad, the second time someone had saved my life.

"Huh?" Ted checked my eyes with a pocket flashlight. "You're not delusional, are you, sky jumper? The ER doc didn't see any indications of a concussion. Guess your head is still swimming from the knockout drops."

I shook my head. It was the only part of my body that didn't hurt or wasn't throbbing. It was the second time death had turned its back on me. I wasn't a cat—how many lives did I have left? This time, however, there'd be a heavy price to pay. I was no longer on the right side of the law. I wasn't a Marine fighting to uphold the rights of a beleaguered country, if that story was, in fact, true. Most saw US involvement in the Vietnam War as political, a war that had no right to take American lives. I was no longer a soldier, no longer a Marine. I was… I shuddered involuntarily as I wasn't sure what I was. I only knew why I was doing what I was doing. But the authorities wouldn't be interested in any of that. Having lived in Cape Coral my entire life, I was aware that the authorities track record for apprehending drug runners was piss poor. An embarrassment. They knew it. Everyone did. They had something to prove, and it didn't take a ton of smarts to figure out that they were about to use me to demonstrate to the higher-ups that they weren't completely inept.

He checked my IV again and flicked the clear plastic bag with his finger. "You've had plenty of fluids. You shouldn't be dehydrated. How do you feel?"

"Like I've been worked over with a meat tenderizer."

"Could've been worse. They X-rayed you from head to toe—you didn't so much as chip a fingernail. Don't misunderstand me, your spine is stuck together with spit and chewing gum, and I've never seen so much scar tissue in my life. But still."

"Then why do I hurt so damn much?"

He folded his fingers inward and admired his manicure momentarily. "Bruises, contusions, sprains, strains, and what have you. Just because an injury doesn't snap, crackle, or pop like a broken bone doesn't mean it can't hurt. Soft tissue pain can be as intense as any. Besides, you've got a hell of a lot of nuts and bolts holding you together. Maybe jumping out of airplanes isn't the low-risk occupation you think it is." He glared at me. "Guess there's big money in dirty deeds. You ever think about where all that crap goes? Kids. Moms and dads doing their best to deal with all the shit life throws at them. Families busted all to hell."

"It's not what you think."

"It never is." He pursed his lips, "Go ahead, plead your defense. What was it then? Deputy Drake said he had to lug a big old bag of narcotics out of the swamp with you. Are you telling me you're some kind of pro bono night jumping commando risking life and limb for indigent drug lords?"

It wasn't the time or place for explanations. He didn't understand. Couldn't. Not that I blamed him. He didn't know how bitter the truth would be. Why lay it on him?

"That's exactly what I thought," he said, playing off my silence in an uppity tone. "Catching a drug runner is big news in a little town like this. I suspect you'll become a local celebrity, an urban legend of sorts…before they haul you off to prison that is."

"I guess that's not an equal opportunity smiley face button you're wearing."

Mr. Congeniality scowled and left the room. It felt as if the temperature had warmed up ten degrees in his absence. Left alone with my aches and guilt, I pictured my mother, the look on her face when she heard the news. Her suspicions would be confirmed. Her son was a criminal. As my stomach twisted into knots, I instinctively raised my left hand to where it would fit on the neck of a guitar. With my right hand tightly shackled to the bed frame, I couldn't mimic playing a guitar. I wanted to pick one up and play away my remorse. I want to belt out soaring riffs, slashing away at the strings with all the pent-up angst that was gnawing through me. Wild rollercoaster divebombs would reverberate in my ears until I'd exhausted myself and my torment had finally waned. Then and only then would I play soothing blues and lull myself to sleep.

A law officer walked into the room. His head was shaved smooth, his dome gleaming under the fluorescent ceiling lights. He was stocky. I don't imagine he had any trouble hoisting me over his shoulder. Unlike meeting John Roswell for the first time, I felt in my gut that this was the man who had carried me out of the swamp. He saved my life and would likely be the one providing the momentum that would send me to prison. Weighing the pluses and minuses, I guess I was way ahead of the game. There might be a life after prison, but even a fool knows that there's no coming back from the dead.

He didn't look friendly. Scratch unfriendly. He seemed hard-edged, as if you couldn't cut through his veneer with a diamond. He pulled up a chair and tossed one leg over the other before making eye contact. "You flunk out of jump school, Rojas?" He opened a folder and scanned the contents, flipping page after page for heightened drama until he got to the end. No doubt he knew every word in the file.

"Good reading?" I asked, knowing what was coming, the we've-got-you-dead-to-rights speech. We're gonna throw the book at you.

"Yessir. Been through it three or four times," he said.

"A real page turner, is it?"

He flipped it closed and weighed it on his open palm. "It's a little light—not exactly *War and Peace*. I tell you what, for such a pissant, you've seen a whole lot of shit." He flipped the file open again, then closed it. "Why, you're just a few days shy of your twenty-second birthday. I should've brought you a cake."

He was right about all the trouble I'd encountered. Hitting the ground in the Vietnam jungle was only the start of my descent, the beginning of things going wrong.

"Being a local, you probably know there are more drugs coming into the country right here in Cape Coral than practically anywhere else along the southern border."

I suspected he was going somewhere with the conversation. Where, I didn't know. Not much chance he was going to let me off with a slap on the wrist. He seemed cool, as if his pulse rate wouldn't break sixty while wrestling a grizzly bear.

"We're gonna take the contraband you landed with and throw it in the evidence locker with all the rest of the garbage we confiscate, and it'll sit there until a judge sends you away for a decade. Then it'll be incinerated. Up in smoke." He looked into my eyes but was seeing deeper, searing straight into my soul. "Just like your life."

He continued to stare, his gaze a clenched fist, reaching down deep, twisting my gut. I'd never had this conversation with a cop before because I'd never been caught before, but sensed he was about to lay it on thick, the reality of prison life, the loss of liberty, beatings, and worse. Then the knockout punch, that mine would be a lifetime of shame, not only mine but for the good, hardworking folks that had raised me. *Say it already. Say it and let's get on with it.* But he stayed silent, playing it to the hilt, allowing time for my psyche to crumble. Impatience was not going to work in my favor. I'd heard from a guy who'd done time that his days behind bars were the longest and slowest he'd ever endured. The creeping clock was the real hell within hell, the constant reminder of how slowly a prison day dragged.

"You have any idea what that shit is you brought into the country?"

I knew what it was named. I knew what it did. That was the extent of it. I shook my head.

"Well, it's not coke, and it's not heroin. It's in an evidence locker right now, but it'll be going to the state crime lab so we can figure out what it is."

"So, why am I handcuffed?"

He laughed. "Because, man, I figure you didn't jump out of an airplane after dark to smuggle Brioschi into the country." He raised his eyebrows. "Paratrooper, huh? I couldn't do that shit—got an awful fear of heights. I read that shit went sideways for you jumping into the Quế Sơn Valley. Is that right?"

Why did he ask? His questions had nothing to do with me smacking down in a Florida swamp. *Stay out of my head.* "Why do you care?"

"Hey!" he boomed. "I saved your goddamn life, Rojas. You owe me better than that." He bit his lower lip and his right hand balled into a fist. For a moment, I thought he might haul off and slug me, but as the moments ticked by, it became clear that wasn't what he was thinking (or had somehow found the strength to stand down). He leaned forward and extended his hand. I looked at it for a long while, unsure of what kind of game he was playing, then took it with the paw that wasn't handcuffed to the bed. "Butch Drake," he said. "Company D. 1st Battalion."

The abrupt change of direction stunned me. "Marines?"

"Oorah!" he shouted with a fist pump.

I felt calmness spread through me. Why? I didn't yet comprehend. Drug runners were looked upon as the lowest of the low, a mere ladder rung above rapists and child abusers, scum-sucking leeches on the asshole of humanity. Yet somehow I understood that I wasn't being judged. Not by him. Somehow, he didn't see me as the night jumper who parachuted to the ground with a duffel stuffed with drugs. Somehow, respect was still there. "Semper fi, brother," I said. "How long did you serve?"

"One hitch. I've been back a little more than a year now."

"Nothing broken?"

He shook his head. "Not mind nor body," he humbly admitted. "One of the lucky few."

I felt my throat clench and had to remind myself that Marines never cry.

Chapter Forty-Three

I was pumped up with pools of pain medications, anti-inflammatories, and muscle relaxers, and yet I still felt beaten up, sore, and bruised. Nevertheless, it was a miracle that I didn't crumble like a house of cards when I smacked down in the Florida swamp. Somehow, the fall didn't set me back to how I was when I landed on my back in Vietnam. Inconceivably, the pieces the army docs glued together had held. I couldn't say that I was able to move without pain, but I wasn't in abject misery. Tethered to the side of the bed, I had a limited range of motion. I tested the positions I was able to get into with my wrist shackled and didn't hit a spot that had me screaming in agony.

A day and a half had passed since Officer Drake paid a visit to the hospital. Despite the bond we shared, I knew he'd be back as soon as the lab confirmed that the substance in my duffle bag was Sublimaze, a potent synthetic opioid. Next stop, prison, and not for the small amount of drugs I was caught with at JFK when I returned from London. The quantity I attempted to smuggle into the country for Serna would send me away for many years if Roswell didn't intervene on my behalf. I wasn't sure he would. Not now, not after bungling the first mission Serna had sent me on. Guzman, whoever he was, was very important to Serna, someone Serna took very seriously. Someone he feared enough to summon his hired guns to provide protection.

Nurse Ted strolled into my room. He was out of uniform, in khakis and a Hawaiian shirt, his smiley face button absent. Seeing him in his civies was puzzling—I had no idea why he'd returned.

"This is goodbye," he said with a casual wave. "I'm off the next two days. I doubt you'll be here when I get back."

I couldn't say we'd bonded, but the man had been attentive to my needs. Although unwelcoming, he was professional, and had a good reason for not getting cozy with me. "Thanks, man, for all of your help."

"I hate this," he said. "Do you think you're going to jail?"

I bunched my lips. "That's a pretty safe bet."

He glanced at the floor, and when he looked up, he had a hangdog expression on his face. "I'm sorry to hear that. I have the feeling you're not one of those dyed-in-the-wool drug runner types. Then again…what the hell do I know? I'm a shitty judge of character. Just ask anyone I've had a relationship with." He snickered. "Relationship, that's a good one. Anyway, good luck. I guess you'll need it." I gave him a thumbs-up, and he turned to leave just as Drake walked through the door. "He hasn't been released yet, Officer," Ted said.

Drake seemed focused, stern. I doubted he would enjoy arresting me, but I knew he had a job to do. He directed his question at the nurse and didn't make eye contact with me. "Who do I have to see to get the patient signed out?"

"Dr. Kalman," Ted said, "but I don't think he's in the building. Maybe you ought to try again tomorrow. The patient isn't strong enough to leave, anyway." He turned to me and winked. I grinned.

"Who does Kalman report to? This man is coming with me. And I mean now."

Ted gave me a gloomy shrug. "Alright," he said with a sigh. "Come with me." He trudged out the door with Drake behind him.

This is the way it goes, I thought. I was in a bad spot for a poor reason while serving my country and trying to do the right thing. Serna wasn't paying me to smuggle drugs. He was extorting me with the threat of killing my parents. I was only trying to keep them alive.

I heard voices in the hallway. One of them sounded like Drake. The other was unfamiliar. He must've located Dr. Kalman or someone of authority who could clear me to leave the hospital. They left me alone in my room for about thirty minutes before an unfamiliar nurse entered the room. She was the straight-down-to-business type. After telling me her name, she said that she would help me with the discharge procedure. She hustled through the paperwork, explaining it without frills or candor. Probably didn't like the duty she'd been assigned. A large plastic bag contained a set of blue scrubs, which I'd shortly exchange for orange prison coveralls. A second bag contained a pair of canvas boat shoes. I didn't ask where my clothes and gear were. I knew they'd been impounded. Even if they hadn't been confiscated, they had to be filthy and saturated with swamp mud.

"The officer will be with you shortly," she said and about-faced without offering a farewell. I assumed there'd be more of that kind of treatment from here on out. Warmth and friendliness were to be a thing of the past.

When Drake came back into the room, he uncuffed me without saying a word, then leaned against the wall while I got dressed. So much for our military camaraderie. He cuffed me again the moment I was dressed, took me by the arm, and led me down the hall. Again, waiting for the elevator, he was silent. That changed when we got out of the elevator and walked across the lobby to the exit door.

"You might've said something," he said.

"About what?"

He shook his head with disappointment. "Forget it, man. What's the point?"

The hell is going on? The driver's door of the car parked next to Drake's cruiser flew open as we approached, and Roswell jumped out.

"Here you go." Drake unlocked the cuffs. "Good luck, Marine," he said and ducked into his car.

"What's that about?" I asked. "Up until now, he was as nice as pie."

"Feds," Roswell answered with a smirk. "No one likes us."

"So, I'm not being charged?"

"Nope, not being charged," he confirmed with raised eyebrows. "Get in."

Chapter Forty-Four

Drake must've been torn, happy that an ex-Marine wasn't going to jail but pissed that his big narcotics bust had gone to shit and that the feds were behind it. Roswell and I jumped on State Road 41 and headed south. Roswell seemed unexpectedly chipper and handed me a fountain cola in a to-go cup. "You okay?" he asked.

"I'm pretty damn sore, but the doc said I didn't break anything new. Somehow, my spine is still in one piece. Near as I could figure, my chute got caught on a tree limb, and it broke my fall. The soft, muddy swamp didn't hurt either. Officer Drake found me. Probably the only reason I'm alive."

"You must be immortal."

"Yeah, well, you can forget that shit because I'm out. We're just minutes out of Cape Coral. You can drop me at my folks' house, then forget we ever met."

"About that," Roswell said with his eyes pinned to the road. "I'm not sure that's the best idea."

"I don't care how good an idea it is. It's what's happening."

Roswell pulled off at the next exit, found a strip mall parking lot, and turned off the engine. He turned to face me. I sensed what was coming and wasn't happy. "Sonny," he began, then cleared his throat. "You're not off the hook yet."

"Bullshit, John. You want to throw me in jail on that bullshit possession charge, have at it. Otherwise, I'm walking away."

He gritted his teeth. "You don't get it, Sonny. It's not me. It's Serna. You jumped out of his plane with a fortune worth of narcotics and haven't been seen or heard from since. A man like Serna isn't going to let that go."

"Jesus, John, what is this Sublimaze shit anyway? What makes it so goddamn important?"

"Sublimaze is the registered name for a substance called Fentanyl. They first synthesized it about ten years ago, and the FDA just approved it for use as an analgesic. It's one-hundred-times stronger than morphine, so—"

"Yeah, I know the rest—ounce-for-ounce it's worth a fortune and much more valuable than heroin. I don't care—make it seem like I died making the jump. Serna can't kill me if I'm already dead."

"He's going to want to see proof, your dead body. Maybe your severed head. Something that can't be faked. This isn't the movies, Sonny. A swindle like that isn't as easy to sell as you might think." He reached over the back seat and lifted the black duffle I jumped with. "You and the package are still in play. Get word to Serna that the cops were all over you when you landed, which is kind of the truth. From what Drake told me, he scared off your meetup crew when he arrived on the scene. That's a story Serna will believe. When you make the delivery, tell Guzman you had to lie low for a couple of days but that you've still got the package and are ready to deliver it. We'll surveil the drop off and have eyes on you the entire time."

I felt my temple throbbing and sweat ran down the back of my neck. "Where are my folks? Are they somewhere safe? That's the only thing I care about."

"We're still looking for them, Sonny. I wish I had better news.

Roswell had stripped me of my free will, the ability to make my own choices. My life and my parents' lives were in jeopardy and would remain so until Serna had been shut down. It felt like a life sentence without the possibility of parole. "This is a nightmare. Where are you taking me?"

"A safe location. You're in kind of deep, Sonny—make the drop off. Then tell Serna you're finished. You'll be a hero because you got his drugs to their intended destination and did so at considerable risk. That's got to be worth something. Maybe he'll let it go at that and release your folks. We'll put you and your parents into the Witness Protection Program. Relocate all of you somewhere safe."

"Well, doesn't that sound grand? You want to rip my folks away from their family and friends and stick them where, some godforsaken shithole in the middle of nowhere? And what about my career? Good luck getting back into professional music with a bounty on my head."

I could see he didn't have an answer for me. The reality of the situation was that the situation sucked. He might be able to keep us alive, but life as we knew it, as we wanted it to be, was over. He started the car.

There was nothing more to say. My mind scrambled, trying to find an acceptable way out of the awful mess, but it was a waste of time. Every scenario I considered ended in disaster.

We got off an exit I was unfamiliar with, and within minutes were traveling into cattle country. Outsiders don't expect to see cows in Florida, but the state is lousy with cattle ranches, cows as far and wide as the eye can see. Roswell navigated into a community of small homes, one-story structures with metal roofs on minuscule lots. He pulled into a driveway and killed the engine. Having clearly exhausted our conversation, we'd traveled in silence for several minutes. Any attempts at restarting it would've been futile.

The area was damn quiet. There were plenty of matchbox houses with cars in the driveways, but I didn't see a soul outside. No kids playing. No one coming or going. No mailman making the rounds. My folks had been part of the same eclectic community for decades, with lots of friends with thriving families. Kids went to school. Men and women went to work. There was life everywhere. This must be where people go to die. It was nowhere, as bleak and lifeless as any place I've ever seen.

"Let's go," he said as we got out of the car at the end of a cul-de-sac. A house was surrounded by giant arborvitae and well hidden from the street. I jumped out and followed him. He knocked on the door. Two knocks, then one, then three. It appeared to be a prearranged signal. I saw the curtain behind the door-side panel move a bit. I couldn't see a face, but someone was checking to see who was at the door. I heard the clack of the deadbolt, then the door opened partially. Roswell stepped in, and I followed. By the time I got inside, Roswell was lying on the floor, his throat slit, blood everywhere.

Chapter Forty-Five

"You have Serna's stuff?" Jacobo said in his deep accent. He grabbed a kitchen rag from the counter and wiped Roswell's blood off his knife, then stepped over Roswell as if he were a doll a kid had left lying about.

Roswell gagged and gurgled as life fled his body. I was trembling as I knelt next to him, unsure of how to help as blood ran from his slashed throat. I was stricken and helpless, unable to think for what seemed like an eternity. Moments passed before I could look around for something I could use to stop the bleeding—I grabbed the same rag Jacobo had used to clean his knife and pressed it to the wound, but it immediately became saturated with blood. Roswell was no longer choking on blood. I could just distinguish the faint sound of air wheezing through his throat. And then it stopped.

"It's too late for him," Jacobo said. He pulled a gun from his shoulder holster under his jacket and glared at me. "Well? I'm waiting. Where's Sr. Serna's merchandise?"

I felt sick to my stomach as I got to my feet. "You bastard—why'd you kill him?"

He cracked his neck and continued to cut me with his gaze. "Do. You. Have. Serna's. Stuff?"

"Fuck Serna's stuff," I screamed. "Where are my parents? Where the hell are they?"

"Not here," he finally offered. "Where's the stuff?"

"Where? Where are they?"

"Safe. For now." He gestured with an open palm. "The stuff?" His eyes flashed a warning. "You want to see your parents alive? You'd better talk, and I mean right now."

I clutched my gut, then leaned over and vomited. Damn close to a minute must've elapsed before I wiped the dribble from my mouth and had the presence of mind to answer. "It's in the car, you piece of shit. It's in the fucking car."

I immediately heard the front door open and slam shut. Roswell's body had fallen in an odd position, head down and tucked into his chest. His jacket no longer covered his torso. The grip of his automatic was visible, protruding from a waist holster. I stared at the gun for long moments before removing it from the holster. Racing outside, I saw Jacobo leaning into the back seat of Roswell's car. As he pulled the duffle out of the car and straightened up, I pressed the barrel of the gun to his temple and pulled the trigger.

Chapter Forty-Six

With his soldier dead and his drugs missing, Serna would never let my parents go. He'd hold them hostage and use them to manipulate me as long as it served his purposes, as long as he could squeeze me. With his Sublimaze in my possession, I had something to bargain with. Or so I thought.

I walked back into the house and found two dead FBI agents, one in each of the two small bedrooms. I used the house phone to call the local FBI office.

I expected to hear hysterics on the other end of the line when I told them I was reporting the death of multiple Bureau agents, but that wasn't the case. I was put on hold for what seemed like ages before someone came on the line, asked for the address, and instructed me not to leave.

It was a solid three-hour drive from southern Florida under the best of circumstances. They arrived almost four hours later, a caravan of four cars carrying a total of ten agents. It must've taken them a while to mobilize the troops, far longer than it took Robert Stack to rally his TV team of incorruptible G-men on The Untouchables. I figured a tactical van was still en route.

I waited for them outside on the front porch because I couldn't stomach the idea of being in the same house with three corpses. I was surprised that the sound of gun fire and a murder victim lying in the driveway hadn't attracted lookie-loo neighbors. That would all change with the arrival of the FBI caravan.

The lead agent was thick, not fat but thick, with a buzzed haircut and wire rim glasses. Agent Cutter introduced himself and showed me his credentials. He was somber and got right to it. "Where are our men?" he asked.

"Roswell was killed as he went through the front door. The other two were already dead in the back bedrooms," I said and pointed through the screen door to where they could be found.

I saw his lip curl. "And that's the doer lying on the ground next to the car?" I nodded. "Are you the law-abiding citizen who settled the score?" he asked with a raised eyebrow. I nodded again. "Christ, what a fucking shit show." He rubbed his chin. "You were sure the agents were dead, right? You didn't miss the opportunity to call an ambulance?"

"Not a chance, Agent Cutter. They were dead. Very, *very* dead."

"Alright. Sit tight. I want to check the crime scene, then I'll come back and we'll talk." He didn't wait for an acknowledgement but moved past me and disappeared into the house with two of his men.

Cutter appeared at the door and motioned for me to come inside. He hadn't been inside very long. As I entered, one of his men got on the phone, requesting crime scene personnel and various special teams.

Cutter sank into a chair at the kitchen table. I didn't wait for an invitation and sat down across from him.

"The fucking drug business," he began, "it's a goddamn plague on humanity." He got quiet for a moment, then focused on me. "Roswell is based out of the New York office, and I wasn't able to reach his supervisor, but I'm reasonably versed on the case." He pulled out a pad and pen and laid them on the table. "Can you take me through it? Just the broad strokes."

"I'm a musician, a guitarist actually."

"I know that. Just bring me up to date."

"He recruited me to get close to a Colombian businessman, an oil exporter he suspected was smuggling drugs into the states, a guy named Serna, Gage Serna."

"More recent, the last month or so. Do we know for sure that Serna is running drugs? Roswell's notes don't mention that's been proven."

"He most definitely is." I pointed to the duffle bag lying on the floor in the corner. "That bag is filled with Sublimaze."

His brow wrinkled. "Subliwhat?"

"Fentanyl."

"Shit-what? Not coke or heroin?"

"Nope."

He jumped out of his chair and called over one of the agents. "Take that bag outside, bag it, seal it, and I mean immediately," he barked. "I don't' want to see it until it's wrapped in fifty layers of plastic. It contains hazardous material."

"Got it," the agent said and removed the duffel bag at once.

Cutter sat back down. "That crap is deadly. You're lucky as hell that shit didn't get airborne, or it would've been like an exploding narcotics bomb. Lethal as hell in even the smallest quantities. The techs wear HAZMAT suits to work with it in the lab." He pulled out his pocket square and dabbed his forehead. "You don't have any more surprises like that for me, do you?"

"No. I didn't know how toxic that stuff is. Serna didn't mentioned it."

"Of course, he didn't—drug lords don't have the highest regard for the well-being of the hired help. So, this guy Serna had you smuggle that stuff into the country. How? How'd you get it in?"

"I jumped out of a plane with it two nights ago. Roswell and I served in Nam together. I'm a trained paratrooper."

"Yeah, that was in the file, but I wasn't sure how it figured in.

"My big concern is that Serna's holding my parents hostage. The corpse outside by the car was his right-hand man. His name is Jacobo. I don't know his last name. I figured Serna would never let my parents go, that he'd hold them hostage to get me to do whatever he wanted. That's why I shot Jacobo with Roswell's gun. That oversized fucker killed a fellow Marine. I figured Serna might swap my folks for his bag of dope. Roswell told me that crap is worth a fortune."

"I believe it is. Although, we don't know a lot about it yet. It's just beginning to make its way onto the streets. The local dealers use it to cut the crap out of heroin. They blend heroin with a flyspeck of Fentanyl and a shitload of anything cheap, like talcum powder, baking soda…rat poison. The street-level dealers aren't picky."

"What do we do now?" I asked.

Cutter seemed deep in thought. "I'm not sure. I have to run this mess by the Director and loop Roswell's CO in as well. We'll put you up in a safe location until we can sort out the details."

"Oh, really, a safe place like this one was supposed to be? No, thank you. Tell me how to reach you. I'll fend for myself."

Chapter Forty-Seven

I'd lived in Cape Coral, Florida, most of my life, but had only ridden the Captiva Island Ferry a handful of times. Captiva was a resort town, and I'd never lived a resort kind of life. Mine had been a life of school, music, and part-time jobs. The last few years had taken me all over the world, from the sewer that went by the name Southeast Asia, to London, then Cartagena. With the many changes of location, I'd almost forgotten Cape Coral existed. It certainly didn't occupy a prominent place in my mind. On the occasions when I thought about my hometown, I thought primarily about my parents and visualized the house I'd grown up in. With my parents missing, Cape Coral didn't seem like home any longer. At the moment, it was a rendezvous point with the feds and nothing more, a place to meet with Cutter, lay out a plan to locate my parents, and return them to safety.

I'd managed to stay off the radar since the altercation at the FBI safe house, moving from one motel to the next every day, watching TV and eating at diners. Each motel was a slight variation on a pedestrian theme, cinderblock buildings painted flamingo pink and constructed in a horseshoe configuration around a pool. The interior walls were painted coral and turquoise. There must have been a closeout sale on bathroom shower curtains. If they weren't identical, they were similar enough that I couldn't tell them apart, nautical themed prints with starfish, seahorses, and sand dollars.

Sleep was practically nonexistent. Not knowing where my parents were or what Serna was doing to them was tearing me apart. And when I did manage to doze off for a short time, there were the recurring nightmares, flashes of Roswell's throat being slit and him collapsing onto the floor. John Roswell had been at the very top of my shit list since the moment he waylaid me at JFK Airport, banished me to Cartagena, and made me his undercover slave. But I never wished him dead and never wanted him to be murdered in such a vicious manner. The idea of him or anyone else getting murdered never seemed a distant possibility, until it happened. Now, with murder on the table, I imagined a short future for myself. Thoughts of rock and roll stardom seemed as distant as the most distant star. All that mattered was rescuing my mom and dad. Beyond that, I'd accept any consequences that came my way.

The sky was clear, but the morning air was chilly as the ferry crossed the Pine Island Sound, raising goosebumps along my arms and at the base of my neck. A pod of bottlenose dolphins swam parallel to the ferry. Periodically, a pair would jump at the same time, and I could hear them whistling and clicking when they breached. Their playfulness pervaded me with a temporary sense of calm. Was there a way out of this mess? I wanted to believe there was, though in my heart I doubted it. The pod veered north as we approached the landing on Captiva Island. It almost seemed as if they were repelled by the presence of the federal officers waiting for me onshore.

Chapter Forty-Eight

Captiva Island was a five-mile stretch of sandy beaches, filled with snack bars, bait and tackle shops, and stands offering equipment rentals for every manner of watersport imaginable. Cutter and Petraglia waited under a shady portico for Sonny Rojas to arrive. The shade didn't prevent them from sweating through their shirts.

"Thanks for making the trip," Cutter said to Petraglia as they stood waiting.

"Did I have a choice? This entire operation is a cluster fuck. Roswell is dead, the kid's parents were abducted, and this mission is headed down a swirling toilet."

"I suppose not. How'd you get dibs on this assignment anyway? New York is the other end of the country. It should've been assigned to the Florida office from the get-go."

"Except it wasn't," Petraglia said. "And Roswell was the one who put it all together, connecting Serna Oil using their barges to shuffle narcotics into the country. There wouldn't have been a mission without his insight and due diligence."

Cutter swiped the back of his wrist across his sweaty forehead. "Roswell did that, did he? Go figure. I spent ten minutes with the guy, and as far as I could tell, he was nothing more than a hot-tempered prick. I guess I was wrong."

"You're fucking A, you were wrong. Roswell was a dedicated agent and a military hero. You know how he first met Rojas?"

"Of course I do—I read his file cover to jacket cover. He rescued the kid. Rojas was flat on his back in a stream after he smashed the shit out of himself

"

during a night jump that went terribly wrong. Roswell brought his helo down in VC territory, risking his life to save Rojas."

Petraglia looked away, his face mired in disgust. "And he died in the line of service. So, unless you've got something good to say about the man…" He checked his watch. "When do we expect Rojas? I feel like a roasting turkey waiting for the pop-up timer to pop."

Cutter checked his watch. "Elvis should be here any minute."

"Elvis, huh?" Petraglia turned away from Cutter, his eyes looking out past the peer. "Is that the ferry off in the distance?"

Cutter strained his eyes. "Looks like it."

"Good," he said as he wiped the back of his neck with a handkerchief. "Play nice, Cutter. We need this kid a hell of a lot more than he needs us. He's making night drops for the cartel, and his parents are God knows where. He's in way over his head and in real danger. Maybe give your piss-off-the-Pope-attitude a rest before the kid takes a hike, and both of us are standing around with fingers up our asses."

Chapter Forty-Nine

Standing on the dock, Cutter stood out like a sore thumb. He wore a button-down shirt with gray slacks in a locale where sun-faded t-shirts and shorts were standard gear. The man with him was dressed a little smarter, in a white short-sleeve shirt and tan slacks. His suit jacket was slung over his shoulder. Dark sunglasses would've helped him blend in if it was possible for a fed to do so. He had that G-Man look a pair of shades couldn't disguise.

"Agent Petraglia flew down from New York to join us," Cutter said. "He's… he was Roswell's commanding officer."

"Rojas," the man began, acknowledging me. His hand shot out quickly. "We appreciate everything you've done for us, Sonny. You've done your country proud."

Cutter didn't offer to shake my hand. I wasn't offended.

"There's an outdoor café just there," Cutter said pointing to a luncheonette facing the water a short distance down the wharf. Pink and turquoise umbrellas were open over circular fiberglass tables. Flamingo colors were everywhere in southern Florida. They were as inescapable as the ever-present heat and humidity. If you were repulsed by Florida hues, your only choice was to pack a bag and head for parts north.

Petraglia and I grabbed a table while Cutter ordered sodas at the outside counter. "You and Roswell knew each other in Nam, I understand." He tilted his glasses and peered over the top of the frame. His eyes were two different colors, one brown eye and one that was sort of a mottled blue. It shouldn't've bothered me, but it did, and I was happy when he put his sunglasses back in place. "I believe that's what he told me when he briefed me several months back."

"John saved my life."

"I know. John was a modest man—didn't talk about it a lot, but it's in your file. Something about a bad jump?"

"Awful jump. I landed flat on my back in a stream in the middle of the night. I would've died there if John hadn't landed his helo and flown me out. Not long after, he was in the bed next to mine in a field hospital. Got to know each other pretty damn well. I can't say that things were the same for us the last several months. Still, I can't believe he's gone."

"You know, I tried to talk him out of this Serna investigation. He had lots of assignments to choose from, and I tried to strong-arm him in another direction, but he was so dammed committed to this op I couldn't get him to change his mind. It was his baby, you know. Put it together all on his own. I told him it was gonna be an absolute shit show, and now it is."

I felt my throat tightening. "Was he married? Have any kids? I was so angry at him for sucking me into this mess, I never thought to ask."

"No, he was married once, now divorced and single. No kids. I guess that's a blessing."

I only knew Petraglia for thirty seconds but had the sense that he was sincere. Of course, he was a Fed, so it all could've been a veneer, and he was playing a predetermined role he thought would get the most out of me. The small dose of the FBI I'd been exposed to was more than enough to make me cynical.

Cutter returned with three bottles of Coke, caps off. He took a swig and smacked his lips. "I love this shit. Refreshing as hell every time."

"Too bad we're not sitting here in 1894," Petraglia said. "Cocaine was one of the ingredients in Coca-Cola when it was first formulated and it was legal. If it still was, we wouldn't be chasing Serna, and Roswell might still be alive." He picked up the bottle and toasted us. "Here's to John Roswell." He gulped the soda and placed the bottle down on the table. "Well, young man, I imagine that tracking down your folks is point number one on your agenda. It is for us as well. How do we reach out to Serna? I don't suppose you've got his phone number."

I'd asked myself the same question over and over again. As much as I hated the idea, I knew I had to go back to Cartagena. Palms upturned, I sighed, indicating that I knew what I had to do.

"Here's the rub," Cutter said. "You mentioned that you wanted to barter Serna's Fentanyl for your parents' lives, but we don't see that playing out the way you want it to. You think you've got him over a barrel, but you don't. He'll torture your mother and father until you give him what's his. At the very least, he'll threaten to, and it'll tear you apart."

"Or he'll kill one of them and tell you that you can save the other by giving up the contraband, which is a deal he'll never honor," Petraglia said. "If we go in with your barter scheme, you *and* your parents are fucked." He put his hand on mine. "Trust me, Sonny, it won't work. Fortunately, there's another way."

"Instead of going head-to-head with Serna and becoming his enemy, there's a way to endear yourself to him," Cutter said.

"Why the hell would I want to do that? I'd already told Roswell I'd quit. I don't want to get any deeper into this than I already am. I only want my parents safe."

"And this is the way we do that," Petraglia said.

I felt my heart pounding. "I'm listening." Truth was, I wasn't so much listening as being patient. Any deal they laid down would suck me deeper and deeper into Gage Serna's grasp.

"An informant has given us Guzman's location," Petraglia said. "We give the duffle back to you, and you deliver it to Guzman as Serna intended all along. Do that, and you're golden."

"What? How does that make any sense? We know that Serna's already heard I didn't make the drop. He sent Jacobo to find the drugs and complete the delivery."

"We don't think he knows everything," Cutter said. "We checked the phone records at the FBI safe house, and there were no long-distance calls to Colombia. And with this Jacobo character dead…how could he know?"

"But I shot him."

"You're not thinking clearly, son," Petraglia said. "Once again, Serna doesn't know he's dead or who killed him. He only knows he hasn't made contact recently. The only people who know that you shot Jabobo are sitting at this table. All you have to do is deliver the drugs and go back to Colombia. Once you're back, you tell Serna that the police were on top of you when you landed, and your connection took off. All of that is true, so if he checks into it, you'll be golden. The pilot who shoved you out of the plane will confirm the Coast Guard was onto you from the very start. Tell him you had to lay low for a couple of days to make sure you weren't being watched before making the drop off to Guzman. He doesn't have to know that you were picked up by the police or that you and Roswell went to the safehouse. It'll fly, Sonny. I know it will."

"And how did I know where to find Guzman?"

"Oh, yee of little faith," Petraglia began with bravado. "You're working with the FB-fucking-I. We've got you covered."

Chapter Fifty

The FB-fucking-I, my ass. Sitting in the back of a van with a sack over my head and my wrists tied, I wondered if Petraglia's masterstroke was going to plan. Just minutes earlier, I'd been sitting on the bed in my motel room watching The Mod Squad when two armed cabróns kicked in the door. One of them grabbed the drug-filled duffle, and the other yanked me to my feet, tied my wrists behind my back, and dropped a burlap sack over my head. They were in and out in thirty seconds with me in tow.

To be fair, Petraglia told me to expect someone to contact me, a guy he said was his confidential informant, someone who worked for Guzman and went by the name, Ralph. Despite all the nasty shit I'd recently been exposed to, I wasn't yet adept at playing by drug runner's rules. I should've known better. Droguistas don't hand you an engraved invitation and politely ask you to join them for a ride to the kingpin's house. I was so naïve, a total shit-for-brains rookie.

Whoever was at the wheel drove slowly, and I was able to sit on the floor of the van without being jostled or rocked side to side. I suppose that was to be expected, as they had a shit ton of narcotics in the van with them and didn't want to attract unwanted attention. *Do they know how lethal the Sublimaze is?* I wondered. A mere uncut fly speck was enough to off the three of us. The FBI had doubled the plastic wrappings around the product and told me it was safe to transport. That's what Cutter told me—for what it was worth.

I was still hooded and bound, but approximated that half an hour had passed when the van came to a stop. The hood remained in place as they led me toward a house. It was brightly lit, and its likeness shone through the coarse weave of the burlap hood. I didn't have a clear picture but could appreciate that the structure was immense.

Once inside, the lighting was dim, and I couldn't tell which room I was in. I heard men speaking Spanish. "¿Este es él?" one of them said, asking, This is him?

"Sí, Jefe."

"Bien." Someone snapped their fingers, followed by a popping sound, something akin to the sealing of a Tupperware container. With the hood ripped off my head, the lighting stung my eyes. We stood in the center of a large foyer. The duffle bag was now enclosed in a translucent plastic bin and sealed with a snap-on lid. The two badasses who paid me a visit at the motel stood on either side of the man I imagined was Guzman. They were armed, their guns in hand.

Guzman didn't introduce himself and looked nothing like the way I expected him to. He was slight with short, well-groomed hair and a thin mustache. He was pale for a Latino living in southern Florida and wore black Buddy Holly glasses. He looked more like a CPA than a drug czar. "Rojas?" he asked.

I nodded and kept my mouth shut. Despite his refined appearance, I was sure he'd have me killed if he suspected anything or if I didn't smell just right.

"I've been expecting you," he said, then turned and left the room.

One of the cabróns pressed his gun on my spine, where I was still sore from the bad jump. I winched and he laughed as he nudged me into the adjoining room.

"Machista," he said, snickering as he sarcastically insulted my manhood.

I entered what was certainly Guzman's office. He sat behind an opulent desk. I'd learned enough about carpentry from my dad to appreciate the quality of the rich wood and the hand-turned carvings on the legs. The walls were paneled in oak. Landscape paintings were ornately framed. The cabrón pulled his gun away and pushed me into a leather chair that was as soft as a baby's behind.

"I don't think we need guns," Guzman said, then turned to me, eyebrows peaked. "Do we need guns, Rojas?"

"No, Sir."

"Excellent. No guns." The cabróns holstered their sidearms.

"I'm glad that you were able to make the delivery even if it took longer than expected. My men told me the police made an unexpected appearance at the site where they were supposed to meet you." He leaned forward. "An unexpected coincidence?"

"Yes. As I descended, I could see a police car parked off the road on the other side of the median where your men were supposed to pick me up. I think it was a speed trap."

He adjusted his gaze and leveled it at one of his men, who nodded. "You were lucky not to get picked up with the merchandise. I presume you ran?"

"I did. I stayed at a motel nearby and asked around, hoping to contact one of your men."

"And how did you accomplish this?"

"Serna's pilot gave me a wad of hundred-dollar bills just in case things didn't work out and I had to get a flight back to Colombia afterward. I spread the money around at bars and strip joints. I didn't know what else to do."

"Not very original, but it worked. I'm overjoyed to learn that my men frequent such highbrow establishments," Guzman said as he clapped his hands. "Bravo, Rojas. Bravo. I'm glad you were so committed to accomplishing your task. Is it because Sr. Serna threatened the lives of your mother and father?" I was shaken by his frankness, and while I deliberated on what to say, he let me off the hook. "It's alright, Rojas. Gage and his Papa, as the saying goes, the apple doesn't fall far from the tree. I know how they operate."

By badmouthing Serna, it almost seemed as if Guzman was sucking up to me, but I knew it was bullshit and that Guzman was one-hundred-percent capable of doing terrible deeds exactly as Serna had done. Possibly worse.

A glass of red wine sat on his desk blotter. He picked it up and took a small sip, then set the glass down once more. "Now that I have my package, I'll reach out to Gage. I'm sure he'll be relieved to learn that his merchandise has arrived, and about the great efforts you made to honor your obligation."

I ached to ask if he knew where my parents were but didn't think he knew or would tell me if he did. I had no choice but to bear the pain and anguish until I could talk to Serna.

"You'll stay on the grounds in my guest cottage until arrangements can be made for your return to Cartagena." He took another sip of wine. "Under supervision, of course. I'm sure you'll find your new accommodations superior to the fleabag motel you were staying at." He turned to the man on my left. "Good job, Ralph. Take young Rojas to the cottage and make sure he has something to eat. After all, rock star paratroopers are hard to come by." He winked at me, then picked up the remote control and turned on the TV.

Chapter Fifty-One

Ralph, if that was his real name, was a tight-lipped son of a bitch, the Latino counterpart to The Addams Family's Lurch. He was tall, sullen, and spoke only when necessary. In his case, necessary meant next to never. His silence bothered me at first, but I quickly came to appreciate that he was more than Guzman's henchman. He was also an FBI informant and was smart enough not to compromise himself lest he end up a fatality. I doubted a man like Guzman was kind to rats and swift to hand out death sentences.

There wasn't a single cottage on Guzman's property, but three, and mine was far from shabby, with a hot tub and an outdoor shower. I couldn't say I felt safe living in Guzman's world. The mattress in my cottage was so soft it felt as if I was sleeping on a cloud. I got a great night's sleep, showered, dressed, and was wondering what to do with myself when Ralph knocked on the door, announced himself with a grunt, and let himself in.

The man was concise, his economy of words breathtaking. "Breakfast," he said and gestured toward the door. I popped out of my chair and followed him to the patio at the main house. The unoccupied table was set with china. A buffet table showcased several chafing dishes, bowls of fruits, breads, and pastries. A maid poured coffee while I waited for others to arrive. Sipping dark roast, I noticed a gardener snipping the ends from perfectly manicured shrubs much in the way a good barber would give a haircut, a snip here and a snip there, grooming the plants until they were perfect. A smaller table was set up at the other end of the patio. Ralph sat down for breakfast with the cabrón who had pulled a sack over my head and shoved me around the night before.

It wasn't long before others showed up. Guzman laughed as he came through the patio door. A young man was a step behind him. I knew without introduction who he was, Gage Serna's younger brother, Thiago. He had Gage's inquisitive eyes and chiseled features, but his hair was long and wavy, whereas Gage's was short and neatly groomed. Thiago was considerably taller and looked wiry.

"We have a guest," Guzman boomed as he sat down. "Thiago, say hello to Sonny. He's a business associate working with your brother."

"Hey, man," Thiago said as he leaned over the table and shook my hand. He sat down and unfolded his napkin. "I'm not going to ask what you and Gage do together. Plausible deniability, right?"

Guzman laughed heartily. "You must watch out for this one," Guzman said. "He's the clever one, numero uno in his class."

"Where do you go to school?" I asked.

"Levin," he said and offered nothing more. He pointed to his coffee cup, and it was immediately filled. Levin College of Law at the University of Florida was one of the top law schools in the country, a tropical Harvard for the rich and powerful. My mother often nudged me, hoping I'd apply there one day, but I had less than no interest in becoming a lawyer and had no plans to attend a college of any type. I'd do my higher learning on the concert stage, studying with rock and roll virtuosos. Guilt washed over me without warning. Perhaps if I'd listened to her, I wouldn't be in the position I was in now, and my parents would be safe and sound in their home.

"Thiago is visiting with me for a while," Guzman said.

"Gainesville's an absolute shithole," Thiago said. "Uncle Renaldo sends his helicopter for me when I need a dose of civilization." I didn't know enough about Gainesville to dispute what Thiago had said, except that there was an up-and-coming local group called Mudcrutch that some of my old bandmates talked about the last time I visited home.

Thiago got up and helped himself to the buffet. Judging by the size of his servings, he had a healthy appetite.

"Thiago and I have business to attend to after breakfast." Guzman sipped coffee. "You and I will talk when I return. I spoke with Gage last night, and he was very pleased to hear about all the effort you put into delivering his product." He leaned across the table and whispered, "Not that you had a choice, am I right?" He sat back in his chair. "For now, suffice it to say that your parents are well."

I was surprised at Guzman's compassion. He didn't have to volunteer that bit of information, but he did. The gears in my head began to turn the second the relief I'd felt subsided. *They need me*, I thought. Serna must've told Guzman to keep me happy. I was certain they'd ask me to make another drop the moment I returned to Colombia. How many drops would I have to make before he released my parents? Would he ever?

Thiago sat down and began spearing large chunks of melon. "How do you like law school?" I asked. Gage Serna's words came back to me, "At this moment Thiago is in Florida working on something for me." Was he here to spy on Guzman and report back to his brother? The possibility seemed more than likely.

"A means to an end," he said. "My brother insists that I obtain a JD before I can take my place as Chief Operating Officer of Serna Oil. He thinks because it was his path that it should be mine as well." He sliced a breakfast sausage. "I don't argue with him. My professors can be quite engaging, and the women…American girls like to have fun." He winked at me. "I'm sure you know what I mean, don't you, Sonny?" He shoveled eggs into his mouth. "Uncle Renaldo tells me you're a talented musician. "What do you play?"

"Guitar and a little bass. Guitar mostly."

"Ah, then it makes sense. My delusional brother sees himself as the next Jimi Hendrix."

He picked a bad example. Jimi was one of a kind. There never was and would never be another guitarist with Jimi's chops. Gage was nothing more than a riff imitator. He didn't have an original bone in his body. "It's always good to dream."

My comment seemed to tickle him. "Very good," he said. "My brother yearns for world acclaim, but what does he need of that world? He's the CEO of one of the largest oil exporters in Colombia. Boohoo. My poor spoiled brother, he has so much to cry about."

Guzman had just filled his plate. I seized the opportunity to stand up and take some food. I knew nothing about Gage's relationship with his younger brother, but it seemed that there was no love lost. Thiago's words oozed envy.

"No interest in music?" I asked.

"This one? No," Guzman said and waved his hand dismissively. "He has the soul of a warrior—runs like a bull on the soccer field. Captain of his team."

I glanced at Thiago. He was grinning even as he chewed his food. "I like music, of course, but—"

"No interest in learning?"

He shook his head. "Where would I find the time? Between soccer, my studies, and women…" He shook his head playfully. "Impossible. My studies could fall by the wayside if they had to, but soccer and women…never!"

A housekeeper approached the table. "Sr. Guzman, your car is ready," she said.

Guzman nodded and took a last gulp of coffee. "Where does the time go? Come, Thiago, the lawyers are waiting for us." He pushed back in his chair and stood. Thiago polished off his orange juice and did the same.

"Nice meeting you," he said.

Guzman called to Ralph at the next table. "Entertain, Sr. Rojas, until I return," he said, then turned to me. "Enjoy your breakfast, Sonny. I'll be back this afternoon."

I laughed inwardly. The thought of being entertained by Guzman's near-mute goon was more than amusing. I soon heard the sound of a car accelerating, then growing quiet as it sped away. Ralph got up from where he was sitting and joined me. The second cabrón had slipped away unnoticed, probably accompanying Guzman and Thiago to provide security.

I made one last attempt at conversation with Ralph. "I never thought I'd meet Gage's brother today. He's kind of full of himself, isn't he?"

Ralph had nothing to say. He ate with his head down, devouring his food.

I wasn't surprised by his silence, but I wasn't ready to give up. I knew he was cooperating with Cutter and Petraglia and was hoping he'd divulge something useful. "Any other VIP guests I should know about?"

Ralph looked up momentarily. Despite his appearance, he didn't have a hint of a Spanish accent. "You don't give up, do you?"

I chuckled. "Your boss told you to entertain me."

He nodded. "Yes, he did."

"So, any other important guests coming, foreign dignitaries or heads of state?"

"Guests?" he laughed. "You don't know who you're dealing with."

"Meaning?"

"Meaning Thiago is no more a guest of Guzman than your mama and papa are of Gage Serna. There is purpose in everything Guzman does."

Chapter Fifty-Two

One sentence from Ralph was all I could handle. He said nothing further but ate enough for two men, then left leaving me to think about what he'd told me. "There is a purpose to everything Guzman does," implying that Guzman had a hidden agenda and that Thiago Serna was being used or would be. The question was, how?

Ralph's lack of an accent and his clear diction also led me to think that he was more than I'd been told. Was he a confidential informant for the FBI, or was he an undercover agent? Was he tongue-tied or was he thoughtful and cautious? The less he spoke, the less chance there was of getting tripped up and saying something Guzman would find suspect. And if he told me nothing, I could repeat nothing. My theory was that he was a pro. His assumption must've been that I was a rookie. He wasn't wrong. I was a fish out of water, floundering at every turn, hooked at the mouth, and doing my best not to get caught in a trap. Another trap. Serna already had me by the throat, a stranglehold ensuring I'd do anything he asked.

Hours later, the closed-mouth enigma of a man once again knocked on the door and entered my cottage. Standing at the threshold, he motioned with his head for me to come with him. I checked my watch. It was after two p.m., and Guzman had likely returned. I didn't bother to ask Ralph if that was the case. A short walk to the main house and Guzman's office confirmed my suspicion.

"Sit down," Guzman said as he looked up from what looked like a ledger book. He picked up his smoldering cigar and took a puff. "Havanas," he began, "still the gold standard. They've become harder and harder to come by since the Bay of Pigs fiasco. So many islands in the Caribbean." He took another puff. "Can you tell me why no one else can produce a cigar to rival Cubans?"

All I knew about cigars was that they stunk. I had to take quick breaths to keep from coughing while his putrid cigar smoke filled the room.

"They have a monopoly, yes? Just as Serna has a monopoly on this Sublimaze. It's an unfair advantage, don't you think? I believe in the free enterprise system. It promotes competitive pricing."

I doubt he was expecting a comment, but I replied all the same. "Do you have a choice?"

His eyes gleamed. "Always, Sonny. Always."

I didn't see that he did, but I saw Guzman as a shrewd operator who was no doubt making moves to expand his business. I couldn't help but wonder how Gage's brother, Thiago, factored into the equation. In my gut, I felt sure he would.

"We all have an agenda, don't we? Yours is to see your parents freed, and mine is to expand business." He leaned back and crossed his legs. "Perhaps our interests can align."

I was once again the fish out of water. What could I possibly offer Guzman, and why would I get involved with him? It was bad enough that I was beholden to Serna for my parents' lives. I needed another criminal entanglement, like I needed an inoperable tumor. These men, Serna and Guzman, were deadly. He fixed me with his gaze while he waited for an answer. "Can you explain?"

His eyes brightened again, equaling the intensity he displayed when I asked if he had a choice of where to buy Sublimaze. "Yes. But first, I want to ask you a question. Why do you think a man like Gage Serna, a man who sits at the helm of one of the largest oil corporations in Colombia, has such a keen interest in drug trafficking?"

I'd asked myself that question several times but had never come close to figuring it out. I assumed it was because Serna was greedy. Although he was very wealthy, he could never have enough. "I have no idea."

"Taxes," Guzman said. "Between corporation and personal income tax, the

Colombian government sucks close to eighty percent of Serna's earnings out of his pockets. Sure, with his team of clever lawyers and accountants, they can hide some of it, but Serna has to share at least fifty centavos of every peso with the government. A small fish can slip through the government's net, but a whale like Serna…? That, Sonny, is a big ugly bite."

Eyes wide open, I nodded. Guzman had painted a crystal-clear picture. Zero taxation on ill-gotten revenue amounted to a highly compelling reason for Serna to be in the illegal drug business. I couldn't condone it, but I sure as hell understood his motivation.

Guzman rested his smoldering cigar in the ashtray, then turned his chair until we were eye-to-eye. "That brings us to me. I am Serna's largest distributor of heroin and cocaine in the United States, and I'm quite sure my appetite for Sublimaze will grow exponentially." He leaned forward. "Do you understand?"

I didn't know what he was trying to communicate beyond what he'd presented on the surface. My blank expression must've been the reason he didn't wait for a reply.

"Serna is as dependent on me for revenue as I am on him for product. Maybe more so. My coffers are full. I have a never-ending supply of customers and Serna…just one outlet to speak of. Who is more important to whom?"

I'd never taken an economics class, but it seemed as if Guzman was in a better position than Serna, and with unlimited resources, he could buy from anyone he wanted to. So, why hadn't he already? "I still don't know where I come in. Serna is going to hold my parents hostage so that I continue delivering product for him. How exactly do we help each other?"

Guzman pressed his fingertips together and chuckled gleefully. "That, Sonny, is what I am about to explain."

Chapter Fifty-Three

Guzman told Serna that offering his jet for my return trip to Colombia was the least he could do after all the trouble I'd encountered to make the Sublimaze delivery. It wasn't the truth. Guzman didn't care if I had to swim back to Colombia as long as it didn't cause a delay with the next shipment of drugs. As Ralph had intimated, there was purpose with everything Guzman did, and my premium accommodation was no different.

"No sense deadheading," Guzman had said with a self-assured smile that day in his office, referring to a trucker driving home with an empty trailer after making a long-distance delivery. I'd delivered the Sublimaze. "Why," he continued, "go back empty-handed?"

In Guzman's eyes, there was no good reason. Forty kilograms. Eighty-eight pounds. Fifty thousand one-hundred-dollar bills weighed a hell of a lot more than I imagined, but its true weight couldn't be measured on a scale. It sat next to me on a seat on Guzman's private jet. He and I were new partners, and a cash payment of $50,000 was now sitting in my safety deposit box back in Florida. He assured me it would be the first of many.

"I'd never had that kind of money before. I'd never even dreamt of it. Growing up in western Florida, I never considered my family poor, but we were far from comfortable and never had more than the basic necessities. Twenty round-trip missions would put a million dollars in my bank vault. My mind swam on the fantasy of the life that money would provide for me and my parents.

"Serna sees himself as the dog and me as the tail," Guzman had said. "He's arrogant and soon, as they say, the tail will be wagging the dog." Guzman's appetite had grown beyond Serna's ability to keep him satisfied. While he was monopolizing Serna's production, he was also adding new suppliers. The cash I carried was an initial payment to a cocaine lab located in the jungles of Colombia.

Guzman's cigar sat smoldering in the ashtray as his plan unfolded. "And when I control Serna and not the other way around, I'll be in a position to make demands, demands such as the release of your parents. This, Sonny, is how your plans and mine align. You continue to deliver Sublimaze and carry back cash. Soon, your mama and papa will be back home, and you'll be a very wealthy man."

Cutter and Petraglia were thrilled to hear that Guzman was flying me back to Colombia for another run. Did I tell them I was getting paid for the trouble? Not a chance. What had the FBI done for me other than put a gun to my head and compel me to spy on Serna? They couldn't even keep my parents safe and put me in a position where I was forced to commit murder, an enormously bitter pill I was still choking on. They hadn't developed a plan to rescue my parents from Serna. From where I stood, it was a one-sided deal, and I was on the short end.

Guzman had told Serna the date I'd return to Colombia, a date five days later than my actual arrival date. The jet landed in Cali, more than a thousand kilometers from Cartagena, Serna's stomping grounds.

Guzman arranged for me to be met at the airport for a drive into the Colombian jungle. What he didn't tell me was that I'd be accompanied by five armed mercenaries in camouflaged military gear. I began to regret my new partnership the moment I met Guzman's mercenaries. Twenty trips back and forth and a million dollars in wealth now seemed unattainable.

The point man was named Parra. He was compact but looked powerful. His musk was strong, putrid, verging on lethal. Scars on his face evidenced he'd been in more than a brawl or two. He and I drove in the middle jeep. There were two soldiers in each of the front and rear jeeps.

"Five soldiers necessary?" I asked as we headed away from the airport.

"No," Parra answered in broken English as his cheekbones rose. "Ten would be better." He waited until the shock on my face faded. "You have any idea what the guerrillas will do to get their hands on the money you're carrying?"

"I'm beginning to."

"Multiply what you're thinking by a hundred." He reached into his pocket and pulled out what looked like a chunk of dried beef, then tore off a piece with his teeth. "There's food and drink in the cooler," he said, and motioned to where I could find it. "Help yourself."

It had been hours since I last ate, but I was without appetite. "Maybe later." It was so goddamn hot and humid I couldn't even think about eating. Too bad he didn't have a portable shower.

He pointed to a canteen on the floorboard. "Very hot in the jungle. Drink," he said. There was only one canteen, so I guess we were sharing. An empty plastic jug rattled around on the floor. He pointed to it and said, "Baño."

I didn't want to relieve myself in front of him, but figured when the time came, I'd do what I had to. "How long will it take to get there?"

"Sr. Rojas, it will take what it takes." He slapped my knee. "Relájate, amigo. Enjoy the view."

There wasn't much else to do. Parra wasn't exactly a chatterbox, but each subsequent message he spoke gave me greater cause for distress. We were off-road within minutes of him telling me to relax as we entered a lush forest with foliage I was unfamiliar with, massive ferns and broadleaf plants, dazzling blooms of bright orange and yellow. The path was nothing more than a clearing through the forest where tires had eroded the ground covering until the brown earth showed through. The jeeps had raked suspensions and were able to cross the shallow rivulets that traversed the path in front of us. Tropical birds were everywhere. Progress was slow. We just barely rolled forward over uneven ground littered with large rocks and dead tree limbs. It was like a rollercoaster as the jeep rocked and swayed over obstacles.

"Is this the best route?" I asked.

Parra grinned. "You value your life?" he asked. I nodded. Every word he said spoke of impending doom. "Then this is the best route." He pointed to the plastic container, and I handed it to him. He managed to unzip and whiz without taking his left hand off the wheel, then handed back the jug. I held my breath and quickly capped it. For an average-sized man, he held a lot of water. I don't know why he didn't just jump out and hug a tree, but I suppose he didn't want to hold up the convoy while he dropped trou. I had difficulty determining how far we'd traveled and didn't have the faintest idea how far was left to go. Parra was right, the jungle was terribly hot and humid. I wasn't thrilled about sharing the same water supply with him, but my throat was as dry as gravel. I grabbed the canteen and poured water into my mouth without putting my lips on the neck of the bottle. God only knew the last time he brushed his teeth or the disgusting places his mouth had been. Having served in Nam, I wasn't squeamish, but my guess was that Parra wasn't big on hygiene, oral or otherwise.

I didn't hear anything other than the jungle sounds that had filled the air for the last few hours, but something seemed to have caused the lead driver concern. He raised his hand, and all three jeeps came to an abrupt stop in a marshy area.

"Stay in the jeep," Parra said as he reached behind his seat for a rifle.

"What's going on?"

"I'm not sure. Wait here and don't be a hero. This area is crawling with fer-de-lance and caiman."

"Huh?"

"Pit vipers, poisonous snakes, and crocodile." He handed me an automatic handgun. "You know how to use a gun?" I nodded. "Anything moves—you shoot it. Good?" My head bobbed once more. He shouted to the men in the rear jeep in Spanish. "They'll stay with you to protect the money."

Sure. Protect the money. Don't worry about me. I'll be fine.

Parra joined the men from the first jeep. I watched as they slogged through the shallow stream, then vanished into the jungle. From the corner of my eye, I sensed something moving above me, glanced upward and froze. A snake was hanging from a tree limb just above my head.

Chapter Fifty-Four

I gasped. My lungs seized. A snake dangled from a tree limb no more than a yard above me, jaws wide, fangs bared. As it came for me, I heard a noise like slashing through the air. I stiffened as it fell past my eyes and landed in my lap, cut in half, dead, its guts oozing onto my jeans. Panting and trembling, several moments raced by before I gained a sense of what had happened. One of Parra's soldiers stood over me, machete in hand, the snake's blood dripping from the steel blade onto my shoulder. I grabbed the severed snake lying on my lap and flung it into the brush. The two soldiers laughed hysterically.

"Yeah, funny, real-fucking-funny!" I said, refueling their hysteria. They were both out of their jeep, rifles on their hip as they perused the area. "What's going on?" I asked.

"FARC," the snake killer said in a muffled voice and placed a finger across his lips, signaling for me to be quiet.

What the hell was FARC? My heart rate raced even faster than it had when the dismembered viper fell into my lap. I watched as the snake killer scanned the clearing in front of the jeep. The second soldier scrambled into my jeep. Standing behind the wheel, he placed his rifle barrel on the windshield frame and used the rifle scope to scan the area. He took his eye off the scope, presumably satisfied that he hadn't picked up any activity.

"What gives?" I asked.

"Guerrillas," he said and pressed his eye back against the scope. I felt my heart flutter nervously. Although we were in the jungle, I understood that he sure as hell wasn't talking about apes. He was talking about rebels,

Colombian insurrectionists. The fantasy of becoming a millionaire and my parents being brought safely home vaporized into thin air. It was just that, an illusion, a pipe dream. I heard the crack-crack-crack of rifle fire in the distance. At that moment, I knew I'd be lucky to make it out of the jungle alive.

The snake killer pointed to my handgun, then mimed a gun with his free hand, signaling for me to get ready to use it. He then gestured for me to lower my head and hunker down as much as I could. "Quédate quieto," he said. I spoke fluent Spanish but *stay put* required no translation.

The two soldiers moved off and slipped into the foliage. I heard cracking twigs and displaced brush, but it only lasted a moment, then everything was silent until rifle fire rang out again. I heard the flapping of panicked wings as a flock of birds took to the sky.

Scrunched below the base of the windshield, I pressed the automatic against my belly, waiting. Waiting for what, for a squad of rebels to discover me? Not a good idea. Five million was five million, but it wasn't worth my life. I certainly wouldn't lose it to protect Guzman's money. He'd have to consider it the cost of doing business and should've told me what I'd be up against, the full picture. What was described as a simple drop-off was in reality, a dangerous military operation. Let the guerrillas find the jeeps and the money. I wasn't waiting around to become a casualty. No fucking way.

As I tucked the gun into the waistband of my jeans, I prayed that the gunfire had the same effect on the snakes and crocs that it had on the birds and that they, too, had cleared the area. As I slithered out of the jeep into a muddy bog, water wicked up my jeans. The bog was just deep enough for me to slog through it with only my head exposed for air.

Rifle fire continued in bursts, both single shots and multiple discharges from semi-automatic weapons. I heard no voices and no grunts, which I prayed meant that casualties were few on our side. I traveled into a dense area where large trees grew out of the bog, their trunks saturated with water at the bases. I knew firsthand that snakes climbed trees, but figured it was better than waiting in the bog for a croc to come up behind me. I found a tree with coarse bark and low-hanging limbs. One limb at a time, I climbed the tree and didn't stop until I was well-hidden in the thickest cropping of leaves, a good fifteen feet above the water. Paying careful attention for snakes that might easily blend in with the foliage, I checked the area around me and didn't see anything moving. Finding a limb thick enough to support my weight, I sat down with my back against the main tributary. I didn't realize that I'd been so tense that I was holding my breath, which became obvious when I finally exhaled. The air rushing into my lungs felt restorative, and I breathed deeply, in and out for what seemed like minutes before settling into a semi-natural rhythm.

After hearing shots close by, I did my very best to stay calm, taking long, deep breaths. Since climbing the tree, I'd heard three low, guttural moans and wondered which of Parra's men were still alive. How many guerrillas had they encountered? How many remained? The sky had darkened considerably. As night fell, I wondered how long the skirmish would last. Knowing that many predators were nocturnal hunters, I performed another reconnaissance of the tree I was in as well as the surrounding trees. I didn't see anything in the nearby vicinity, but in the fading light, it became difficult to see into the many shadows. Minute by minute, the world darkened around me. I felt relief in the fact that I was better hidden in darkness than I was in the light of day, but at the same time grew tenser at the prospect of what night in the jungle might bring.

One more exchange of gunfire and another failing gasp. If I was right, four men were dead. At worst, Parra or one of his men was still alive. At best…? I saw the full moon rise through the tree canopy above me. Its light pierced the tree covering and fell on my face. As the wind whistled, a bird with a massive wingspan swooped down and perched on the tree's highest limb. Wings fully extended, the creature must've been ten feet wide—it completely blocked the moonlight. The enormous wings finally retracted and allowed light to shine through once more.

Another torrent of bullets, then two solitary shots and a splash. I counted five dead and wondered what I'd do if Guzman's mercenaries didn't return. I knew I'd never find my way to the drop-off location, but would I be able to find my way back to Cali? Guerrillas, poisonous snakes, and man-eating beasts lay in both directions, but doubling back seemed more doable and certainly more feasible than pressing on to God knows where and encountering God knows who.

Then, an unexpected sound, the rumble of a jeep engine coming to life. I heard sloshing sounds in the bog below me. "Rojas," someone called softly. There was just enough light for me to make out the figure searching below. It was Parra.

"Up here," I said. He came to a stop and looked up, searching the canopy for the source of my voice. I began my descent. Grasping tree limbs, I found branches with my feet, one at a time, until I was once again knee-deep in the bog, face-to-face with Parra. "Thank God," I said. I knew there were fatalities. Still, there was hope. "Are your men alright?"

His expression grim, he shook his head and held up three fingers. "Tres muertos." The whites of his eyes flashed in the moonlight, and his mouth fell open. He righted his rifle and, without warning, fired into the air. I heard wild thrashing just behind me as a long, spotted tail whipped across my leg. Head spinning, I caught a fading glance of a fleeing jaguar. The big spotted cat leapt over a fallen tree trunk and bounded into the jungle.

Chapter Fifty-Five

I lurched forward, practically jumping into Parra's arms, my heart pounding so hard I thought it would crack a rib. In my mind, the beast had pounced on me, buried its fangs in my neck, and dragged me up into a tree where it would slowly devour me over a series of days. I shuddered uncontrollably. Parra slapped me hard across the face. "Estás vivo, Rojas. You're alive."

Yes, I was alive but not in any manner I'd known before. I'd stopped shaking, but my nerve endings were on fire, every one of them sizzling as if I'd stepped on a train track's third rail. My neck twitched. My teeth rattled.

"Unusual," Parra said.

"Unusual? What the hell are you talking about?"

"Jaguar no prey on man. Must be her bebés nearby. She feel…amenazado."

"Threatened? *She* was threatened? How the fuck do you think I felt?"

His eyes were lifeless and had nothing left for me. With three of his men dead, he simply turned and lumbered back toward the jeep. When we arrived, the snake killer was behind the wheel of the lead jeep.

"Money still there?" Parra asked. I checked the jeep and nodded. The duffle bag was exactly where I'd left it. "Bien. No deliver. No get paid," he said and pointed to the passenger seat of the jeep we'd traveled in before the skirmish.

"You're kidding. We're actually going through with this? This is crazy. Loco."

Parra said nothing. He scavenged through the supplies the dead men wouldn't need and stuffed them into our jeep.

"Seriously," I said. "This is too dangerous."

He pointed to the dead men's empty jeep and shrugged. "Don't go. Still plenty gas." He got behind the wheel of our jeep and cranked the engine. "You come, or you stay?"

Who was I kidding? Guzman would have us killed if we came back without making the delivery. At least with the jungle and the Colombian guerrillas we stood a small chance. As we rolled slowly through the jungle, I wondered how far we were from the cocaine lab. I wouldn't waste my breath asking. As Parra had said before, the trip would take what it took.

He reached into the cooler and grabbed a bottle of beer. Using the windshield frame for a bottle opener, he popped off the cap. "Help yourself," he said. We have food and drink for six. Only three mouths to feed."

The man was demoralized and exhausted. "I can drive," I said. "Close your eyes."

He turned to me, his expression showing that he was too tired to argue. "You just follow, Salazar. You can do?"

I nodded. *Salazar,* I mused. *The snake killer has a name.* Parra stopped the jeep, and we traded seats. I'd only driven a stick shift a few times but knew the basics, and he hadn't gotten the jeep out of second gear even once since we resumed the trip. I figured I could handle the job. In the time it had taken us to jockey positions, Salazar hadn't gained more than a hundred feet. I accelerated until our jeep was just ten feet off his back bumper. When I turned my head, Parra was sound asleep.

Chapter Fifty-Six

We rode through the night and arrived at the cocaine lab compound around mid-morning the next day. Parra slept until dawn, his head folded into his neck, bouncing with every obstacle the jeep rolled over. When he woke up, he was in a foul mood. He had all the reasons in the world—three dead comrades were on his conscience. I didn't know what his relationship had been with those men. I didn't know if they'd only been hired for the mission or if they'd been working together for years. He wouldn't talk about his skirmish with the guerrillas and wouldn't say how many they'd encountered or how his men had died. "Ninguno capturado," was one of the few comments he made; none captured. I knew from my tour in Nam how strongly soldiers dreaded capture, and I doubted the guerrillas were more humane than the Viet Cong. He crossed himself. "Mejor morir," he said. Death is better.

Delivering payment to the cocaine lab was the least dramatic part of the mission. We met in a tent with a folding conference table, three droguistas, and no chairs. The compound had a high perimeter fence and lookout towers. There were no man-eating animals or poisonous snakes hanging from trees. They checked the payment in the most casual manner possible, fanning a few bundles to make sure they contained all hundred-dollar bills, and rummaged through the large duffle bag to ensure that there were no surprises. I'm sure they'd go through the payment bill-by-bill afterward, but for the moment, my only interest was in a mattress to pass out upon. I was tired beyond words, mentally and physically exhausted. The concentration required to drive through the jungle at night had drained me more than a week of sound sleep would make up for.

I slept until midafternoon when the sound of a blast launched me straight out of bed. The explosion was nearby, close enough that I felt the pressure waves pass through my canvas tent. I stepped into my boots and took off running without lacing them up, then flew out of the tent opening and onto the compound grounds. A large military vehicle had rammed the tall, barbed-wire fence, flattening it. Men and women were scattering, desperate for cover. I felt a hand on my shoulder, turned, and was face-to-face with Parra. "FARC?" I asked.

Parra nodded, grabbed me by the shirt, and led me behind the latrine building. The guerrillas must've found their murdered comrades and picked up our trail leading to the compound. My assumption was that they'd come seeking revenge. But now that they'd located the cocaine lab, they'd be back to milk the cash cow. The guerrilla's main focus was government rebellion—all terrorist factions need funding, and drug money was as good as any.

"¿Cuántas?" he asked. How many?

It was easy to differentiate the men with guns from the others. I held up four fingers. One of the guerrillas was down on one knee, aiming at the sentry in the closest guard tower. His bullet was true. It hit the sentry squarely in the chest, who staggered backward, then collapsed forward over the tower railing. His body hit the ground with a dull thud. As the shooter got to his feet, Parra pulled his gun, stepped out from behind the small outhouse building, and shot him through the mouth.

"Three left," I said.

Parra pulled a second gun and offered it to me. "You can kill?"

The answer was no, but I said, "*Yes.*" I'd kill if it was a matter of a guerrilla's life or mine. Beyond that, I didn't see myself as a killer. This wasn't my war, and I didn't want another life on my conscience unless there was no other way. Jacobo had murdered Roswell, an ex-soldier and brother in arms. It was my duty as a Marine to put the bastard down.

"The others must die. You understand?"

I did understand. I understood instantly. If any of the guerrillas survived, they would assume control of the lab and confiscate all the cash. It wasn't our fault that we'd been ambushed and that the rebels had followed us back to the compound, but Guzman wouldn't see it that way. He'd kill us all and not lose a moment's sleep. Conversely, if all the guerrillas were put down, the lab could be relocated. It would return to business as usual, and Guzman would be an extremely happy camper. I nodded. Parra chambered a round before handing me the gun.

A second sentry took down a guerrilla with a shot to the center of the back. The fallen soldier was face down on the ground, writhing. I didn't know if he was dying or if the bullet had hit his spine and paralyzed him. A second bullet from the tower sentry put the guerrilla down for good.

We saw the third guerrilla enter the packaging house. Parra pointed to him, then gave me a push on the shoulder. "Mátalo!" he ordered. Kill him! There was still a fourth guerrilla. Without notice, Parra took off, presumably to find the last soldier. In his absence, it took a full minute until I was able to resign myself to the task, then I took a deep breath and pushed forward, across the compound to the building I'd seen the guerrilla enter.

My heart was beating far faster than my apprehensive pace across the grounds. I'd covered half the distance when I heard shots being fired within the building. I froze dead in my tracks, closed my eyes, and squeezed the grip of the gun. Sweat ran into my eyes, the salt stinging them. I rubbed it away with my bare wrist and continued on. One more shot, then another. I refused to let the gunfire slow me down. I came around the building to the door, then pried it open ever so slightly. A man in his underwear was on the floor with a bullet wound to the chest. Packagers in drug operations routinely worked with minimal clothing or completely nude to prevent theft of product. This man would weigh cocaine no more. A shot rang out, and the wooden door splintered a few inches from where my hand rested against it. I dove to the ground and rolled under a table. A second round punched through the wooden-topped table and ricocheted off the floor near my left boot. I saw the soldier advancing and took aim. *A little closer*, I thought. *Just one more step*. The moral compass that told me I wasn't a killer had now swung one-hundred and eighty degrees. As my aim improved, so would his. I squeezed the trigger and fired before he had the chance.

My bullet tore through his upper leg just below the hip. The soldier hit the ground, and I saw him grab at the entry wound. I could see him grimace in pain and knew that I had to finish him before he was able to defend himself, but I couldn't. I was frozen, my heart racing, my throat knotted and locked. It didn't take the soldier long to shake off his wound. We were both on the ground facing one another, and he had a direct shot at me. He grabbed his rifle and raised it to his hip.

Now, I thought. *Hurry, or you'll lose your—* He was about to squeeze off a shot when the door creaked behind me. I saw the soldier's aim travel from me to the doorway. As he did, a bullet blew a chunk of meat from his forehead. The door pushed wide open, and Salazar, the snake killer, stepped in. He glanced at the fallen guerrilla, then at me, and gave me a thumbs-up.

Chapter Fifty-Seven

The return trip to Cali was a blur. The rush of adrenaline that charged my veins didn't dissipate until we were hours into the jungle. I vaguely recalled our journey coming to an end at a hovel located off the central road. The sight of a landing airplane indicated the Cali airport was nearby. Inside, there were cot-sized mattresses on the floor. The kitchen counter was well-stocked with rum and tequila. I drank both and passed out.

I think it was Parra's rancid body odor that woke me up the next morning. If he stunk on the way out to the coke compound, he now stank three times as bad. My first impulse was to retch, but I grabbed a mug of burnt coffee and drank it outside, watching the sunrise. Whatever the ask was, whatever Guzman promised, it wouldn't be enough. I'd never make another trip into the jungle. I'd ferry cash back to Parra in Cali, but that's where my services would end. If Guzman had a trust issue with Parra delivering the money, he'd have to send someone else to make sure the money was delivered as promised. No way in hell would I ever do it again.

I walked out into the adjacent field. Standing tall, I let the morning sun warm my face as only the sun could. Its rays imbued me with a sense of hope. I didn't think for a moment that the feeling was genuine. It was simply my preservation instinct grasping at straws. I wanted to see my folks safe and an end to my entanglement with the world of narcotics trafficking. I sat down and crossed my legs. Inch by inch, the sunrays swept over me, moving across me from shadow to light, until I was fully illuminated. The vista was breathtaking with lush trees and rolling hills. The land was so beautiful, but the reality was sad. Colombia was a land of devastating poverty and a class system with only the very, very rich and the very, very poor. The country churned with civil and political unrest, with guerrilla hit squads and government-sanctioned murders. And then there was me, a pawn being manipulated by the FBI and a pair of drug kingpins who dictated whether my parents would live or die.

I was somewhat rested but emotionally drained. Still, I knew what I had to do. I had to confront Serna and demand to see my parents. I knew he wouldn't set them free, but I had to know that they were okay, see them for myself. I closed my eyes and let my mind wander. I must've dozed off because when I opened them, the sun was no longer sitting on the horizon but high up in the sky.

Dusting myself off, I made my way back to the hovel. I expected minimal activity inside, Parra and Salazar easing into the day. I hoped they'd be preparing to drive me back to my apartment in Cartagena. As I approached the door, I heard a rhythmic thudding coming from inside. I opened the door and looked in. Parra and Salazar had women pinned up against the wall, jackhammering their pent-up frustration like a pair of barnyard animals. *Those poor women*, I mused. *I hope they're wearing nose plugs.*

Chapter Fifty-Eight

We were on the road for three days getting back to Cartagena. The roads were shitty, and Parra was in no particular hurry. We'd travel in two-to-three-hour clips. He knew every watering hole along the way and was determined to stop at every one of them. The jeep broke down in Taraza, a town about halfway between Cali and Cartagena. A blown water hose took most of the day to fix, a repair my dad and I could've made in thirty minutes with a rubber patch and a pair of hose clamps. But this was Colombia, where no one hurried.

Parra had a pair of sleeping bags, and we slept in the fields off the road both of the two nights we traveled. Falling asleep under the stars was pleasant, waking up not so much. The temperatures dropped precipitously overnight. Three days of bouncing around in a jeep with a concrete-like suspension didn't help my fragile back. I woke up shivering and my back aching like hell. All things considered, it could've been worse. I never knew what to expect with my back. There were times it took punishment like a champ, and other times when the smallest movement sent it into spasm. Pain was a hell of a lot better than spasm. Spasm was misery of unknown duration, days bent over at a right-angle and sleepless nights. Pain could be managed, and I'd learned to overcome muscular distress without drugs. I was off everything except aspirin and Doan's Pills, no doctor-prescribed pain medication, no heroin or methadone, no nothing. I'd beaten the beast and had control over my body, but not my life. Too many players had their hands on my puppet strings. I didn't know how to sever them but desperately needed to.

I'd never used the tub in my apartment for more than a shower, but the grit and sweat of living like an animal was so deeply embedded in my pores that I needed to flush it all out. I filled the tub with hot water, grabbed a fresh bar of soap, and dunked my entire body before lifting my head to breathe. There was no time to waste, but I couldn't spend another minute with caked-on filth and sweat. I took a few minutes for the hot water to loosen the grime, then went at it with soap and a brush. With each whisk of the brush, I felt as if I was scraping away not only grime, but the anguish and tension I'd endured.

Dripping wet from the bath, I'd wrapped a towel around my waist when I heard a knock on the door. I didn't know who to expect. Roswell was dead, and I hadn't spoken to Cachumbo in a long while, nor did I know if he was still working for the FBI. I threw on some clothes and answered the door. Opening the door a crack, I peered out. But that rickety door wouldn't have kept any of Serna's men at bay. Willow stood outside, holding a plant.

"I missed you," she said. "Can I come in?"

It took a second for the tumblers to click into place. *She is not who you think she is. She is not a local woman who fronts for your band. She is a spy and not to be trusted.* "What's your real name?" I asked.

"Cayetana," she said apologetically and offered the plant she was holding. It was a beautiful peacock plant with green and white leaves, so striking that they looked as if they were hand-painted. "I brought a plant because flowers didn't feel right. They're more for a woman, yes?"

"Do I have to check it for bugs?" I wasn't referring to insects, and she knew it.

"No, no listening devices. I swear."

"Thanks." I took the plant and set it on the windowsill.

"You've been away a long time."

"I haven't been home an hour, and you knew I was here. Who told you?"

"We know these things," she said unashamedly. "This is what we do."

I had no idea how she knew my whereabouts. Parra had dropped me off and immediately set out in search of the nearest unclaimed saloon. Was he playing for both sides or was my apartment being watched? "You heard about Roswell?" She nodded. "So, what do you want?"

"I'm just touching base, Sonny. We've been talking to Cutter. We know your parents are being held by Serna. Cabrera and I would like to help if we can."

I'd never been the callous sort but was now finding it easier to be cold. "What's in it for you?"

She took the insult in stride. "The same thing you want, Sonny, your parents safe and Gage Serna in prison. What else is there?" She sat down on a chair and crossed her legs. She didn't try to play up to me with her soft brown eyes, nor did she play with her ringlets. She was direct and straightforward, earnest. "I'm not a monster, Sonny, but I've got a job to do. I'm sorry I had to deceive you, but that's the way the game is played. Our goals are aligned, and we can do more together than you can alone. The ICPO is very eager to deal the drug trade a crushing blow." She paused for a moment, then continued. "We believe narcotics are being offloaded from Serna's tankers and from there transferred to ships traveling across the Atlantic to Europe. We're hoping you can help put a stop to it."

"I'm kind of tied up. I'm sure Serna will want me to continue dropping his merchandise into Florida, and that's going to take up all my time. You know about Guzman, I'm sure."

"Yes, Cutter filled us in on everything. How did the drop-off go?"

So, she didn't know everything. That somewhat eliminated Parra from suspicion of being a leak. Had she talked with him, she certainly would've known the shit show we endured over the last five or so days. "A nightmare. A fucking nightmare. I'll never do that again."

I suppose she found the report exciting because her leg began to pump. "I hope you didn't encounter resistance fighters."

"Resistance fighters, snakes, swamps, and one man-eating jaguar that almost had me for dinner. I got the full experience. Three of our men were killed, and I just pulled a pair of bloodsucking leeches off my ass."

I didn't mean to be funny but wasn't surprised when she laughed. "I'm sorry," she said. "It's just…" She drew a deep breath to push the smile from her face. "When does Serna expect to see you?"

"Guzman told him I'd be landing in Cartagena today, but if he's got someone watching the airport the way you and Cabrera are watching my apartment, he already knows that's a crock of shit."

"I understand his man, Jacobo, was killed. I'm sure Serna will want an explanation."

"I have none to offer."

"You're sure he doesn't know the FBI intervened after you were apprehended and were moving you to a safe location? Jacobo might've informed him of that."

She was right, it was a worry I'd had since putting a bullet in Jacobo's skull. "I'll deny knowing anything. If he suspects that the FBI is involved…there's nothing I can do about it. Apparently, he's known all along who I was and that our meeting wasn't a coincidence. He played along until he was ready to use me. I guess he'll keep me alive as long as I'm of value to him. Beyond that, all bets are off."

"What's your next move?" she asked.

I shrugged. "Wait for Serna to contact me and pray he lets me see my folks. I won't do anything to jeopardize their safety and he knows it."

"I know Serna has you on a tight leash, but if you learn anything that might be useful to us… Poor, Sonny," she said and rose from the chair. "Not what you signed up for, is it?" There was a look on her face I didn't understand. I thought it was pity, not because that's what it looked like, but because it would've been appropriate. She took a step toward me, her posture and movements revealing her intentions. In her wedge sandals, she was just a few inches shorter than me and put her arms around my neck. I didn't stop her from kissing me, because I was desperate for what she had to offer, the embrace only a woman could offer. Her voice was breathy and suggestive. "Surely there's a little time for just you and me, no?"

Was she playing at something else now, or was this still espionage, seduction to break down my resistance? Seduction to make me compliant? I didn't care. One more kiss, then another. She nuzzled my neck. "What are we doing?" I asked.

"It's called foreplay, Sonny," she said as we tumbled onto the bed. "I'm sure you can figure out what comes next."

Chapter Fifty-Nine

Serna generously gave me a day to rest, one whole day, then sent a car for me the next morning. It seemed odd to see someone other than Jacobo behind the wheel of the big Benz, and it triggered a twinge of guilt. I'd never killed anyone before, but Jacobo had slit Roswell's throat in front of my eyes. That pang of guilt was short-lived; the duration of its existence was infinitesimal.

Serna owned many homes. I thought I'd visited all of them, but I was wrong. We traveled quite a distance south of Cartagena to yet another waterfront property located on Casa Mar Beach. Like all his other homes, this one was opulent but in a different way than the others. It had a laid-back vibe with palapas on a private beach and glass-walled rooms that opened to the ocean. An American muscle car was parked in the driveway that got me excited in a way the tank-like Benz never could. It was a purple Hemi Cuda that I knew pumped more than four hundred horsepower. It had an air intake protruding through an opening in the hood and pins to keep the hood from becoming unlatched at high speeds. I didn't consider myself a gearhead, but that purple beast really got me going, and the thought that I had enough cash to buy one thrilled me. I took a moment to look it over, memorizing every detail, so I'd be able to order one just like it if I ever had the chance. Now, if I could only negotiate my parents' release and stay alive long enough to buy one. One day at a time.

Like the others, Serna's beach house was staffed with servants. I noticed the gardener and pool boy straight off and saw several other members of his workforce coming and going, although I'd yet to determine what they did.

Serna was dressed in a cabana set when he entered the large room, a print swimsuit, and a terrycloth-lined matching shirt. He was deeply tanned, and his hair was damp as if he'd just taken a swim. He'd entered with another gent, who definitely wasn't a servant, a guy whose skin was genuine shoe leather, his hair salt and pepper. He looked rough, as if he'd been scraped off the hull of a ship along with barnacles. He was in jeans and a well-worn shirt. They stopped by the opening that faced the beach and chatted. The room was so large and the winds off the beach so loud that I couldn't hear what they were saying, but their conversation seemed cordial. Whatever this man did for Serna, he must've done it well. Serna grinned and slapped the man on the shoulder. They shook hands, and he left.

Serna walked over to the bar and poured a drink before acknowledging my presence. "Sit down," he said without looking at me and pointed to a chair at a large rattan table. I was surprised to hear the rumble of the Hemi Cuda's powerful engine as it roared to life. I figured the muscle car belonged to Serna, one of his many playthings. The man who'd just left didn't look as if he could afford a car like that, but I'd obviously misjudged him. All of these droguistas had more money than God, and I supposed Leather Man was no exception. I didn't know what he did for Serna, but it was obviously lucrative, and I'm sure he did it well. Of what I knew of Serna, he was intolerant of mistakes. I wondered how he'd approach our conversation. My delivery of Sublimaze had more than its share of hiccups.

Serna finally sat down at the table with his drink and a bowl of strawberries. They were deeply red and immense in size, as if they'd been hand-selected and were the best of the very best. No surprise—a man like Serna didn't eat day-old fruit. They were probably rushed to the table directly from the strawberry field, just minutes after being picked. He plucked the largest and reddest berry from the bowl and ate it whole, leaves and all. "I'm glad you're well," he said as he picked a piece of fruit from between his teeth. He'd yet to look me in the eye. "I understand things did not go smoothly."

"Could've been better. The police were on site when I landed. I was lucky to get away without getting caught."

"Yes, yes. Sr. Guzman relayed all the particulars. I was happy to hear how resourceful you were and that you managed to deliver my merchandise as promised." He finally looked up and locked his gaze on me. "Personally, I didn't think you possessed such skills. Did you have help from anyone?" he asked pointedly.

Serna was clearly fishing, trying to determine if the FBI or any other law enforcement agencies had assisted me. "Just a few bartenders and their regular customers. It was a good thing you gave me emergency cash. I had to stay in a motel a few nights while I tried to connect with Guzman. It helped me to grease the wheels."

"Who'd have thought you were such an expert wheel-greaser?" he said and picked up another strawberry. "Sonny, did you know strawberries are not berries at all?"

I shook my head. "They're not?"

"True berries have their seeds on the inside, but strawberries…" He pointed to the many minuscule seeds on the surface. "Strawberry seeds are on the outside. They are not what they appear to be." The meaning of his metaphor was clear. He stared at me in a telling way, driving home the masked allegation that I might not be what I seemed to be. He then examined the strawberry, put it down, and selected another. "Like these berries, which ones are sweet and which are bitter? You can't tell just by looking at them." He nibbled the fruit. "Ah, a good one," he said with a grin. "Now, there's the matter of my man, Jacobo. I sent him to Florida to look for you, to lend you a hand." His gaze turned cool. "He hasn't returned. Did you have any contact with him?"

Contact? I shot the fucker dead and wished I could do it again. "No. I didn't know he was there."

"Pity. He could've been helpful to you. I'm worried the American authorities arrested him, or worse."

"Worse?" I knew exactly what he meant. I'd delivered worse to the son of a bitch, deservingly so.

His expression showed remorse, but it didn't last long. Three seconds of sympathy, and he was done with his period of mourning. "Your next drop is in two days. Same arrangements as last time. I trust you will not encounter the complications you did on the initial run. I wouldn't want to see any harm come to you. My people will be in touch." He pushed the bowl of berries to the center of the table, stood up, and turned to leave.

"My parents," I blurted.

He stopped mid-step and turned back. "What of them?"

"I need to know that they're alright."

He grinned in a carefree manner. "They're alright."

"I want to see them."

He had turned away and was exiting the room when he said, "Complete the next delivery with no complications, and we'll talk about it…perhaps."

Chapter Sixty

It was the night before my second jump. My backpack was crammed with every essential I'd need for the jump into Florida. I headed over to Señor Whisky Bar for a badly needed drink. I'd been sick to my stomach since meeting with Serna. He was a man who did whatever he wanted and only what he wanted. It seemed clear he wanted to behave like an animal and didn't care how badly it troubled me or how it affected my loved ones. And with that enormous weight heaped onto the burden I already carried, I needed to perform a perfect night jump into Cape Coral. The duffle bag full of Sublimaze would kill me instantly if the inner packaging ruptured. Piece of cake.

Cabrera had replaced me with the guitarist I'd replaced all those months back. With him leading the band, they were fair at best and rarely deviated from their canned set list. They were, however, reliable, and for the crowd at Señor Whisky's, reliable was good enough. Not everyone had a discerning ear, and after a few drinks, even those with better taste in music became far less particular.

It was early evening, and the bar was far from packed, which was good because I wasn't in the mood for all the noise and commotion a full house at the bar was capable of. Most of the customers got a thimble full of Jack in their cocktails, but I knew the bartender well and saw that he was pouring heavy. Oddly, I'd had two Jack and Cokes and didn't feel the slightest buzz. I ordered a third, hoping I'd feel something soon, because I didn't want to drink enough to get hungover and didn't want to sack out too late. Serna's men were going to pick me up for the ride to the airport at six a.m. sharp and hand off the duffle bag of Sublimaze. I'd be flying to Jamaica, then onto Cape Coral for the drop with the same charming pilot I'd traveled with the first time: the same humorless asshole who shoved a gun in my face and forced me to jump while taking evasive maneuvers to shake a pair of US Coast Guard planes. I was truly overjoyed at the prospect.

Cabrera made a rare appearance in the club and sat down alongside me at the bar when he saw that I was there. "Sus bebidas corren por mi cuenta," he told the bartender, who confirmed with a thumbs-up.

"That's not necessary," I said. "I can buy my own drinks."

"Please allow me," Cabrera said. "It's the least I can do." He put his hand on my shoulder and ordered a beer for himself. "How soon do you go back?"

"Tomorrow morning. Six sharp. Same exact gig. Let's hope things go better than last time."

"Yes, let's hope." He took a swig of beer, then leaned closer. "Any luck seeing your padres?"

"None. Serna was as cold as ice. I think he suspects he's been lied to."

"This is the problem—at the drug lord level, you're dealing with intelligent, capable men. And Serna, with his Ivy League education and everything he learned from his papa, is a true force to be reckoned with. I'm sure the G-men told you it wouldn't be easy."

"Actually, they told me practically nothing. Roswell, my former comrade in arms, coerced me into working for him. He didn't tell me anything more than he thought I needed to know. He didn't say it wasn't going to be easy, and he didn't tell me it was going to be brutal and illegal. God rest his soul, Roswell completely underestimated Serna, and now he's dead."

Cabrera shook his head sadly, then crossed himself as he peered upward toward heaven. "I know Cayetana told you we'd do anything we could to help you, did she not?"

Indeed, she did, the message signed, sealed, and delivered along with a passionate boink to make sure I'd remember the promise she'd made me. I knew the night we'd spent together was nothing more than a good time, a tension-breaker when I needed it the most. I'd become cynical and felt that, down deep, she gave herself to me for a reason. She knew who I was and what I was, a wet-behind-the-ears pawn being forced to do something I didn't want to do. She knew I wasn't cold or callous and that the sex would mean something more to me than what it was. How right she was. I continued to think about what she'd asked, to help them get information on the large-scale drug transfers from Serna's oil barges. I had the sense I knew something that might help them and decided to offer it to Cabrera.

"This could be something or nothing at all, but when I was at Serna's beach house, this guy was there, and he didn't look like your typical cartel killer. He had skin like tanned cowhide, and my sense was that he spent his life on the water."

"You mean a sailor?"

"I think so. A sailor or some kind of maritime profession. It might be a lead worth looking into."

"Were you introduced?" he asked eagerly.

"No."

"So, you don't know his name or where we can find him?" Cabrera seemed mildly disappointed.

"Not directly, but maybe this will help." I grabbed a napkin and scribbled down a series of letters and numbers. "He drove an American Muscle car, a purple Plymouth Barracuda, and this one was top of the line, what they call a Hemi Cuda with a large, powerful V-8 engine and lots of high-performance equipment. You do have the equivalent of the DMV down here, don't you?"

He looked at me quizzically. "D-M-V?"

"Department of Motor Vehicles."

He grinned. "Si, El Ministerio de Transporte."

I slid the napkin toward him. "This is the license plate number. You might be able to track him down from this."

He picked up the napkin, studied it quickly, and stuffed it in his pocket. "We'll check it out, Sonny, and we appreciate the information."

Nothing ventured, nothing gained, I thought. In the back of my mind, I toyed with the fantasy Willow had cultivated and the possibility of getting together again if I made it back to Cartagena alive.

Chapter Sixty-One

If the first drop into Florida was pain, the second was pleasure. The Coast Guard didn't pick us up on the way onto the southern peninsula, nor did the pilot point a gun at me and force me out of the plane. The police were not on the ground waiting for me to land, and I didn't hit any trees on the way down. Guzman's men were waiting for me exactly as they were supposed to. I handed off the package and was delighted to be rid of it.

I showered and went to bed in Guzman's cottage. He was waiting for me on the patio for breakfast the next morning, reading the local newspaper and smoking a Havana cigar. He glanced over the top of the newspaper as I approached. A pleased smile surfaced on his face, his cheekbones rising for perhaps the first time since I'd met him. He gestured to an open seat across from him at the table and waved to his housekeeper to pour coffee. I hadn't expected the first-class treatment—it caught me off guard.

He continued to scan the paper as he talked. "I got a full report from Parra about your excursion across the Colombian jungle. He was rather insistent that I hire someone better qualified to chaperone the money to the compound."

What a relief. I'd been rehearsing what to say to Guzman to remove myself from the grueling chore. I knew I needed to be firm with him, but careful not to be insulting. Rehearsing the appeal had kept me up half the night.

"Parra said that keeping you alive was a chore in itself. He thought a trained commando would be better suited to the task." He flipped the page of his newspaper. "I agree. When you head back, you'll be free to go as soon as my plane touches down in Cali. Or, if you prefer, you can take a commercial flight back to Cartagena. It's your choice." He took a bite of toast and washed it down with coffee. "I'm sure you're relieved. I heard you had a run-in with an angry jungle cat." He laughed. "I hope you didn't shit your pants."

I felt worlds lighter and was actually beginning to feel like things were going my way, that rescuing my mom and dad was possible. Guzman changed in the next moment, his eyes flashing fiercely.

"I should kill you here and now."

What? What happened? The change in his mood was as sudden as the flipping of a switch. He snapped his fingers. Ralph approached and placed a round disc on the table. I knew at a glance what it was.

"Your FBI cronies sewed a tracker into the lining of the duffle bag you first delivered." He rose suddenly, formed a fist, and pulverized the small electronic wafer with the side of his fist. "You led them to my home," he roared. "My fucking home." He picked up his coffee cup and smashed it on the ground. "Did you know? Did you know those federal bastards put a tracker in the bag?"

"No," I said as genuinely as possible. It was the truth. Neither Cutter nor Petraglia mentioned what they'd done. I was innocent in that regard, but guilty as hell because I was working with the FBI. I felt cold, and my arms went limp. *This is it,* I thought. *This is where I end.*

His chest heaving, he swept his arm across the table, sending plates and glasses crashing to the ground. "You made this delivery for free, and I want the names of the agents you worked with so that I can neutralize them." He gritted his teeth. "I'm so angry, so fucking angry. If I didn't need you, I'd cut you into pieces and feed you to the dogs." He shook his head, then sat down. The housekeeper hurried over with new plates and silverware. She filled his empty cup with fresh coffee. A second servant rushed over with a broom and dustpan. The storm had passed. He picked up the newspaper and began to scan it once more. "Eat something," he said. "You look pathetic."

My throat was knotted, my stomach upside-down. The best I could do was to slowly sip coffee and hope that my innards would unwind.

He snapped his fingers and told the housekeeper to put food on my plate.

I said nothing. I needed time to process what had happened. Fucking Cutter and Petraglia had almost gotten me killed. Roswell had railroaded me into service, but I don't think he lied to me and believe he cared about my well-being. These other two didn't give a rat's ass about me or my parents. A valuable lesson learned, more accurately, reinforced—the FBI had lost my trust, and it would never be restored.

I was able to eat some fruit after a few minutes. Guzman noticed and put down the newspaper. "Serna offloads large quantities of cocaine from his petroleum barges in the Panama Canal. It's taken from there to the port of Valencia in Spain for distribution throughout Europe. Aside from the business he does with me, it's his largest source of revenue."

How did he know that, and where did his information come from? Had Thiago sold out his brother? I had difficulty accepting the idea of such deceit.

"I am going to commandeer this transfer vessel and bring the cocaine into Florida. Serna will be out fifty million in revenue and lose the confidence of his European customers, a crushing blow." He looked at me pointedly. "And you are going to play a pivotal role in Serna's downfall."

I was sinking deeper and deeper into this drug dealer's pile of shit. The coffee and fruit I'd swallowed were fighting their way to my mouth, but I managed to choke them down. "Me? What can I do?"

"You, Sonny," he began, "will do exactly as you are told, or I will inform Serna of your duplicity, and he will surely slaughter your parents. I believe that is a fate worse than death, far, far worse."

Thiago Serna bounded out the patio door dressed in tennis whites. He beamed brightly as he sat down. Apparently, he was unaware of the wrinkle in my cover story. "Ah, Sonny, good to see you again," he said in a congenial tone. He glanced at Guzman. I trust Uncle Renaldo is taking good care of you."

"Like royalty," Guzman said, then turned my way and shot a dagger through my heart.

Chapter Sixty-Two

It was early in the morning four days later, much too early for any of Cabrera's staff to have arrived for work at the bar. Willow and Cabrera were there waiting for me when I arrived. I was still tired from travel and stress, but they seemed bright-eyed and eager to talk. "You have an ally," I said the moment I sat down at their table.

They looked at one another, their curiosity piqued. "Enlighten us," Cabrera said. "Please."

There is an ancient proverb that goes, "The enemy of my enemy is my friend." I never really appreciated what that saying meant until now. "Guzman wants to destroy Serna. He wants to seize his entire business and run it as his own."

"How can he do that?" Willow asked. "He has no bearing here in Colombia. Taking over Serna's drug empire will never happen. He's too well insulated."

I looked at her pointedly. "I believe he can."

"What are you telling us?" Cabrera asked.

"Line of succession," I said. "I have no proof, but I think Serna's younger brother Thiago is working with Guzman. He was at Guzman's home both times I visited, and they went to see a lawyer while I was there the first time. It may mean nothing, but Thiago seems very at home around Guzman. I think Thiago wants to take the reins from his brother, and with Guzman on his side, he can do that."

Willow leaned forward in her chair. "That's an interesting piece of news, Sonny, but how does that help our cause? Whether Gage or Thiago sits at the helm of Serna Oil, drugs will still flow into Europe."

"Maybe. Maybe not." I had so much to tell them, news that would delight them and infuriate the FBI, but the FBI had done nothing for me other than deceive me and drag me into a sewer filled with killers and drug lords. I owed them nothing, nothing at all. If Guzman was being straight with me, Cutter and Petraglia might already be dead, and my association with the Feds was over. "Were you able to track down the owner of the purple muscle car?"

From their expressions, I could tell they thought the conversation had gone in a strange direction. Cabrera nodded. "Yes. His name is—"

I filled in the blank. "Diego Dumas."

They appeared surprised. "Yes, that's right," Cabrera said. "How do you know?"

"He pilots an ocean-going vessel for Serna. His ship trails Serna's barges into the Panama Canal, then pallets of cocaine are offloaded from the barge onto Dumas's ship and taken to Valencia, Spain."

Willow elbowed Cabrera. "Valencia. See? I told you."

He rolled his eyes. "Yes, Cayetana, you're a genius."

"It makes sense," she said. "The port is large enough for a small vessel to berth without scrutiny, and the security is the most suspect in all of Europe."

"Do you know Dumas's address?" I asked.

"We do," Cabrera said. "What does that matter?"

"Because Guzman will pay him fivefold what he gets from Serna to transfer the shipment to the Port of Miami."

Willow gasped. "Five times? That's got to be hundreds of thousands of dollars."

"Guzman isn't playing games. He wants to destroy Serna's credibility in Europe, and it will cost him nothing. Once he receives the cocaine that was headed for Europe, he'll make a fortune selling it through his distribution network in the States."

"Ruthless," Cabrera said, then applauded.

"He's pretty fucking smart," Willow said. "How do we make this happen?"

"Guzman wants me to pitch the offer to Dumas. I need the two of you to set up the meeting. If I don't do as Guzman asks, he'll tell Serna I'm in deep with the FBI, and you know what that will mean for my parents."

Willow clenched her teeth.

"You mean you want us to grab him? Pick him up off the street?" Cabrera asked.

"However you want to do it, as long as we get him alone so that I can offer the bribe." I cringed before going on. The balance of the requirement was far less savory. "Dumas isn't married and has no kids, but he has a younger sister, and Guzman wants her held hostage to ensure his compliance. I don't think Guzman knows that I'm working with the two of you. He's relying on me to make it happen." I took a deep breath, then raised an eyebrow. "And I'm relying on the two of you, heavily."

The two European spies absorbed the information. They didn't react visibly, but I knew the wheels were turning in their heads.

"The FBI will be furious with you," Willow said. "You're compounding their problem. Not only are you not taking down Serna, but you're diverting additional narcotics into America."

I hated the idea of facilitating the entry of cocaine into the States, but it was only one shipment, and America's hunger for narcotics was huge. It would disappear up the noses of party animals and Wall Street hotshots and be gone in the blink of an eye. Guzman had promised to have my parents released as soon as he controlled Gage Serna's operation. Was Guzman any better than Serna? Would he honor his word, or was I trading the devil I knew for the devil I didn't? I had little choice. With my parents' lives in the balance, I had to roll the dice.

Chapter Sixty-Three

Guzman knew things about Dumas, things he could've only learned from someone that knew the man's routines, someone on the inside. Someone like Thiago Serna. Guzman told me that Dumas was a creature of habit and that there was a pub he liked, one he visited most nights and always on the night before going to sea. Maybe Dumas felt that alcohol would replenish the moisture in his buffalo hide complexion, but more likely the booze was one of the culprits in the tanning of his hide. My Uncle Mateo always had yellowish skin and dark circles under his eyes with red blood vessels visible on his face and neck. Growing up, I figured it was just the way he looked, but I learned the truth when he died of liver cancer. I was betting it was the combination of alcoholism and briny air that made Dumas' face look like a well-worn catcher's mitt. It was an image Willow would have to look past to get the job done.

Cabrera and I waited in a van while she worked her wiles on the man on the inside, tempting him in a way only she could. I'd learned firsthand that she was not only an accomplished seductress but a potent one at that, one that I'd found impossible to resist. I didn't know if Dumas had greater resolve than I did, but I was willing to bet that stronger men had tried to resist her and failed.

"I wonder how she's doing in there," I said as I checked my watch. "It's been a solid forty-five minutes."

"Patience, Sonny. You have to give these things time. You can go in and check on her if you like," Cabrera began, "but it'll be a waste of time, and you may jeopardize the mission."

"I can't go in. Dumas has seen me. At Serna's beach house. Remember?"

"That's right. I could go in and have a look, but I'm sure she's okay. I've worked with Cayetana for more than two years. She's a pro."

Forty-five minutes turned into an hour, then two. She finally appeared. Standing outside the bar, she lit a cigarette, signaling to us that Dumas was on his way out. Cabrera got out of the van and into position. Willow had dressed for the job in a form-fitting mini dress and pumps, not the same one she'd stunned us with at our gig, but one equally potent, her look treading the line between sexy and slutty. Dumas would've needed the resolve of a monk to refuse her. She took his arm the moment he emerged, laughing gayly as she led him to where Cabrera waited in hiding down a darkened alleyway, which led to his home.

Cabrera approached silently, coming up behind Dumas. He slung his arm around Dumas's neck, tying him up in a sleeper hold while Willow muzzled him with a handkerchief she had splashed with chloroform. Cabrera was much stronger than he presented. He hoisted Dumas over his shoulder and carried him over to the van. I got out in a flash and opened the rear doors. He dumped Dumas inside. I got in with him and grabbed a rope to bind him. A hood was draped over his head. Willow and I got back in the van and drove off. All told, the entire abduction took scant minutes.

I had not been informed as to where we were taking Dumas, and maybe it was better I didn't know. I only knew that the destination was an abandoned warehouse out of the way in a desolate area not far from Cartagena. Willow had no difficulty with the directions. As best I could determine, we made it to the warehouse without her making a single wrong turn.

Dumas was already coming to when Cabrera and I carried him into the abandoned building, sat him on the floor, and shackled him to an old sewer pipe. No sooner had we backed away when he started to kick and test his restraints. "What the fuck is going on?" he screamed. "Why am I here, and where's that bitch from the bar?"

I was surprised that he spoke clear English, but not unhappy about it. We were all fluent in Spanish, but some of the local dialects could easily be misunderstood. I pulled over a wobbly old stool and sat down a few feet in front of him. Willow and Cabrera stood off to the side.

"Hey!" Dumas said. "What do you want?"

"I want to make you a very rich man," I said. "How'd you like that?"

"Take off my hood, coward. Look me in the eye."

"When I'm ready. What does Serna pay you?"

"Who's Serna?" he said.

Cabrera got in front of him and walloped him in the face. "Don't waste our time," he said. "How much is Serna paying you to transfer the cocaine onto your ship and sail to Spain with it?"

"More than you've got," Dumas said. I heard him spit and saw blood trickle from under the hood.

Cabrera socked him in the stomach with everything he had. Dumas grunted. "You have no idea how much we've got," Cabrera said.

"Kiss my ass," Dumas said between gasps.

It didn't seem as if he was going to give us a figure. I shrugged and looked to my partners for help. "Make him an offer," Willow mouthed.

I nodded, then did my best to calculate what Serna paid him. I multiplied that number by a factor of five. "Half a million American dollars," I said.

He was quiet for moments. The number had obviously given him pause. Hijacking cargo from an oil tanker en route through the Panama Canal and the arduous voyage sailing back and forth across the Atlantic seemed to be a hell of a difficult way to earn money. "Think of all the muscle cars you can buy with that kind of dough. All you have to do is take the shipment off Serna's boat as you normally would and sail it to Miami instead of across the Atlantic. It'll be weeks before Serna realizes anything went wrong. You can move anywhere in the world you want. Live out your days racing cars and drinking beer."

"I've got cars up the ass, shithead. No deal." A moment passed. When he spoke again, it seemed as if the large payout had piqued his interest. "Besides, Serna will track me down and have me killed."

"There are things worse than death," I said.

I reached over and pulled the hood off his head. He blinked a few times to clear his vision, then glared at me. "I know you," he said. "You were at

Serna's house the other day." He laughed. "I was wrong. Serna's not going to kill me, not once I tell him about you. Whoever you are, you're a fucking dead man."

"I don't think you'll tell Serna anything, and I don't think you'll turn down my offer. As I said, there are worse things than death." I stood up and moved my stool out of the way. His vision unobstructed, he was able to see to the far end of the warehouse where his sister Fernanda sat gagged and bound to a chair.

Chapter Sixty-Four

It was going to take quite a while for the shit to hit the fan, over two weeks' time, but once the plan was in motion, all we could do was wait. It was a relatively short voyage from the Colombian port to the Panama Canal, where the cocaine shipment would be offloaded from Serna's oil barge onto Dumas's ship as it traveled through the canal. Dumas would follow the oil barge into the canal, then come alongside while the big barge waited to go through one of the locks. The drugs would be transferred and shipped to Miami, where Guzman's men would wait to take it to an undisclosed location. In the meantime, a cross-Atlantic sailing from the Panama Canal to Valencia, Spain took roughly thirteen days. It would be over two weeks before Serna's European buyers realized that something had gone wrong.

Willow and I stood on the pier as Dumas's ship prepared to launch. "Everything is in place," Willow said as we waved to Cabrera, who stood on the deck of Dumas's ship. Cabrera and a squad of enforcement agents were accompanying Dumas to make sure he didn't pull a fast one. We'd given Dumas half the money up front, a good-faith payment to ensure his compliance. Willow would deliver his sister, Fernanda, to Dumas in Miami, along with the remaining two hundred fifty thousand dollars, once the cocaine shipment was delivered to Guzman. Where Dumas and his sister went from there was anyone's guess. I presumed it would be as far away as possible. I doubted we'd ever see them again. With the 500K he was going to receive on top of any money he had already stashed away, his options were limitless.

We watched the ship chug out to sea until it was only a speck on the horizon. Willow put her arms around me. "I've got nothing to do but babysit Dumas's sister until he arrives in Miami three days from now. You're not making another jump until the end of the week. How do you choose to spend your time?" she asked with a playful lilt in her voice. "I have a few ideas."

"Do they all involve a bed?"

"A bed, a tabletop…maybe the shower." She shrugged. "I'm not picky."

"I like that about you." There was nothing I'd rather do than spend time with a beautiful woman, and I'd assuredly indulge her request. Serna implied he might let me see them after I made the next Sublimaze delivery. I'd made that drop, and he'd offered nothing.

She must've read my expression. "It's like dominoes, Sonny. One has to fall before the next one can tumble. The shipment to Valencia will go missing, his buyers will react, then Serna will become vulnerable. He'll be distracted, and we'll be in a better position to rescue your mama and papa."

"Cabrera isn't alone on that ship. He took several men with him." I looked directly into her eyes. "You've got more resources than you let on. Meanwhile, my parents are locked up, and no doubt scared shitless without any word from the outside. The FBI was supposed to keep them safe." I shook my head. "What a joke they are. Roswell is dead, probably Cutter and Petraglia as well. I've got to find out where they're being held."

She kissed me lightly on the lips. "You have been a true friend to us. We'll do everything we can. I promise."

I wasn't going to mention it, but Willow and Cabrera must've looked like heroes in the eyes of their supervisors. A major drug shipment intended for distribution to the European market had been diverted. They most certainly owed me big time.

"I know you're worried, Sonny. Surely, there must be something I can do to distract you. Hmm?" She stared into my eyes, and I stared back. Who would blink first? A moment passed before I succumbed to her winning smile.

I took her hand, and we set off. "Yes, distract me," I said. "Distract me until I'm unable to stand."

Chapter Sixty-Five

Two weeks later

By my third jump into Cape Coral, I was actually getting good and was pretty much back to the form I'd mastered in jump school a million years back. Directing the rectangular parachute, I was able to split two rows of palm trees down the center and hit my target on the money. Feet and knees together, I hit the ground, then fell to the side. Then, while on one knee, I reeled in the parachute, bundled it, and hid it beneath a pile of fallen palm branches. I got to my feet and heard a car engine idling while I unclipped the heavy duffle bag filled with Sublimaze. More important than the expert landing, the duffle bag had not been breached—the deadly substance within was still intact. I crossed myself, attuned my ears, and listened for the sound of police sirens. There were none.

Ralph and the cabrón appeared from between the palms. I hadn't heard them approach—they simply appeared and sauntered casually toward me.

"Skydiving looks like fun," the cabrón said. "Maybe I try someday." He snatched the duffle and whipped it to his side in utter disregard of the danger the unleashed substance represented.

"You best be careful with that," I said. "It's deadly if you breathe it in."

He ignored my warning. "How hard it is, the skydiving?"

"Not hard if you've got the balls to jump out of a plane."

Ralph was his usual silent self. He didn't weigh in on the conversation but turned and began back in the direction he'd come from.

"Balls? I got big balls." The cabrón grabbed his nut sack and gave it a manly tug. It was his right as a Latino man to proclaim his virility. "Where you learn?"

"In military jump school."

"The army?" he scoffed. "Fuck that shit. I pay for lessons, from a professional." He turned and followed Ralph out of the clearing. Their car was less than twenty yards away, where it sat idling on an unpaved road. The cabrón was scary slow on the uptake. He popped the trunk and tossed the duffle into it, which landed with a thud but didn't burst. He got behind the wheel and pulled the door shut, then leaned out the window. "Next car, sky jockey," he said.

"Huh?"

"Next car," he repeated, then dropped the shifter into gear and rolled off, leaving me baffled. The evening grew quiet as their car disappeared. I listened closely for the hum of the aforementioned next car. I thought I heard the rumble of another engine, but wasn't sure as the sound I picked up on was displaced by the rustling of palm leaves in the evening breeze. A moment later, the growl of a car engine became distinct as it drew closer. Within a few minutes, I heard the telltale sound of car tires crunching over uneven terrain. The approaching vehicle was wide and low. I'd seen several of them in London but very few of them here in the States, a Jaguar XKE convertible, white with a tan interior, absolutely gorgeous. Moonlight illuminated the driver's face. Thiago Serna sported a broad grin as he piloted the car alongside me.

"Get in," he said, booming loudly. "Uncle Renaldo said nothing but the best for our hero, Sonny Rojas." He slapped the passenger bucket seat. "Come on. Let's go."

I was stunned and unsure of what to make of the new development but shrugged it off and walked around the long hood to the passenger door. "What's going on?"

"You and me, that's what's going on, my man. Tonight we celebrate."

"Celebrate?"

"That big shipment of cocaine you diverted to Miami—it's gonna make bank on the street. All profit."

The cocaine we had stolen? His brother's cocaine? He's happy about that? *What the hell?*

"I've got the evening all planned for us. Uncle Renaldo's got a place on the beach. It's fully stocked with lobster, booze, and sweaty chicas. We're gonna party like rock stars." He slapped me on the knee. "You're a rock star, aren't you, Sonny?"

Not really. I'd never been closer to center stage than off in the wings, twenty feet from famous, as they say, a studio musician and friend of the band. But party like a rock star? No problem. I'd spent time with Keith Moon of The Who and lived the life of a party animal. My heart was still pumping adrenaline, and it washed away the worry I'd been dragging around for weeks without relief. *Have fun tonight,* I thought, *and take up the crusade in the morning.* I'd return to Cartagena as soon as possible and press Serna to let me visit my folks, press him harder than I'd ever pressed him before.

"Have you been to Uncle's beach house?" I shook my head. "You'll love it. It's fabulous, and the view of the gulf is breathtaking." Thiago went on and on, rambling about the night and the women, "Cuban women," he said. "So hot. So incredibly hot. Have you been with una cubana?" He reached over and patted my cheek. "A pretty boy like you, they'll eat you alive."

I suspected Thiago's involvement but hadn't been sure if he knew about the cocaine heist. Now, there was no doubt. He'd referred to the heist and seemed thrilled about it, about ripping off his brother Gage. So much for brotherly love. It cleared up a lot of confusion—Thiago had joined forces with Guzman one-hundred percent. All of the lawyers I'd met were sleazy, opportunistic bottom feeders. Thiago was a few years from taking the bar exam and becoming a full-fledged shark but seemed to fit the greedy mold perfectly. What else were Guzman and Thiago scheming, and what would their new partnership mean for me? It hit me days before, while I was still in Colombia. I had to stop relying on the promises of criminals and became consumed with a plan to take my life back, a plan I'd already set in motion and was watching unfold.

Chapter Sixty-Six

A nudge on the shin awakened me. Eyelids lifting, I turned left, then right. Both women in bed with me were still sound asleep, their tan, naked bodies soft in the morning light that filtered through the window shades, painting their skin in stripes of light and dark. Each had been magnificent, each a treasure that revealed her sexual prowess moment by moment, touch by touch, throughout the night. Now, each looked innocent as they slept, their sculpted faces in profile with long eyelashes and gently sweeping noses.

"Sonny, get up. We have to go," Thiago said. Standing at the foot of the bed, he looked freshly groomed, his wavy hair styled, and his clothes crisp. "Playtime is over. Uncle Renaldo is waiting for us."

"Huh?" I was still in a fog, still half-asleep and hungover, still reveling in the sexual fantasy I'd been awarded. If only temporarily, the evening at Guzman's beach home had blotted all the pain from my mind as well as the plan I'd committed to before leaving Cartagena. It too had been blotted away momentarily.

Why was Guzman waiting for us? I wondered. I'd never been told any more than I absolutely needed to know. Now, suddenly, I was showered with luxury and taking part in the kingpin's plans. Why had the dynamics of our arrangement changed so dramatically?

Thiago glanced at his watch. "You look like shit, Sonny. Take a quick shower and grab what you need from my closet." Thiago was taller than me—I wasn't sure how well his expensive threads would fit.

I took a hurried shower and was back in Thiago's Jaguar thirty minutes later with a container of coffee and a grilled sandwich that Guzman's cook had prepared for me. Thiago was at the wheel, his head swaying to the music playing on the radio. Free's "All Right Now" was blaring from the tiny car speaker. I'd met Paul Kossoff, the lead guitarist, during my London days, and had learned to mimic his vibrato technique. It wasn't something I used often, but it was one of the weapons in my string-bending arsenal that I pulled out when required. I breathed a despondent sigh—getting back to my guitar seemed a million miles away. My passion for playing music was beyond my grasp for the moment.

"You must feel like a king," Thiago said. "Those girls were crazy, were they not?"

Crazy wasn't the word that came to mind. Those two women were not strangers to each other and quickly became adept at pleasing me in a way I'd never experienced before. They were unrestrained, impassioned lovers. "They were wild. Now, if only my head didn't hurt so damn much."

"I always say that a hangover is our way of remembering how much fun we had the night before. It sounds like you had more fun than you can handle. But I'm sure you have no regrets." He slapped me on the knee. "An amazing night, yes?"

"Yes."

"You earned it. Uncle Renaldo is very pleased with you."

Amazing was the only word that summed up those hours between arriving at Guzman's beach home and blissful unconsciousness that settled over me many hours later. I gulped coffee from the container. It was hot and strong. "Where are we going?" I asked.

"You'll see," he said in a gleeful tone. "A big surprise, Sonny. Very big. Drink your coffee and return from the dead. You'll want to be alert when we get there."

"Get where?" Get fucking where? I was so sick and tired of being led around by the nose, tired of being manipulated by Guzman and Serna.

"Patience," he said with another pat on the knee that really pissed me off. The gesture was obnoxious and patronizing, a practice the polished ass-kisser seemed to have already mastered in his crusade to become a lawyer.

"About thirty minutes more." The way he was pushing the Jag, thirty minutes meant at least forty miles. I glanced over at the speedometer, and the needle was over eighty.

I knew the road we were on—it led away from the coast to central Florida. "I don't like all this mystery. Just tell me where the hell we're going."

His head swiveled forty-five-degrees, his eyes deadly serious. "Mystery is better than death, Sonny. Drink your coffee and enjoy the adventure." He turned back to the road, and we drove in silence the rest of the way.

Chapter Sixty-Seven

I couldn't appreciate the size of the structure that lay before us until we were directly in front, an enormous one-level building so wide I couldn't take in the two ends of it without turning my head from one side to the other. Polished metal letters stood out prominently against the building's brick surface, that read: Árbol de la Vida Meats, which translated meant Tree of Life Meats. Of what I'd learned of Guzman, I doubted fruit of any variety sprang from the flowers of this tree. I was sure time would prove me right.

"Impressive, no?" Thiago boomed with yet another annoying slap on the knee. If there was any more than a micron of room in the Jag, I would've moved my legs out of harm's way. "One million square feet," he boasted. "Gage toured this building some time ago and frequently confided in me about what he could do with such a facility. Between you and me, I think he's envious."

I concurred with an absentminded nod. Thiago confounded me more each day—where did his loyalty lie? Did he get off knowing he and Guzman were about to topple Gage's empire? How could he be so two-faced? "I didn't know Guzman was in the provisions business."

"He has interests in numerous areas," Thiago said. "Many different kinds of consumables." The word consumables made me laugh on the inside. Up the nose or in a vein were the kind of products Guzman dealt in, nothing a mother would ever serve her children for dinner.

He whipped the Jag into a parking spot and popped out immediately. Checking his watch, he motioned for me to move quickly. "Uncle Renaldo is expecting us. Let's go."

Chapter Sixty-Eight

Thiago was exactly right—Renaldo Guzman waited just inside the entranceway, wearing a butcher's coat. It was pure white and pressed as crisply as a tailored dinner jacket, not a spot of animal blood visible anywhere. "Señores, come in," he said. His voice was robust, exuberant. "Welcome to Árbol de la Vida Meats, where we package and distribute the finest cuts of meat in the state of Florida."

Package and distribute, I mused. These were two areas in which Guzman undeniably excelled.

"I'm quite proud of this facility, Sonny. I'll take you on a quick tour before we get down to business."

Getting down to business was code for, I own you and I'm going to tell you how I'm going to control your life. Still, this was a different Guzman than I'd previously seen. He played the role of a proud papa and the meat packaging plant, his infant child. Gone was his calculated indifference. His demeanor was warm and personable. I couldn't imagine how much this change would cost me or what would be demanded of me next.

Guzman turned and began moving down a long, wide corridor. "Have you ever been to an abattoir, Sonny? It's quite impressive." He glanced at me for an answer. I shook my head. I'd no idea what the word meant but assumed it meant slaughterhouse. Pushing through a set of metal doors, we entered the butchering area where cow carcasses hung from meat hooks and large cuts of meat were chopped and sliced before moving onto a conveyor belt. I couldn't believe Guzman actually operated a meat packaging plant, but suspected it was a front for one of his illegal enterprises.

I envisioned the slaughterhouse late at night, the day's meat processed and the butchers sent home for the night…his henchmen dragging their trophies into the room, the corpses of men and women Guzman had marked for assassination. They'd be hacked up and ground into chopped meat, then extruded into buckets before being dumped at sea. Sharks would do the rest.

"I import the finest meats from all over South America, everything from Brazilian picanha, what Americans call sirloin cap, to Colita de cuadril from Argentina. Or as we call it here, tri-tip. Only the best of everything. Which do you prefer, Sonny? I'll have some prepared for you to take back to Cartagena."

His generous offer meant he'd keep me around to complete additional missions. Was this good news or bad? "I truly appreciate your generosity, Sr. Guzman, but the only thing I want to take home is my mother and father."

Guzman put his hand on the back of my neck as if he were fond of me. "We'll discuss that matter shortly," he said. "You don't have to worry about that anymore, Sonny. I'll take care of you. You're one of us."

Chapter Sixty-Nine

"One of us," he said. Who was us, Guzman, duplicitous Thiago, and his network of murderers and drug dealers? What an esteemed body of notables to be included among. "You were instrumental in redirecting Serna's cocaine shipment to Florida," Guzman said. "To show my appreciation, I've tripled your fee for the last delivery of Sublimaze. It has already been deposited into your safe-deposit box."

I glanced at Thiago. His brother's cocaine had been stolen, and he didn't so much as bat an eyelash. What made him tick? I already knew he was in league with Guzman but found his double-dealing unnerving. He was a true schemer in the making, an unparalleled piece of garbage. How ambitious can a person be to cut his brother off at the knees? I was brought up understanding the value of family. Thiago, it seemed, had missed that lesson.

"This is just one of the butcher shops, Sonny. There are eight more, each specializing in a different meat product, everything from smoked specialty cuts to the garbage that goes into dog food. But I won't bore you by taking you to see all of them. I have more important things to show you."

We exited the butcher shop and took an elevator down to the basement. The doors opened onto the lower level, where a pair of guards stood sentry with automatic rifles and handguns. Guzman grabbed a pair of respirator masks and handed them to Thiago and me. "These are necessary," he said, then fitted a third mask over his face. He gestured for the guards to open a locked steel door. One of them inserted a key into the lock as instructed, then held the door for us to enter.

The large masks covered most of our faces and made it difficult to understand what Guzman said. I listened carefully as we entered a spotless packaging facility where mostly naked men and women measured and packaged what I assumed was cocaine. The workers eyed us warily as they went about their business under Guzman's acute eye. How many of them had made a late-night trip to the slaughterhouse for stealing a smidgeon of cocaine? How many had become chum for the sharks that inhabited Florida's coastal waters?

"Witness the fruits of your labor, Sonny. Gage Serna's cocaine being made ready for mass distribution. The return on these drugs will be several million dollars." I'd seen drug cutting operations in the movies and on TV. They were usually small mom and pop operations located in neighborhood slum houses. The drug kingpin patted me on the back. Maybe the triple payment he'd added to my safe-deposit stash wasn't enough. Based on the titanic scale of his operation, it seemed he'd been downright miserly.

"Not too shabby," Thiago commented. Opening his trap for the first time since we'd entered the complex. He was such an obvious piece of shit. I physically ached to rap him in the mouth, knock out a few of his perfect white teeth. As Guzman walked among his employees examining the goings-on with a discerning eye, Thiago studied the women's naked breasts, winking at the women whose anatomy he found pleasing.

Guzman spent a significant amount of time at the weighing table, checking to make sure the small glassine bags were not being overfilled. Finally satisfied, he motioned for me to join him in front of a second metal door. "Make sure your mask is snug," he said, and waited for Thiago and me to check our masks before opening the door. "This, gentlemen, is where the magic happens."

Chapter Seventy

This room was much smaller, perhaps only twenty feet square. If, as Guzman said, the magic happened within, there was no magician in sight. No swarthy sleight of hand conjurer was in attendance. No disappearing rabbit. No top hat and cane. Instead, the Sublimaze-filled duffle bag I'd landed with sat dead center upon a large steel table, enclosed in a Plexiglas box like a rare antiquity on display at a museum. Half a dozen workers stood around the table, wearing white vinyl suits and hooded respirator masks. Guzman nodded, and the Plexiglass box was removed. One of the men leaned across the table and slowly unzipped the duffle bag. He peeled back the bag, revealing the small plastic-wrapped packets of Sublimaze within.

"I have this to thank you for as well, Sonny. This one small parcel will yield more revenue than all the cocaine you saw outside. You have truly proved your worth to me, and I will soon demand that Serna release your mama and papa. Consider it my first order of business. All I want in return is your promise to go on delivering this precious material. Can we agree on this?" I didn't hesitate to offer my hand. He took it immediately and seemed elated—I could see sparks crackling behind his eyes, flashes of greed-charged electricity. The man's appetite for money was insatiable.

One worker lifted the drug packets while the other pulled the duffle off the table and deposited it within an airtight container. My eyes were pinned on the sachets of Sublimaze. Knowing its deadly potential, I couldn't wait to leave the room. Apparently, Thiago was on the same page. He made his way to the door and slipped out. Had he witnessed the process before, or was he simply scared shitless?

Seeing Thiago leave, Guzman said, "It's time we did the same, Sonny." He pointed to the door. As he turned, the worker who'd disposed of the duffle, pulled a small pistol from where it had been tucked behind the elastic cuff of his vinyl suit. He fired at the Sublimaze bundle, rupturing it. As the room spontaneously filled with the deadly airborne powder, he yanked off Guzman's mask. Grabbing him by the hair, he drove Guzman's head face-first into the ruptured package. Guzman struggled to hold his breath but was pinned in place until his lungs filled with a lethal dose of the drug. I was stunned and petrified, unable to move as the others fled the room.

"Get the hell out of here," Guzman's assailant said. "Run!"

Chapter Seventy-One

I staggered from the room, still immobilized by the sight of Guzman being murdered before my eyes. Knowing just how potent a depressant Sublimaze was, I was sure the Florida kingpin's heart had already seized. I heard a machine gun blast fill the air, then someone grabbed me by the scruff of the neck and yanked me forward.

"Move quickly," the man said behind the hooded mask. "No one will be left alive."

Manhandling me, he pushed me through the large cocaine packaging room and out the door. Then, down a corridor, he led me in the opposite direction from the elevator. We were at the far end of the hallway, a good twenty yards away from the packaging room, when my escort yanked off his hooded respirator mask. I'd never seen him before. "You can take yours off as well," he said.

I didn't. We were in an underground facility where the air must've been fed through an enclosed ventilation system. I had no idea how far it might carry the lethal drug.

"Did you hear me?" he said.

"I'll keep it on."

"Whatever," he said and led me to a staircase. No longer dragging me along with him, he took off up the stairs, and I followed as machine gun blasts continued to ring out intermittently. My assumption was that a kill squad was going area-by-area within the structure and assassinating everyone they encountered, drug packagers, butchers, everyone on Guzman's payroll. No one would be spared.

As I followed him out the stairwell and down yet another long corridor within the monolith, I thought about who was capable of ordering such brutal mass-scale genocide, an example that would resonate throughout the enormous drug-trafficking world and send a crystal-clear message, "Don't fuck with me."

Guzman's murderer picked up his pace and was running at full stride as the sound of machine gun torrents drew nearer. I finally found my legs and paced him until we reached an exterior fire door. Bounding outside, I found freedom and the answer to all of my questions. As I pulled off my respirator mask, the rear door of a large sedan opened and Gage Serna stepped out.

Chapter Seventy-Two

Serna was immediately surrounded by his security detail, five men armed with shotguns and automatic rifles, all with their backs to him, watching for a possible attack coming from any direction. I doubted the US Secret Service was capable of more decisive action.

There were jeeps everywhere I looked, parked outside all the building entrances. Although I couldn't see all of the entrances in the enormous building, I was sure that every chink and crack in the facility was covered. It must've cost Serna a fortune to assemble the army I saw before me.

One of the men gripped me by the arm and dragged me in front of Serna. "We've come a long way from guitar instructions, haven't we?" Serna said. He seemed hardier and more self-assured than I'd ever seen him before. Had they already reported that Guzman was dead or was he fully confident of his plan's outcome? It seemed he'd already accepted victory.

Just then, the Jaguar pulled up. Thiago seemed calm and collected. The top was down, and his wavy hair was flowing in the wind. He gave his brother a double thumbs-up, then got out, hugged his brother tightly, and gave him a kiss on the cheek.

Shit! I'd been wrong about Thiago from the very start. He wasn't a turncoat, nor was he focused on the reins of Serna Oil. He was Gage's spy, a masterclass actor in his brother's grand production. Guzman had thought himself a cunning opponent, but Serna had checkmated him with one blazing move.

Serna saw my expression and smiled. "Sonny, you can't be surprised that blood is thicker than water. Certainly not Serna blood."

"Had you fooled, didn't I?" Thiago said. "You must've thought I was a backstabbing weasel."

"Not exactly. I thought you were a piece of shit." Gage hadn't revealed the identity of his secret operative. He never mentioned that Thiago was under deep cover. I was naïve to believe that Thiago had missed the lesson on the value of family. To the contrary, he knew the curriculum inside and out.

The brothers laughed. The fact that gunfire was still audible didn't seem to faze either of them in the slightest. An empire had changed hands, and men were being slaughtered by the dozen. Gage Serna, the conqueror, took it all in stride. On the chessboard of criminal enterprise, he was already onto his next victory, many moves ahead of his competitors.

Chapter Seventy-Three

The moment of truth had come when I realized the FBI wasn't going to do diddly-squat for me. They weren't going to lift one goddamn finger. Whatever influence I had with the FBI died along with John Roswell. A large shipment of drugs destined for Europe had been diverted to the United States. Best I could tell, the FBI was less than enamored with me. I also saw that Guzman couldn't be trusted and saw only one way to save my parents. That's when I rolled the dice and confided to Serna that Guzman was planning to hijack his shipment. Serna was able to scramble and, by airlifting a replacement cocaine shipment, was able to meet his obligation to his European buyers.

"Guzman was going to take what was mine, but now my cocaine is here in Florida, and I've taken what was his," Serna said. "His operation is now my operation, his entire distribution channel. He thought he was clever, but he proved himself a fool, an overconfident buffoon."

"You've done your job and then some, Sonny," Thiago said. "It's time for us to leave."

"But what about my parents?" I said.

"I gave you my word when you revealed Guzman's plan," Serna said. "Yes, Thiago had already given me the broad strokes, but he didn't have the specific details. We knew that Guzman was focused on hijacking a shipment, but we didn't know which one or how he planned to pull it off. Your information gave me the specific information I needed to take him down. I began mobilizing a strike force immediately. Your mama and papa are already waiting for you at home. They were never more than a few miles away." His expression straddled the line between craftiness and indifference. "I thought withholding the location added a heightened sense of jeopardy."

Heightened sense of jeopardy, my ass, you fucking prick! I would've strangled him on the spot if his men weren't armed with AK-47s.

Thiago will take you to see them right now," Serna said.

You bet your ass he will. I was emotionally spent, devoid of any strength. For a moment, I thought my legs would buckle. My pulse rate skyrocketed at the thought of returning to my family. My mouth opened, but I had no words to speak nor air in my lungs to give them life. The thank you I knew Serna was expecting was wedged down deep and couldn't worm its way past my lips.

"This is a reprieve and nothing more," Serna said. "Your obligation to me is far from over. One day I will call on you again, and when I do…"

My heart sank as his mouth twisted into a mocking grin before turning away. He'd had the last word and was done with me. For now. His insidious shadow would hang over me until he ended me or I ended him.

It was time for me to regroup, to hug my mama and papa and bask in the love and warmth of my family. I needed to think clearly, to get my life back on track, and organize my thoughts. I had to outmaneuver Serna, but how? As I got into Thiago's Jag, I saw Gage's men carrying bodies out of the building, far too many to grind into chum. It served as a brutal reminder of what Gage Serna was capable of, and it chilled me to my core.

Chapter Seventy-Four

1971

My mom always forgot something when she was invited to a family function. Sometimes it was a bottle of sangria chilling in the refrigerator or the Tarta de Queso she'd stayed up until midnight baking the night before. Regardless, my parents never made it out of the driveway on the first shot. There was always that quick return to the front door, my mom frantic to retrieve the forgotten item. "I'd forget my head if it wasn't attached," she'd say, followed by a mad sprint to the kitchen. "We're late," she'd continue. "Your father is going to kill me. You know how he hates to be late to Uncle Pedro's house." I'd always pitch in, retrieving the Tupperware cake carrier from the highest shelf in the pantry, the one she couldn't reach without a stepstool. My efforts were always rewarded with a hug and a kiss. I couldn't get enough of them. What is it they say, "You don't know what you've got until it's gone?" I appreciated them more than ever now that they'd been returned.

The weeks of peril they'd faced was probably the reason Mama was more forgetful than ever. Neither of my folks were sleeping the way they used to. I'd hear them whispering in the middle of the night and playing gin rummy until they couldn't keep their eyes open. And though I was to blame for what had happened to them, they never blamed me. Telling them the truth was the hardest thing I'd ever had to do, but I came clean and prayed for their forgiveness. Months had passed, and my father still seemed to look at me differently than he used to. A specter of distrust was always there in his expression and might always remain. I knew he'd need more time to get over what had happened. But a mother's love knows no limits—she was as warm and caring as she had been before the abduction and rarely spoke of her time in captivity. There was a lot I could criticize Gage Serna for, but he'd treated my parents well. Although he'd hijacked their freedom, he never took their dignity. Those who oversaw their stay treated them with the utmost care and respect.

"Are you sure you don't want to come?" Mama asked, already marching toward the front door with her cake in tow. "Your aunt and uncle are dying to see you."

I shook my head. "I'm not ready, Mamá."

I noticed her eyes were damp as she hugged me again. "Maybe soon?" she asked, her words both sad and optimistic.

"Maybe." My reply was noncommittal. I was riddled with guilt over what had happened to them and wouldn't be ready to face the family for a long while. The horn honked out in the driveway.

"Aye yai yai," she said with a hand to her cheek as she vanished out the front door.

I heard my father yelling, "What took you so long? We'll be the last ones there." I didn't like it when he hollered at her but smiled on the inside. Things weren't quite back to normal, but they were getting there slowly. As they say, one day at a time.

Chapter Seventy-Five

Music was once again soothing my soul. I was practicing regularly and had found an intense passion I hadn't felt in a long time. The things we experience change us. The blues were born out of pain and anguish, suffering and torment. It began in the deep south as the lament of slaves and the impoverished. Those people who truly knew pain. At long last, I was beginning to get in touch with mine. My playing had become angrier and more soulful, with an intensity I'd never exhibited before. My hands were on the guitar all the time, and when life got in the way, I played guitar in my head because life seemed to get in the way far too often.

That threat named Gage Serna was ever-present, lurking in the background, stalking me. I knew the day would come, the phone call or unannounced visit. I never knew when one of his minions would knock on the door and say, "Let's go! Señor Serna is waiting for you. Get your shit. Make it fast." How would my parents live through that again? How would I? I'd disappear again. To where? For how long? Would I ever return? My parents knew I could've died serving time in Vietnam but dying for your country and dying because I was obligated to a drug czar were two horribly different things. And in my heart, I knew I was incapable of killing Gage Serna. Yes, I had killed, but shooting Jacobo had been spontaneous, a knee-jerk reaction to Roswell's murder. It wasn't in me to plan and carry out Serna's death. It just wasn't. Yet somehow I knew I had to keep my parents safe and isolate them from him.

My dad's age had caught up to him. Though he objected, Mom wouldn't let him climb the tall ladder to paint the outside of houses anymore. So, while he painted the insides, I worked the outsides. My hands weren't on a guitar, but my time away from the fret board didn't annoy me the way it used to. Twenty feet in the air, I painted a chord with every stroke of the paint brush. The altitude seemed to help me work out harmonies and phrasing that I put into practice the moment I got home. I remembered every note and chord, the soft touches as well as brash slashes at the strings. About the only thing that drove me crazy was caulking, filling the spaces around windows, and the gaps between siding panels, getting that maddening white glue on my fingers and under my nails, that infuriating white paste I'd have to scrub like hell before I picked up my guitar to play.

Most importantly, house painting gave me the opportunity to spend quality time with my dad, time to mend fences and close the wound I had torn open. The delight I saw on my mom's face when she saw the two of us walk through the door at the end of the day was second to none. Neither believed I was going to abandon music, but life was sweet in the interim. My life was expendable. Theirs' wasn't.

Chapter Seventy-Six

May 1971

Nailfile in hand, I had the pointed edge under a nail, cleaning away the last bits of caulk and dried paint hot water and soap couldn't remove. Mamá and Dad were once again at Uncle Pedro's having dinner, leaving me to fend for myself and taking the evening to decompress. Fending for myself meant peanut butter on crackers. Sure, I could've easily prepared a healthier meal, but I didn't want to take the time. I'd worked out a tasty riff while painting the gable of an old colonial and was keen to test it out and build it into a full solo. Having just plugged my guitar into the amp when the phone rang, I was eager to get my fingers on the guitar and unhappy about being interrupted.

The voice on the phone sounded distant, but I knew in an instant who it was. "Sonny, it's George, George Harrison."

I know. Believe me, I know. "George, it's so good to hear your voice."

"Sonny, I got your note and tape recording, and there was so much I loved about it. Your playing, it's changed quite a bit. You must've found some new influences."

I wanted to tell him what those new influences were: drug czars, FBI agents, and international spies. George was not judgmental, and I knew he'd accept the information in time, but not now, not after such a long silence. It was way too soon. "I've grown a bit, I think."

"I felt something, something that wasn't there before, angst, I think. Lad, are you okay?"

"Yes. I am now." I wasn't sure if I'd hear back from George. It had been such a long time since we worked together, and he was, or rather had been, lead guitarist for The Beatles. The Lads from Liverpool had disbanded more than a year earlier, and Harrison was now doing his own thing. He'd released "Times They Pass," and the triple-album was a highly acclaimed success. I was thrilled for him because I knew just how good he was, and the solo album showed the world that George Harrison was as great an artist as John Lennon or Paul McCartney, a genius in his own right. I'd hoped to work with him again and sent him some tracks I'd been working on. I led off with an ample dose of rockabilly because I knew he loved that style of playing, then exploded into hot emotional riffs.

"Your style, it's more aggressive," George said. "Kind of raw, actually. Where did you pick it up?"

"I was in South America for a while, but as you see, I'm home in Florida now."

"South America. *Oh!* You'll have to tell me all about that one day."

"I've been listening to your new album nonstop. It's everything you talked about doing and so much more."

"Thank you, Sonny," he said with an appreciative lilt in his voice that reminded me he was a genuinely kind-hearted person. "I'm starting to kick around ideas for the next one. Would you like to come over and help me work on it?"

Come over wasn't exactly the house down the street. Come over meant London. He must've really enjoyed my tape because he had access to the best musicians in the world and thought enough of me to invite me to contribute. My mom and dad wouldn't be happy to see me leave again, but this was an offer I couldn't pass up. It was an opportunity to get back to the thing I loved most, get back to who I was. Hopefully, I'd be smart enough to not repeat the same dumb-ass mistakes a second time. The condition of my back was and would always be an unknown quantity, but I was off painkillers and hopefully not susceptible to the lure of drugs. "Sure," I howled. "When?"

"My friend Ravi Shankar asked me to arrange a charity concert for the people of Bangladesh at New York's Madison Square Garden. It's set up for August 1. Why don't you come up to New York, see the show, and we can fly back to the UK after the concert? Eric will be there. I'm sure he'd love to see you."

"Yes, yes, yes, count me in. Yes!"

"So good to reconnect with you, Sonny. I'll have someone ring you up with the details. Bye now."

"Bye, George."

The line went dead, and my heart sprang to life. After hanging up the phone, I went straight back to my room and picked up the guitar. It became alive in my hands, just as it had before all my troubles began, before the arrest, before Roswell, and before Gage Serna and Renaldo Guzman.

I practiced for hours, smoking the fret board, too consumed with making magic to break for food or drink. I hadn't noticed that it had turned dark outside when I heard a knock at the door and finally set down my guitar. My fingertips were sore, and my knuckles ached. Family get-togethers at Uncle Pedro's usually went on late into the night. I checked my watch, and it seemed much too early for my folks to come home. I hurried to the front door, opened it, and gasped. With her big brown eyes and round cheeks, Willow was the last person I expected to see standing outside my door. Her smile lit me up like a flashbulb, and it took several moments for the thought process to override the surge of hormones rushing through my veins. *What does she want?* I wondered. *Why is she here?* We'd managed to divert a boat shipment of cocaine from reaching Spain, but Serna had duplicated the shipment when I leaked to him what was going down. She, Cabrera, and the ICPO couldn't have been happy about the way things turned out but I didn't think they suspected I'd leaked the plan to Serna. I didn't like playing the role of a double-dealer, but didn't see any alternative. Then again, I was too naïve—they were spies, and it was their job to know such things. I wasn't privy to the plans and workings of the intelligence agency she worked for. What else didn't I know about Willow, Cabrera, and the ICPO? What would my ignorance cost me?

"Hi, Sonny," she said warmly. "May I come in?"

This is not Willow, I thought. *This is not the innocent girl you met in Cartagena. She's Cayetana Blanco, seductress, spy, woman of countless faces. She's not innocent. You know better.*

I should've said no, no to whatever she had to offer. I should've shut the door and locked her out forever, but the look of wanting in her eyes and the promise of adventure proved more than I could refuse. I stepped aside and let her back into my life.

Sonny Rojas will return

A Note from the Author

Free Fall is a work of fiction and the character Sonny Rojas purely a product of my imagination. Throughout this book, Sonny interacts with real-life individuals of great renown. These situations are fictitious. The interactions and conversations between Sonny and these real-life individuals never occurred. Some of the conversations between Sonny and these celebrities are actual quotes from the celebrity but have been used out of context, shared in this novel to impart the personality of said celebrities. To imbue the story with a sense of authenticity, much effort was employed to place Sonny at genuine historic events where he would have had the opportunity to interact with these real-life celebrities. Based on extensive research, the celebrities Sonny interacts with in the book actually participated at these events. However, their descriptions and the actions of these individuals in the story may be based partially on fact but also derived from traits and actions these individuals have exhibited and become known for over the course of their public celebrity. As an example, in Chapter Four a fictitious character refers to Keith Moon's use of fireworks backstage at the RKO Theater in New York City on March 26, 1967. No evidence exists to support this stunt ever took place and is merely indicative of Moon's well-documented history as a prankster.

A Short List of Electric Guitar Techniques

Rhythm Techniques:

- **Power Chords:** *A chord or combination of notes used in rock music and typically selected to sound good at high volume and high levels of distortion.*
- **Palm Muting:** *Resting the picking hand on strings near the bridge for a percussive "chug".*
- **Down Picking:** *Using only downstrokes for aggressive, consistent rhythm.*
- **Barre Chords:** *Using one finger to fret multiple strings.*
- **Octave Chords:** *Playing two notes an octave apart, often used in punk and rock.*
- **Strumming/Picking Dynamics:** *Varying intensity.*
- **Pick Scrapes:** *Dragging the pick edge along the wound strings.*

Lead and Articulation Techniques:

- **Bending:** *Pushing strings to raise pitch (full, half, quarter tones).*
- **Vibrato:** *Oscillating pitch for expression.*
- **Slides (Glissando):** *Moving from one note to another along the string.*
- **Hammer-ons & Pull-offs (Legato):** *Playing notes without re-picking.*
- **Double Stops:** *Playing two notes simultaneously.*
- **Unison Bends:** *Bending one string to match the pitch of a higher, unbent string.*
- **Pre-bends:** *Bending the string before picking it.*

Advanced and Expressive Techniques:

- ***Tapping:*** *Using picking-hand fingers to fret notes.*
- ***Sweep Picking:*** *Dragging the pick across strings for fast arpeggios.*
- ***Harmonics (Natural & Pinch):*** *Creating high-pitched "squeals".*
- ***Whammy Bar Techniques:*** *Dive bombs, vibrato, and pitch scoops.*
- ***Tremolo Picking:*** *Rapid, repetitive picking on a single note.*
- ***Hybrid Picking:*** *Using a pick and fingers simultaneously.*
- ***Volume Swells:*** *Using the volume knob or pedal for violin-like effects.*
- ***A Dive Bomb:*** *is an electric guitar technique where the player strikes a note or harmonic and immediately pushes the tremolo/whammy bar all the way down, causing the pitch to drop drastically, mimicking a diving airplane or bomb.*

Acknowledgments

Anyone who says novel writing is a lonely pursuit is a bald-faced liar, a fraud, a sham-dealer, and a ruthless prevaricator. Sure, the project may begin in a singular mind but from there on the initial draft passes through so many hands it's practically impossible to give proper credit to one and all. But I'll try. First and foremost I must recognize my wife, Isabella, the unsung hero of my work who reads quietly late into the night making sure that each and every one of my books is the best it can be. At a time when good people can be particularly hard to find, this author has struck gold with Shawn, Deb, and the fabulous team at Level Best Books—thanks for going the extra mile. Many thanks to Lynn and Karen, the ladies who critique my poorly formed word-muddle and help shape it into something moderately enlightening.

About the Author

Lawrence Kelter hails from New York but now calls North Carolina his home. He is the bestselling author of more than thirty mystery and thriller novels, including the Stephanie Chalice Mystery series that has topped bestseller lists in the US, UK, and Australia. In 2017, he penned *Back to Brooklyn*, the studio-authorized sequel to the cult comedy classic *My Cousin Vinny*. Early in his writing career, he received direction from literary icon Nelson DeMille, who edited portions of his early work. Well before he said, "Lawrence Kelter is an exciting new novelist, who reminds me of an early Robert Ludlum," he said, "Kid, your work needs editing, but that's a hell of a lot better than not having talent. Keep it up!"

AUTHOR WEBSITE: http://www.lawrencekelter.com

SOCIAL MEDIA HANDLES:
~~Follow Larry on Facebook at https://www.facebook.com/larrykelter
~~Follow Larry on Twitter at https://twitter.com/larrykelter

Also by Lawrence Kelter

My Cousin Vinny Humorous Thrillers
My Cousin Vinny
Back To Brooklyn
Wing and A Prayer

Level Best Standalone Thrillers
Beyond The Veil
Into The Groove

Gina Marie Cototi Thrillers
Man-Killer
Lady-Killer (2027)

Stephanie Chalice Thrillers
Don't Close Your Eyes
Ransom Beach
The Brain Vault
Our Honored Dead
Baby Girl Doe
Compromised
Out of the Ashes
Righteous Collars
Making Her Bones
Nonna's Cosa Nostra

Chloe Mather Thrillers
Secrets of the Kill
Rules of the Kill
Legends of the Kill

Lawrence Kelter has published more than thirty novels. For his stand-alone books and collaborations, please visit the author's website: lawrencekelter.com.

www.ingramcontent.com/pod-product-compliance
Lightning Source LLC
Chambersburg PA
CBHW031529150726
47990CB00001B/110